Champagne Friday

Champagne Friday

A Novel

Brian Boger

ISBN-13: 9781718963030

FOR MY GRANDCHILDREN

Acknowledgments

WE DO THIS writing, this excruciating, painful, all-consuming storytelling, alone. We do it in early mornings, long before sunup or late at night when the characters won't let us sleep. When talking with other people who write, the subject frequently comes up: why do we do something so aggravating, so frustrating, so exasperating? The answer comes pretty quick: because we have to.

But as any writer knows, no man is an island. We need, we crave, and are inspired by human interaction—at least I am. The people who have helped me along this journey with *Champagne Friday* are too many to thank, but my editors have been invaluable: Erin O'Donnell, Bill Simpson, Harry Goodheart, Gail Russell, Judy Steenstra, Allison Tocci, Sara Printz, Rebecca McGuire, and Cameron Vogt. They encouraged me (beat me up) and gave direction to this novel. My good friend and fellow writer, Norwood Holland, was a constant source of inspiration and support.

I wish to thank the city of Aiken and all the good folks at the Aiken County Historical Museum. The townspeople of this fine city were a great source for research and a proud, deserved, sense of history. Aiken is truly one of the most unique places in the South. Judith Burgess's family has lived there since the late 1700s—she took us on a tour that lasted most of the day. When it was over, I wanted to do it again. Thank you, Judith.

Big kudos to Steven Whetstone, the talented artist who painted the cover for this book. He is an original.

Finally, I want to thank my family. My wife Ellie tolerates my writing obsession with grace. My children Jayne, (her husband Chad) Tommy (his wife Lindsay) and Greg have been more than supportive. I couldn't have finished this book without them.

Part One

Chapter 1

WHEN HUGH BUNCOMBE found ten thousand dollars in cash on federal land he had one thought: *It's mine.* Then his brain kicked in: *It's not mine; it belongs to the government.* A third idea hit him: *I'll ask my dog who owns it.* There he stood, on a moral and legal cliff. He also stood with hundred-dollar bills stuffed into every crevice of his clothes. Bailey, a six-month old black Labrador barked. That was enough; Hugh stepped off the cliff. "That's what I thought, Bailey. It's my money."

The money was scattered all over Rhodes Field, the only baseball field in Ellenton, South Carolina, a town that was taken by condemnation by the United States of America when it needed to build atom bombs during the Cold War. The village was only a few miles from Aiken, where Mr. Buncombe lived, working as a chemist at the Savannah River Site until he retired. Because he had worked at the bomb plant, he still had his security clearance and could walk Bailey within a thirty-minute time limit on the abandoned, eerie streets of the condemned land.

Before the government took the town, Ellenton was a small farming community of eight hundred good souls, a drug store, a restaurant that served breakfast and lunch, and a one-pump gas station. Like any village in America in the 1950s, it had a baseball field. After the town was moved (the new town being New Ellenton, only ten miles away), nature slowly reclaimed the land, the roads, the abandoned houses, everything but the clay infield of Rhodes Field. The field was so compact, so hardened by the pounding of little feet over eighty years of use, nature ignored it as a lone, red-clay, diamond reminder of man's influence on *that* spot on earth.

The cash was all over the ball-yard, scattered like litter by the wind into the tall grass of the outfield, tossed up against the rusting fences of the dugouts, and into the woods where crumbled wooden bleachers once stood behind home plate. When Hugh saw the money, he looked around to see if anyone else was there. He looked up. Maybe there was a drone watching him. No such thing.

Knowing he was close to his thirty-minute limit, he used every second of time, stuffing the money in his pockets like a madman. He retrieved every bill, hopping around the field like a kid chasing ground balls, putting the money here and there until he got it all. Bailey thought it was a game, running back and forth with Hugh as he collected the treasure. And then, making sure he didn't leave one single bill, Hugh turned around and looked. Rhodes Field stood in fallow silence, the little pitcher's mound almost flat, home plate and the bases long gone. Again, he looked. Nothing.

Three minutes later Hugh walked around the "road closed" barricade and strolled by Wendell, the guard at the entrance to the Savannah River Site. Hugh threw his hand up in a thankful, perfunctory wave and mumbled something about seeing him tomorrow.

Sure enough, the next morning, Hugh and Bailey went past the gate after making small talk with Wendell. Hugh headed straight to Rhodes Field where he found two more one-hundred-dollar bills near center field. And he found six more the next day. And every day after that, he found at least one bill. Hugh had enough sense not to spend the money; it was found on forbidden federal land. Things could go wrong if he started slinging cash around Aiken like a rock star.

He was right not to spend the money. Hugh Buncombe, the retired, unassuming scientist, had stumbled into one of the largest financial scandals in American history.

Chapter 2

BY THE END of the first month, Hugh had collected over twenty-five thousand dollars. He put the bills into one of those purple cloth bags that Crown Royal gives out with the purchase of their whiskey. He felt like some sort of bank robber, storing cash, occasionally opening the bag and making sure it was still there. He didn't have much going on in his life except the painful loneliness that filled his time, day and night, since his wife died of a sudden heart attack a year before. Bailey was a great companion and the dog had become the only living thing with which Hugh communicated during his self-imposed mourning. Hugh was happy with his seclusion; he'd been a quiet chemist who'd spent his life making sure the atom bombs were safe in their silos until they were needed. He had few friends. Those co-workers he counted as buddies had either died or moved away from Aiken when they retired. Hugh, however, chose to stay in Aiken, South Carolina because it was too much trouble to move. He didn't like change.

Hugh's wife Michelle taught third grade elementary students for forty years before her heart attack. They had no children of their own, Michelle often saying she'd raised a few thousand kids in her long career.

When Michelle died, Hugh hired Calhoun Cooper to handle the estate. Cooper was a well-respected lawyer who Hugh knew from Rotary. And six months after Michelle died, good old Cooper croaked in the middle of the night—a victim of a stroke, also unexpected.

Calhoun Cooper had his legacy in Maxwell Cooper, a good-looking young man who'd been at Calhoun's side since Calhoun's wife died of breast cancer when the little boy was only eleven. Max had been reading complaints, answers, interrogatories, reviewing depositions and listening to legal arguments and theories since he was old enough to hold a crayon in his little fingers.

Calhoun told stories about his boy all the time. Maxwell was supposedly smart, like all fathers say, but in this case, it was true. Young Max was not only a good-looking young devil with dark hair and gorgeous bedroom-blue eyes; he was also extremely bright. He was blessed with a photographic memory, finishing at the top of his law school class at the University of Virginia. When the offers poured in from corporate firms promising a fat salary and a signing bonus to join their ranks, Maxwell turned them down and returned home to practice with his dad. A year and a half later, Calhoun was dead and Maxwell was managing a monster.

He was capable, but with grief in the foreground, Max struggled between dealing with the loss of his dad, his love of practicing law, and his second love: women. He had several women he was seeing—none seriously. He had a favorite cougar and four or five other lovelies at his disposal. His sexual appetite and the attempt to satisfy it helped him forget the pain he felt.

Hugh Buncombe made an appointment to see Max. After picking up his cash, Hugh arrived at the offices of Cooper and Cooper—an office that Calhoun had converted from an old dilapidated house into a four-thousand-square foot workplace with a spacious lobby, three conference rooms, four large offices, and two bathrooms. It was where Calhoun spent most of his time and his digs had been comfortable.

Young Max was happy to see Mr. Buncombe, who showed up fifteen minutes ahead of schedule. Max greeted Hugh in the lobby where Hugh had been sitting on the burgundy leather couch reading *Popular Mechanics.*

"Let's go back to the small conference room," Max suggested.

"You know I thought the world of your dad," Hugh began as they walked down the hall. "He and I sold Christmas trees for the Rotary Club every year. He was a smart guy."

Max didn't like talking about his dad.

"I miss him every day." That was all Max would yield to most people.

Hugh figured the young man was tired of hearing clients talk about his father. They sat across from each other at a sturdy rectangular walnut conference table with room for six. Hugh didn't waste time getting to his problem.

"Look, the reason I wanted to see you is I have found some money, some cash. I don't want to say where I found it, but let's just say it's on federal property. It's in the thousands of dollars. It's all one-hundred-dollar bills and all the bills are old. They're not the same as the new hundred-dollar bills. I'm afraid to spend the money. It's not really my money and I don't know what to do about it."

Max didn't say anything.

"And the thing is, I find more every day. I know the money isn't mine. Should I spend it? Should I take a trip? Should I report it to the police? I don't know what to do."

"How much have you found?"

"Let's just say it's close to thirty thousand dollars."

Max's left eyebrow raised up just slightly as he looked at the ceiling. "If you deposit over ten thousand dollars in cash, the bank will send a report to the Internal Revenue Service with your name on it. If you spend that kind of money around town, especially the old bills, it will eventually come back to you. The banks have a duty to retire the old bills. If they keep retiring a bunch of old bills from Aiken, sooner or later you'll be the target of an investigation by the Secret Service and the IRS. Oddly enough, the Secret Service is the agency in charge of matters involving United States currency. This is an interesting problem." Max sat back in the navy-blue leather chair that tilted for comfort.

"It's the kind of problem that drug dealers have."

"I'm not a drug dealer!" Buncombe blurted. "I've just got too much cash!"

When Buncombe raised his voice, Max got up and closed the conference room door that had been standing wide open.

After he closed the door, Max whispered, "I didn't say *you* were a drug dealer, I said it's the kind of problem that drug dealers have. They have to launder their money." Max sat back down in his chair. "Let me think about this for a few days. In the meantime, get the money to the bank and put it in a safe deposit box. Pay for the safe deposit box with a check. Don't spend a penny of that money, yet. Let me do a little research."

"How much is this going to cost me?"

"I don't know, but let's put a cap on it so you don't waste a bunch of money on me. I'll get you an answer for three hundred dollars. If that answer means we need more help, then you're only out three hundred bucks. And pay me with a check. I don't want any of that cash. Are we good on that?"

"That's a fair deal," Buncombe said, as he stood up and shook hands with Max. He liked the idea of putting a limit on the legal bill and Max was more than willing to help.

As he walked through the lobby, Buncombe nodded at a very nicely dressed woman; she was about his age, he thought. She sat in one of the wing-backed leather chairs, legs crossed, reading her own copy of *The Wall Street Journal.* She didn't look up when Hugh exited, but she'd heard every word of Buncombe's problem with too much cash and his emphatic denial of being a drug dealer.

That woman was Carla Robeson, the next appointment on Max's busy calendar.

Chapter 3

CARLA ROBESON WAS dressed in a handcrafted Carolina Herrera navy suit and Manolo Blahnik ankle boots that matched perfectly. Max wasn't aware that her dress and shoes cost over five thousand dollars, but he got the sense that this woman wasn't worried about spending a few bucks on a lawyer. Seated in Max's office, she tossed her *Wall Street Journal* onto the chair next to her.

"Your father always handled my rather mundane legal matters here in Aiken with a great deal of skill. I enjoyed our relationship when I was in town."

"I remember that, yes ma'am. What brings you in today?"

"This time it's a very serious matter I want you to handle," she said.

She was in her mid-fifties, Max figured. She had her brown hair in a bun, and while her hair was probably longer than a woman her age should wear, it was well kept and attractive. Her eyes, also brown, had a steely intensity. Her figure was also well maintained; Carla Robeson worked out on a treadmill and did some light weight training to stay in shape.

"What kind of case, Ms. Robeson?"

"Two weeks ago, my father was injured in a horrible accident at the intersection of Hampton and Barnwell streets. An eighteen-wheeler, exceeding the speed limit, ran a red light and plowed into my father's Cadillac on the passenger side."

"Was he hurt?"

"More than hurt. He's been in a coma over at Aiken Regional Medical Center since the accident. I don't know if he'll live another day or another year. It's tragic."

"As you know, my dad and I… I mean we, I mean I, handle personal injury cases."

"I'm sorry about your father. He was my trusted attorney here. What I want is a little unusual. Look—I'm a retired investment counselor; I received my engineering degree from Princeton. I earned my MBA at the Wharton Business School. With my background and attention to detail, I can help with the technical parts of the accident. I need a lawyer who will allow me to do some of the work on this case. I'll pay the costs, up front, which I anticipate being over one hundred thousand dollars. I can write you a check today for that amount to be held in escrow for the costs. I know about the standard contingency fee and will pay you one third of the settlement or of the trial proceeds."

Max looked at the classy Ms. Robeson. He'd heard about that accident. It was a doozy. There was a rumor that the driver of the eighteen-wheeler may have been drinking.

"Well, although my dad is … gone," Max stammered, "I bring the same skill that my father gave your family."

"You can stop selling me, Maxwell. I've checked you out. You try cases. You don't advertise on TV. Your father was one of the most respected lawyers in this community. Three months ago, you won a five hundred-thousand-dollar verdict on a case that could have gone against you. The word on the street is that you were better prepared than the other side and the jury loved you. I want a young, aggressive lawyer. You're the person I want to handle this matter. I just want to help, that's all."

Max smiled. His only concern was having Ms. Robeson do some of the "work." It could be a disaster. He leaned back and pulled out the middle drawer on the right side of his desk and put his feet across it.

"What kind of work can you do? I don't understand."

"I'll hire the expert witnesses. I'll get the accident re-constructionists. I'll find out the physical condition of the eighteen-wheeler. The brakes need to be examined. You write the letters and I'll do the legwork."

"Are you still in the Brunswick ... mans... I mean in the Brunswick home?" Max almost said mansion, which is what home was. It was a forty-room palace built in the early 1900s by the Brunswick clan, the family who would rival Bill Gates' money now.

"I moved here from New York a few months ago. My father has been living in the cottage over on Abbeville Street, not far from Hitchcock Woods, as you know. He needed some help. He's eighty-three and can't take care of the house like he used to. I moved here to help with the cottage and his horses when the accident happened. There aren't enough hours in the day to get it all done. I've hired a full-time housekeeper and a handyman."

Max relaxed. Carla had hit all the buttons. She was still in the mansion, although she called it a cottage. The homes in that part of town were where the robber barons of the 1890s built their castles. And they called them cottages—twelve thousand square foot little bungalows. She didn't say it, but Carla's great-grandfather was none other than Leland Brunswick, one of those men who might as well have invented money. Max had heard enough though. Knowing the case was worth a small fortune, knowing Ms. Robeson was willing to pay the costs up front, Max had one more question.

"The work you want to do on the case–where do you want to do that?"

"I'd like to do it here. I'm going to need administrative staff to handle some things."

"That's what I was thinking."

That was *sort of* what he was thinking. He was actually thinking about his lunch date with Reena, one of his lovers, but having received the answer he wanted from the cold-eyed, but rich, client who knew his dad, Max stood up with his hand outstretched. "We're going to get to know each other, Ms. Robeson."

"Carla," she smiled.

Carla was outwardly calm as they shook hands across the desk, but inside she was thrilled. She'd convinced the bright, young Maxwell Cooper to let her work at his office. Sure, there really was a horrible accident; her father was in a coma and Carla sought legal help from a very competent attorney, but there was more that Carla needed from Max Cooper. In her world, the six-figure fee represented mere pennies.

Carla Robeson's DNA, her genome, was programmed to turn *one* dollar into a million. Some folks *earn* money, some people *find* money—Carla's nature was to *make* money. She didn't need the educational degrees she'd earned. She could, and did, make money in the market: commodities, bonds, stocks, it didn't matter. Her chemistry, her biology, her constitutional makeup was designed for commerce. It was genetically preordained.

As she stood shaking hands with Max Cooper, warm as her hands were, there was a cold calculation spinning underneath her demeanor. She needed an IP address that wasn't her own—and the deal she cut with the unwitting young lawyer gave her that.

While still thinking about his lunch rendezvous, the phone buzzed.

"You remember your court appearance at noon, right?"

"Of course," he fibbed. "I'm on my way."

Chapter 4

MAX HAD AGREED to help Quentin Cleveland try to save his house from foreclosure. Ronnie Avery, a real estate lawyer, begged Max to take it on *pro bono* as a personal favor. Mr. Cleveland's hours had been cut at the plant where he worked—apparently his wife forgot the 'richer or poorer' part of the vows—two weeks later she left him in the house with three payments owed. Papers were served. Cleveland, desperate to save his house, rented out the two spare bedrooms. With a little effort, Cleveland thought, he'd save enough money to make up the back payments.

Two of the three roommates, Derek and Patsy Harnett, were more than despairing. They were a complete mess. They'd already lost their home because they spent house payment money trying to save their seven year-old-daughter, Cleo, from leukemia. The house and Cleo were both gone. Derek Harnett had been clinically depressed to the point of a nervous breakdown. He hadn't worked in seven months; he spent most of his time in bed, sleeping, agonizing over the loss of his daughter. Patsy had been the stronger of the two and worked as an operating nurse at Aiken Regional Medical Center. With only one income, they could only afford to pay Cleveland four hundred dollars a month.

The other bedroom was rented to Jimmy Nash, the most pleasant of all people living. He was a thin, nice-looking, sandy-colored haired man in his early thirties. The only thing wrong with him was his smile. His two front teeth overlapped which made his smile a little awkward. Although he didn't have 'Hollywood' choppers, his friendly eyes and his easy-going, honest manner were engaging. People were drawn to him by his inherent niceness. He had a welcoming spirit that was instantly felt by those with whom he made contact. He'd also lost his job and his little house had been sold back to the bank two months before. Of all things, Jimmy decided to be an organic garbage man. He'd heard about the organic craze one night while watching the news and thought it might suit him. His simple life revolved around collecting the food scraps from restaurants, bars and diners and composting them. The business had just gotten started and Jimmy was making enough to pay Quentin another four hundred for his share of the house.

But Jimmy's dream was bigger than that. He had been given his grandfather's house, a beautiful old Southern two-story white-columned home, but it was condemned and about to be taken by the county wrecking ball. Jimmy had to find a way to save that house.

There they stood, the four of them, each one a little worse than the other, Quentin, Jimmy, Derek, and Patsy waiting for Max outside the courtroom when he arrived.

"The lawyer for the bank just told us the judge is waiting for us," Quentin said. "What do we do now?"

"Give me a minute."

Max approached Henry Stokes, counsel for the bank. They had never met before. Stokes was in his early forties. His navy-blue suit and royal blue tie were perfectly coordinated. He was of medium height, had light brown hair, and a slight paunch. He also had stress written all over his oval, pinkish face. Max introduced himself and informed Stokes that he had never handled any foreclosure cases before and hoped Stokes would help Cleveland with some time to make up the back payments.

"The first thing you need to know, Mr. Cooper," Henry Stokes began, "is there is no extra time I can give your client to make up anything. In case you haven't heard, the answer you filed doesn't have any defenses. It just asks for more time. My Motion for Summary Judgment should be granted today. Your client has no defense to this suit. What you want is more time."

Stokes paused, looked at Max and at then at the courtroom door. "There is no extra time in foreclosure land. We get the bums out of their houses when they don't pay. You've heard the old saying: don't pay, don't stay."

Max looked at Henry Stokes and back at the four of them who were out of earshot. "Look Mr. Stokes, this is a case of real tragedy. Mr. Cleveland's hours got cut. He's now renting rooms to those folks. The couple there has had one helluva time. I didn't want to go all into it, but they lost their little girl to leukemia eight months ago. She was their only child. Mr. Harnett has taken it real hard. He's had a nervous breakdown. Mrs. Harnett is working to make ends meet, but they had some outrageous medical expenses trying to keep their daughter alive.

The other guy is picking up trash. They're all chipping in to make up the back payments. Give Cleveland a little bit of time."

Stokes looked Max square in the eyes. "As I said, there is no extra time in foreclosure land," he repeated. "I've heard every excuse known to mankind. I really don't want to know about their medical bills and people who are sick. It's not the bank's problem."

"Their eight-year old daughter isn't sick," Max said quietly. "She's dead."

"One less mouth to feed. Besides, if they've already lost their house, it'll be that much easier to move out of Cleveland's spot." Henry Stokes turned his back, walked to the courtroom door and opened it. He turned to Max who was standing in the large, open hallway. "The judge is waiting on you." Stokes went in while the door slowly closed behind him.

In his short two years of practice, he hadn't met any lawyer who behaved quite like Stokes. Calhoun sometimes talked to Max about opposing counsel who were assholes, but in Aiken, the lawyers were more civil. They knew they would have to run into opposing counsel in some other arena the next time and it wasn't smart to take pot shots at other lawyers and clients. But Stokes was from Charleston and worked for one of the big foreclosure mill law firms. The banks were winning, the law was on their side, and there was no reason for Stokes to be nice. After all, how many houses could one family lose? Max pondered those things for an instant while he turned his pen in his fingers. He knew better than to explain to his group of four sad sacks what had happened between him and Mr. Henry Stokes. It would be better if he tried his luck with the judge. Max opened one of the double doors to the Master-in-Equity's court, the place where the foreclosures were heard. Max hadn't spent much time in that courtroom before. It was where real estate disputes were heard, and his father hadn't really dealt with real estate disputes. Max was in a foreign land.

As Max entered the room, about a fifty by fifty-foot square, there were four benches, church-pew type, to the left side of the courtroom. The benches were stuffed with humanity. There wasn't one place to sit. Max made a quick assessment of the room. There were at least eighty people crammed on the benches, all of them in foreclosure. No other lawyers were in the room. The faces of the people were empty, frightened, stress-filled, and sullen. Max was accustomed to that look, but it was usually in the criminal courts where he could sense the anxiety. This was different. This is where people lost their land, their roots and their homes. As Max looked up and down the pews, the folks in foreclosure either looked away or stared at him with questioning faces, almost begging. Maybe he could help them? Max turned his attention to the bench. Judge Warren wasn't there. Henry Stokes looked at the bailiff inquisitively.

"He took a pee break," the bailiff whispered to Max and Henry.

Max made his way past the wooden rail which separated the benches from the rest of the courtroom where two large oak counsel tables were positioned about ten feet from the judge's elevated bench. Max knew he had a few minutes to gather his thoughts and design an argument that would grant him more time.

It was true. Cleveland didn't have any real defense to the suit. At this point, he hadn't made six payments. Maybe the judge would let him have some more time if he pled hard enough. He looked at Cleveland, a dark black man, medium height, built like a fullback. He was holding his Bible in his thick hands. Derek Harnett stared straight ahead, not appearing to see anything. Patsy was a pretty woman. Her short-cropped blonde hair was combed smartly. She had a very cute figure; whatever she did to take care of herself, it showed. Although they weren't the owners, maybe the judge would have some sympathy with the tough situation of these hard-working folks.

A loud knocking sound came from the bailiff's knuckles smacking against the dark mahogany walls.

"All rise, the Honorable Walter Warren presiding."

Judge Warren was in his mid-sixties, bald. He wore round spectacles, the kind that people wore in old movies. His face was youthful for his years; his eyes had loads of energy with dancing, dark eyebrows.

"Mr. Stokes, this is your Motion for Summary Judgment. Proceed."

Stokes droned on about how Max's answer wasn't a defense and how Cleveland was six payments behind. He presented an affidavit signed by a bank officer about how the note and mortgage were owned by the bank and blah, blah, blah. Judge Warren had heard these a thousand times and looked bored. When Stokes finished, he took a deep breath and suggested the Motion be granted and the property sold. The judge looked at Max Cooper.

"Mr. Cooper, I'm sorry to hear about the loss of your daddy. He and I were in law school together. A fine lawyer and a good man."

"Thank you, Judge. I appreciate that."

"Tell me why I shouldn't grant summary judgment, Mr. Cooper."

"Your Honor, our answer doesn't contain a defense, but Mr. Cleveland came to me last week and told me that he is now sharing the home with these nice folks and with a little time, the back payments can easily be made up."

"Mr. Stokes, what says the bank?"

"Your honor, the fact remains that he is in default on the payments and in default on this lawsuit. There's no defense, just a request for time. There's a difference between a defense and a request. A request gives him nothing at law. With all of that said, the bank is asking to have the property sold at the next sales day, the first Monday of next month."

Unfortunately, Stokes was right. There wasn't any wiggle room when it came to not having a defense. Judge Warren looked over his spectacles at Max.

"I'm sorry, Mr. Cooper, but I'm going to grant summary judgment in favor of the bank, but I'll put the sale out ninety days to give these folks time to make some decisions. The property will be sold at appropriate Monday auction ninety days out."

Henry Stokes looked over his shoulder at the crowd on the benches. He smiled a wry grin at them all. His look let them know that coming to court with a lawyer was of no use to them, either. While Stokes was gloating, Max stepped outside with Cleveland and his three tenants.

"Is there anything we can do?" Cleveland asked.

"I can file a Motion for Reconsideration after I get the signed Order from the court, but I don't have any basis for it as we stand here today."

"Can you look for something?"

"I'll try," Max said quietly. He knew of nothing he could do.

Chapter 5

Carla Robeson didn't like the chair that was part of the Cooper office furniture, so she brought in her own black-leathered, rolling place of comfort for her to work. She was pleased with the large desk, a top big enough for her to spread things out, and she used one of the computers in the office to which she attached an external hard drive.

She didn't have to share the desk or space with anyone and she made herself at home. Max was fine with all of it. He had the one hundred thousand dollars in escrow, and if the mid-fiftyish Carla Robeson wanted to work, she could work. She phoned the Highway Patrol, scheduled the necessary meetings for Max and generally did everything a paralegal would do.

Before she came to "work" at Max's office, she visited her comatose father at the Bladen Home. She saw him every single day, never missing. Carla, like her dad, loved reading the financial news, so she read to him, out loud, the first page of the *Wall Street Journal.* On the weekends, she read selected articles from the *New York Times.* She believed he understood it. It didn't matter. Carla was going to read to him regardless of what anyone else thought about Leland Brunswick's condition.

She loved her father; her dedication to him was something the nurses at the home rarely witnessed, and they welcomed her every day with hugs and smiles.

Carla worked about three days a week at the Law Offices of Cooper and Cooper. From the very beginning, Max didn't pay much attention to what Carla did. Her enthusiasm, skill, and work ethic were beyond reproach. She stayed out of his way. If she needed to tell him something, she wrote a memo and emailed it to him from her office. On the days she worked, she carried a briefcase into the office and left with it. Max innocently assumed the briefcase contained the file on her father's accident.

It didn't contain anything about her dad's case, but the computer at Max's office made it very handy for Carla to do things that mattered to her.

Chapter 6

HUGH BUNCOMBE HAD already gotten his daily load of cash from the Savannah River Site. This day, a Thursday, he'd gotten six hundred dollars, dirt on the bills, out near left field.

He had a new habit since becoming cash enhanced every day. He got his money and then settled into a wooden chair on the sidewalk at the *New Moon Café*, a popular little spot where office folks stopped for a shot of caffeine on their way to work. It was only a block away from Max Cooper's office and Hugh stopped in, Bailey on a leash, to get a cup of java.

Hugh didn't see it coming, but dogs are magnets for women. It's true. Put any man—old, young, ugly, handsome—it doesn't matter—with a dog somewhere and women will talk to that man. Put the same guy in the same place without a dog—a woman wouldn't think of making conversation. Of course, Hugh didn't know it at the time, and he sure didn't bring Bailey with him to find women, but this day, although it was a day like any other—a day of bright sunshine on a chilly morning in January—turned out to be one of those monumental days when everything changed. And it was all because Hugh brought Bailey to get coffee.

He sat at one of the outside tables under a big red umbrella with the Cheerwine logo on it, Bailey wagging his tail at every passerby. Since finding the money, Hugh had become interested in the history of the Savannah River Site property. This particular day he was reading *The Unexpected Exodus*, a book about how entire little towns were moved from the SRS property in a matter of a few months after the government decided to build its nuclear bombs on the land where small farmers had been successfully tilling the dirt for two hundred years. Hugh thought the book might give him a clue about how and why he was finding cash at Rhodes Field.

Hugh, who was reading and not paying attention to anything but his book, didn't notice the young woman approach. She was young and beautiful, early twenties, big brown eyes, light brown, shoulder-length hair. She wore blue jeans and a thin, large, black sweatshirt with a white Nike logo on it. Her well-figured body was hidden under the big sweatshirt, but it was obvious she had lovely curves.

Bailey wagged his tail with great vigor as she approached.

"Hey buddy," she said, petting Bailey.

Bailey stood up, getting the full benefit of the head scratching she delivered. "He's a good boy," she said to Bailey in a coquettish tone. She turned to Hugh. "College professor?" she asked, looking over Hugh's shoulder at his book.

"Amateur historian," Hugh responded, looking up. "I used to work at the bomb plant."

"Ellenton and Dunbarton were two of the lost towns."

"Sounds like you might have some amateur historian interests yourself."

"I'm a writer for *The Standard.* Lived here all my life. I love the old stories of the plant property. It's too bad some of those towns had to go."

Hugh closed his book and looked at her. He wasn't good at small talk, but she was the prettiest young woman he'd ever laid eyes on—and she didn't have that "I'm too good to talk to you" attitude that so many of the gorgeous ones have.

"What kind of history are you interested in?" she continued with her journalist's curiosity. *She is genuinely asking me questions,* he thought. The curmudgeon in him wouldn't allow him to be exactly bubbly, but she was *so* pretty, he *had* to chat.

"I like all kinds of history. When I retired, I decided to learn about some of the Revolutionary War and Civil War sites around South Carolina."

"That's so cool," she said, as she boldly sat down across from Hugh in one of the other, small wooden café chairs. "I got a degree in journalism and a minor in history a few years ago. There are some great books I could turn you on to."

Hugh smiled. That was an event. He didn't always break into *that.*

"Hey Mandy," a mid-fifties-looking woman said, standing at the door of the café, "I got here a little early. I ordered your coffee and a muffin."

"Thanks Kathy," Mandy said, "I'll get us a table out here."

Mandy took a quick inventory of tables, and seeing none, looked at Hugh. "Would you mind if we joined you? We won't bite."

"Sure," he said. He'd rather have said no, but Mandy had already charmed him.

Mandy helped Kathy bring out their coffee and muffins while Hugh put his book away. Bailey quickly accepted his new friends as any Labrador would, excitedly swishing his tail and loving the new soft hands on his head.

"I don't even know your name," Mandy said, looking up from Bailey to Hugh.

"His name is Bailey. I'm Hugh. Hugh Buncombe." He stuck out his hand like he didn't really want to shake hands. Mandy grabbed his hand and squeezed tight. "Mandy Alexander."

"Hi," Kathy said, standing behind Mandy. "I'm Kathy Gates." She also gave Hugh a firm handshake.

"Oh my god," Mandy said, pulling her chair up to the table, "you're Mr. Buncombe. You're Michelle Buncombe's husband. She was my favorite teacher in the whole world. I came to the funeral."

Hugh was impressed. He looked at Mandy as he tried to remember her. There were so many people at the funeral Hugh didn't know.

"She was a special woman," Hugh said, hoping the topic would go away. He didn't like talking about Michelle with strangers.

But Mandy wouldn't quit. "Mrs. Buncombe made me want to read," she said, looking at Kathy, "she showed me how reading could be fun. She is probably one of the biggest reasons I am a reporter for *The Standard.* This man was married to my favorite teacher." And then turning back to Hugh she added,

"Kathy is my mentor. She recently retired from the paper and she's helping me to be the best reporter I can be."

"She doesn't need much help," Kathy said. "She's nice enough to have coffee with me most mornings while I help her negotiate the politics of the paper and the town."

"My goal is to write books one day," Mandy said, "Kathy is teaching me about the newspaper side of things, but I want to write fiction. I've got goals."

Kathy looked at Hugh, leaned forward and touched his arm. "She doesn't need me," she said, "she's talented beyond my abilities and she's not even twenty-five."

Kathy Gates was attractive—blonde and blue-eyed—with crow's feet around her eyes and little lines on her upper lip. There was not one gray hair in her head. She was tall, not much shorter than Hugh, and slender. And she was touching Hugh's arm like they were old friends.

Mandy interrupted Kathy. "I've got goals," she repeated. "And I've figured out the best way to achieve those goals is with a little help from people who know their way around. Kathy wrote for *The Standard* for twenty years. She knows how to get a story, and she can write."

Kathy had removed her hand from Hugh's arm, but continued to look Hugh in the eye. "Twenty years was enough for me," she said, "now I work at Aiken Saddlery. Selling tack and horse supplies is easier. The pace and deadlines of the newspaper wore me out. So now I work three days a week. And I have coffee with Mandy several times a week to keep up with things."

Hugh looked up from Kathy and spotted Max Cooper walking toward the café.

"Max, how goes it?"

"Hey, Mr. Buncombe. I haven't forgotten that answer you want. Give me a few more days."

"No problem. Take your time," Hugh responded in a friendly tone while Max made his way into the *New Moon.*

"You know him?" Mandy asked.

"Yeah, he's helping with Michelle's estate. Getting me an answer on something."

Mandy couldn't help but comment. "He's a known womanizer. He probably hasn't gotten you an answer because he's been busy with his body parts instead of his brain."

"That seems a little out of character," Hugh defended, "he's helping me with some estate work. I've found him to be very responsible."

"Whatever. I've heard he sleeps with half of Aiken. The other half are men."

"Wow, you have an opinion on *him*, now don't you?

"He's three years older than me. When I was a freshman in high school, he was a senior. He was an excellent student, but I don't think he could throw a baseball. Now he seems to throw himself from one woman's bed to another."

"How do you know all of this stuff?" Hugh asked.

"It's a small town, Hugh," she said, "he sleeps with a neighbor of one of our people in the advertising department. Some forty-year-old divorcée. The employee says he comes and goes at all hours of the night."

"Oh."

Mandy was finished with *that* conversation and Hugh determined to leave it alone. He liked his new coffee mates and didn't want to spend his time defending his decision on his lawyer. All Hugh wanted to do was to find out if he could legally spend the thirty-some-odd thousand dollars he had in his little liquor bags.

As for Hugh, after he finished his coffee, he stood up, shook the hands of his new friends and wished them a pleasant day. He rubbed the money in his pocket as he headed to his truck.

"Nice guy," Kathy said as he walked away, "and damned handsome, especially for a man his age."

"Is that how we define attractive these days? We say damned handsome? I can write that in the paper?"

"Ok, in the newspaper story you would write something like "older man maintained well," she teased, "He seems like a really good guy. Sorry about his wife."

As the women chatted about Hugh's good looks, a beat-up black Ford Ranger pulled into a parking place across the street. Jimmy Nash hopped out of the truck wearing work gloves and carrying a black plastic bag. He walked into the rear entrance of the *New Moon.* At the rear of the store was a sealed fifty-five-gallon drum lined with another thick plastic bag filled to the brim with organic garbage, tossed out bagels, used coffee grounds, eggshells, anything but plastic. Jimmy nodded to some of the workers as he unsealed the drum, picked up the full bag and put the fresh bag into the drum. He then took a rag from his pocket and a spray bottle from his belt and cleaned the top of the drum.

The proprietor of the *New Moon* was trying Jimmy Nash's service that removed the organic trash every day. Jimmy was making his rounds, hoping to crawl out of his own barrel of financial ruin. But Jimmy, typical Jimmy Nash, smiled at everyone and every thing, happy to be making a living doing anything.

Jimmy waved at Max as they both walked away from the *New Moon*. Max also gave a little nod to Mandy and Kathy as he walked by carrying his large cup of coffee. He had just passed their little table when his phone rang.

"Hello."

"Max, Carla here. Do you have any plans tomorrow night? I want you to come to dinner at my house. You can bring a date or a friend. I thought we'd get to know each other a little better. I promise I won't spend all of our time talking about my father's accident."

"Carla. I'll be there. And I've got a buddy."

Times were set and the address given. Max was going to the Leland Brunswick Mansion for dinner the next night.

Chapter 7

MAX DIALED SCOTT as he walked back to his office.

"So that's what you were thinking?" Scott asked. "You were thinking I didn't have a hot date on Friday night?"

"I know you don't have anything to do."

"Right."

Scott Rowan had a degree in art history. Some college students took that course of study because it seemed easy, but Scott loved art. He could draw, and a great way to meet women was to draw caricatures. He loved painting, sculpture, architecture, and ancient pottery, all of it. He liked, and could intelligently discuss, Renaissance Art, the Masters, primitive art, and the most modern trends. It was his passion; selling pharmaceuticals was how he made a living, but his goal was to become a curator of a museum or own his own art gallery. And it didn't hurt that he could paint a little too. He was quite good with a canvas.

Scott was a very handsome man—he had thick blond hair that he kept unkempt. His light blue eyes matched his blondness and with an athletic, thin frame at six feet one, he had no trouble attracting the fairer sex.

Scott and Max had been fraternity brothers at the University of South Carolina. Kappa Alpha had seen thousands of brothers in its long history; many of them became governors, United States senators, attorneys general and other rather important-sounding folks. Max didn't hurt the fraternity's goal to have a high-grade point average and Scott Rowan helped keep the intramural athletic competition strong. They had been roommates in their last year at the university. Three years later when Max finished law school, Scott had moved to Aiken, bought a two-bedroom condo, and was working as a pharmaceutical rep. The two of them were great wingmen for each other. The dating scene is always easier with a buddy and Max and Scott were perfect together.

"The Leland Brunswick Cottage?" he asked Max. "You're kidding."

"Carla Robeson is my client. Her great-grandfather was Leland Brunswick."

"Holy shit. Do you *know* how famous he was?"

Although Max Cooper was a life-long resident of Aiken, he'd never been to a "cottage" that wasn't a museum or converted into a bed and breakfast. The Leland Brunswick cottage was on Russell Street, a broad unpaved avenue. That's another thing about the cottages. The streets aren't paved. That's because the owners have horses and they ride to the polo fields or just down the wide dirt lane to the two-thousand-acre Hitchcock Woods where horses can gallop endlessly without seeing one ounce of asphalt. It was still that way in 2017.

Scott was more excited about seeing the cottage than Max. Scott didn't have to worry about making an impression on Carla and Max knew, he *knew* that Carla's case would come up.

When Max pulled his brown Tahoe into the paved circular drive, Scott looked at Max.

"Wow, dude," Scott said, "this really is the Leland Brunswick Cottage. I've seen it in magazines. This house is where the richest guys in America brought their girlfriends for a month. There were parties here that made Gatsby look like a bantamweight."

Scott opened the car door.

"Don't get out of the car yet, Scott," he said, "*promise* me, look me in the eye and *promise* me you won't start asking about parties. This is a client of mine and she seems pretty stiff. I don't want any embarrassing questions from you tonight."

"Yeah, I understand. But what if she *volunteers* that information?"

"No embarrassing questions. This lady is not one of your widows or pickups. And her dad is in a coma. *And*, I told her you were an Art History major. She invited you because she thinks you'll make conversation about art."

"Maxxy, I just wanna feel the karma of this place. There was probably more liquor spilled in here than I could drink in a lifetime. Maybe I'll just ask about the human sacrifices."

Max looked at Scott with a whiff of disgust.

"There were no human sacrifices."

"I know. But how else can I put you on edge without threatening a little stupidity?"

They were at the front entrance.

The front door wasn't really a door. There were two twelve-foot-tall carved wooden doors with one-foot stained-glass windows on the sides. There was no doorbell, but there was a large doorknocker in the shape of a horseshoe. Before Max could knock, the door opened. Carla Robeson stood behind her housekeeper, a Hispanic woman in her early forties.

"There is no door bell, Max, but the knocker makes it sound like there's been one of those atom bombs exploded over at the SRS. We picked you up on the video cameras when you pulled up. Would you gentlemen like an adult beverage?"

She was wearing a royal blue Eileen Fisher ensemble and holding a crystal tumbler with ice and a circular slice of carved cucumber. Scott knew it was a Hendrix gin and tonic.

"If that's Hendrix," Scott said, "I'll have the same."

"You know your gin." she commented.

"I know Hendrix, and with that carved cucumber, you must be drinking Hendrix," Scott said, feeling immediately at ease with Carla Robeson.

"I'll have a Heineken if you have it," Max said.

"I think we might find a Heineken somewhere," Carla said, strolling through the broad foyer carrying her gin and tonic in her right hand and signaling to her maid with her left toward the kitchen where she knew to wait thirty minutes so the guests and host could enjoy a few cocktails.

The entrance was splendid; there was a curved staircase on the left, a "flying staircase" with no support underneath, that went to the second floor. As Carla walked through the open room, Max realized that the "room" was really the foyer. The floors were broad-planked dark heart pine. Carla turned to the right through a large archway and there stood another room, completely open with a twenty-foot-long white marble bar, liquor bottles behind it, lit up with lights hidden in places that only an electrician could find. There was the bottle of Hendrix by itself, sitting on top of the bar with a bowl of cucumbers soaking in gin. The room was massive, a pool table sitting atop a Persian rug midway through the big room. The sides of the walls, which were white bead board, were lined with tall chairs with all the pool cues and other implements of the game standing at attention in proper racks.

There was a dartboard several feet away from the pool table, the darts in sets of green, blue, red, and yellow on a well-placed table underneath. Nothing was out of place.

Scott chatted with Carla as she poured him a stiff Hendrix and tonic and added the infused cucumbers. Max took in the room. He felt, in a very cozy way, some glorious energy that seemed to ooze out of the walls. It was an awesome bar.

"You play pool?" Max asked standing next to the carved mahogany table.

"No," Carla said, "My father is an excellent pool player. I play darts."

"I play darts, too," Scott said, sipping his drink as Carla handed Max a frosted pilsner glass with the Heineken filled to the top.

Carla gracefully moved to the dart boxes, offering Max the box with the red darts and pointed to the yellow ones for Scott.

"I'm partial to the green ones," she said, "gentlemen, my guests, you play first."

Scott threw four darts, the best one landing in the third rung nearest the center.

Max followed, also not exactly doing well.

Carla Robeson stood at the line, closed her left eye, and threw the first dart that missed the bull's eye by a half inch. She cursed a little under her breath. The next dart hit the bull's eye and the following two missed it by maybe a quarter inch from the top.

"Holy crap, Carla, I mean, Ms. Robeson," Scott said, "That's unbelievable."

"It's Carla, my good friend and fellow gin lover. I've played a lot of darts, gentlemen. A lot of darts."

"Tell me about the parties here, Carla," Scott said, "I've heard some stories."

Max shot a glance at Scott that Carla noticed. She put up her hand at Max's look.

"It's ok, Max," she said, "we're going to get to know each other. And now you know not to play darts against me for money. Let's get another drink and head toward the veranda. We can chat before dinner."

Carla led them out of two large French doors at the far end of the bar which led to a patio where four, large circular teak tables sat with six matching teak chairs with comfortable padded seats. Scott felt like he'd gone to heaven when he sat down.

"This is some place," Scott gushed, looking out, probably three hundred yards past a stand of live oaks and tall pines that defined the border at the rear of the estate.

Carla didn't respond to Scott as she chose the table nearest to the kitchen and waved at the housekeeper who stood at the doorway to the cooking area. She knew what that meant. Dinner would be served on the veranda.

Scott couldn't help himself as he continued, "I mean this place is like a piece of art, Carla. The parties here were beyond legendary. They're a part of American history. Do you have any pictures?"

Max made another face at Scott that Carla noticed but ignored.

"I do have pictures, Scott. They're interesting, you might say, but I'm not into the pictures of what happened here. However, since Max is my lawyer, you both might as well know the truth about this place and my family history, not just the rumors that seem to make things bigger than they were. Some stories have become legendary as you suggest Scott, but I'm pleased that you've heard of my great-grandfather, Leland Brunswick. Of course, the true eccentric was his son, Leland Brunswick, Jr."

Scott and Max nodded to Carla and they sipped their drinks and she continued.

"My great-grandfather built this place. It was much smaller; the bones of it barely exist now. It was my grandfather, who was a bit of a dandy, who really embraced Aiken life. The junior Mr. Brunswick came here to avoid my grandmother who wanted nothing to do with travel or the South. My grandfather liked to shoot quail, doves and wild turkeys. He believed in the life of gentility," she said as she waved her left hand at the rear of the house, "good weather, horses, and excellent liquor. He was a hippophile and a philogynist. Being a lover of women meant he didn't believe in fidelity. He added on to the cottage and made it his own personal getaway. He brought his girlfriends here, sometimes two at a time. He had a gluttonous sexual appetite. His first two wives tolerated his indiscretions, of which there were plenty. His third wife became my grandmother, my father being born when my grandfather was fifty. My grandmother turned out to be a terrific mother who raised my dad in New York and Connecticut, mainly. Although my grandfather was becoming older, he continued his rather unruly, ribald existence, as my grandmother distanced herself from him. This house, this garden, this estate, was a bacchanalian paradise, especially in the fall and spring. And that's why the parties are so well known. They would last two weeks, you know. Guests came from all over the country and rode horses; they fox hunted, drank liquor, and enjoyed the outdoors—and their girlfriends. It was a wild, different time."

Carla stopped for a moment, looking at the expansive estate, focusing on the acreage in the backyard. She continued: "My father is different than my grandfather. My grandmother's maternal instincts were excellent for my father, whom she raised under strict supervision and care. He served in the Army during World War II. My grandmother died of breast cancer while he was overseas. My father barely knew about this place until he was a grown man. He has been a superb steward of my grandfather's property, all of it. My grandfather was an ostentatious, overbearing, sybaritic narcissistic roué who would have squandered his fortune had it not been for my father. I've been very fortunate to have such a wonderful man as a dad."

Carla stopped talking again. She took a deep breath, pushing the air out of her lungs very slowly. "He's in that coma now," she said, "I want him to wake up and come home to me. That's what I want. I don't want him to die until I tell him again how much I love him."

Even Scott knew it was time to quit asking questions about parties. Max and Scott looked at each other as Carla gained her composure. Before anyone could say anything, the maid approached the table with plates filled with food.

"Max said you gentlemen don't have any special culinary restrictions, so I thought we'd have a filet," she said, as the plates of steak, baked potatoes and asparagus were placed in front of them. The maid supplied white-cloth napkins and silverware, *real* silverware, and opened a bottle of Silver Oak, a cabernet sauvignon that Carla had chosen in advance. After patiently waiting for everyone to get their crystal wine glass filled, Carla said, like she was starting an event, "Dig in, gentlemen, I'm glad you got to come out tonight. I'm looking forward to getting to know my lawyer a little better; we've got a long road ahead. I appreciate Max here allowing me to help with the case."

They ate; the young men quietly enjoyed the most tender filet that had ever graced their taste buds. Carla also had little to say as she carefully sliced a piece of steak and followed it with a gentle sip of Silver Oak.

Scott knew that Carla and Max could talk about the terrible accident for the next hour and he wasn't ready to listen to that boring discussion. Scott also knew that it was time to leave Leland Brunswick's memory alone. As any good salesman is keenly aware, people find themselves to be very interesting. He went right to Carla. "Tell me about yourself, Carla," Scott said, "if you haven't been living here, where have you been staying?" Max cut another rough look at Scott. This time Carla didn't even notice it. Scott had struck gold and Carla had just enough gin and wine to loosen her tongue.

"I've been in New York for the past thirty years," she said, "working in the market. After finishing my Master's degree in finance at Wharton, I was given an opportunity on the street. It's hard to believe that thirty years have blown by. I've been married and divorced, no children. My ex-husband and I are still good friends. We didn't see eye to eye because I worked too hard. He's a little lazy, only working sixty hours a week." She stopped for a moment and cut a stalk of asparagus into four small portions. Max looked at Scott and slightly raised his left eyebrow—sixty hours a week was hardly a sign of lethargy. Scott knew that Carla was getting warmed up and waited for her to continue instead of asking another question. He was right.

"I take a little after my Grandfather Brunswick. Although he played hard, maybe a little *too* hard, he worked long hours, sometimes days at a time, sleeping very little. I also worked. I enjoyed the market." If Carla Robeson had been a Stepford wife, Max and Scott would have thought "the market" is where she shopped for cute dresses and fine jewelry, but they knew the market wasn't where groceries and dry goods were purchased. This time Carla took another sip.

"Let me tell you young gentlemen something," she said with a little fire in her eyes, "there is no satiety in corporate America. Every corporation lives by the quarter, constantly chasing the next ninety days' numbers. But even after a company has a record year, doubling profits, exceeding EBITDA by stellar proportions, the market insists that the next quarter be better than the last. There is no satisfaction on Wall Street." Carla was in her own private reverie; she sat back in the big comfortable white-cushioned, teak chair and looked out beyond the croquet court. And then she sat up and drank the last of the wine in her glass. Scott stood up, gently grasped the wine bottle, and filled her glass as Carla waved to the housekeeper for another bottle of Silver Oak.

"In the market today, there are no rewards for doing the right thing. The rewards are only for producing a quarter better than the last one. If the CEO knows something is wrong with their product, he or she spend most of their time covering it up instead of fixing it. Look at the number of recalls by General Motors. Don't you know that *somewhere* in the bowels of GM there is a report that said, "We have a problem?" The CEO then spends all her time in front of Congress apologizing. If they had fixed the problem, there didn't have to be an apology. But corporate America doesn't reward honesty in business. It gives dividends, not medals of Honor. My grandfather, as crazy as he was about women and booze, did the right thing in his business. And since his company wasn't publicly held, he didn't have to answer to anyone. He didn't receive any merits of recognition, but he never had to apologize to America or Congress. He made money and did the right thing."

The second bottle of Silver Oak was open; the housekeeper poured a little more for all three of them. Scott was more willing to ask tough questions than Max, knowing if Max challenged his client on things unrelated to the legal matter he was handling, it could make their future relationship difficult. Scott pushed on. "But your great-grandfather had a monopoly on railroad tracks. He kept competitors from getting into business. It's well documented."

"My great-grandfather and his son were both ruthless businessmen," she admitted, "but they did the right thing by people. My great-grandfather gave his employees the highest wages among the robber barons. He didn't fight the unions because he didn't have to. His employees never joined because his wages exceeded the union pay scale."

She stopped again, this time looking at Scott and then Max.

"What's worse about the market these days is that 'it is what it is' as they say and it's not going to change."

It was quiet again. Carla was finished with her soliloquy. She turned to Max.

"Enough about the past here," she said, "Max, tell me about your family."

"Not much to tell," Max said, "As you know, my father died several months ago. My mother passed away when I was eleven. No brothers or sisters, just me. I'm the end of the line. I am still playing the field. My friend Scott here says he's going to wait until he's thirty. Something about a Bacchanalian Rite of Passage, except on a much smaller scale than your grandfather." Max slapped Scott on the back as Carla smiled.

"I understand," Carla said, looking at the young men.

"And you," she said to Scott, "you're the art enthusiast, right?"

"I love art," Scott said, "but you need to know more about Max than he's letting on. He graduated at the top of his law school class at the University of Virginia. He had offers from every major law firm in America to make a lot of money, but he came home to be with his dad. And he follows your work ethic. He works every Sunday, usually ten hours, to get ready for the next week. You've chosen one good lawyer."

"I know," she said, "I checked him out. He won half million dollars in his first jury trial. People around here know him."

"See?" Scott looked at Max, who had hung his head. He was uncomfortable hearing about himself, especially in glowing terms.

"I was also blessed with a good father," Max said, "I'll try to help you every way I can."

They shifted to small talk for a time and wound up the evening by taking a stroll in the English garden with Carla pointing out the plants and designating them with their Latin names. It was a little after ten when they left, still early for a Friday night for the young men. As soon as they shut the doors to Max's car, Scott sent a text. And he looked at Max. "I think Carla's sorta hot for an older woman; she's got a lot of tenderness underneath that tough armor."

"You are one sick individual," Max said, while he worked his own phone.

"Does she always talk that way—with those big words? I should hang around her just to improve my vocabulary. And I could teach her dirty words. It'd be a match made in heaven."

"She always talks like that. It's just the way she is. And didn't you just send a text to The Widow Amber? Have you no shame? You're already seeing a woman, not *dating* I might add, who is in her early forties. You don't need another old cougar."

"You've got a lot of room to talk; Dharma is over forty."

Scott's phone buzzed.

"I got my Amber Alert."

"You mean your request for sex has been granted."

Max's phone showed a message. Dharma had also confirmed.

The boys were off to their play dates.

As for Carla Robeson, she was pleased with the evening. She retired to her bedroom, putting on her silk nightgown, propped herself into her king-sized bed with a large sham to support her back and opened her MacBook Air. She had some things to check on, in the market. Carla Robeson didn't enjoy television. It was the stock market that she loved to watch.

It's a funny thing about wealthy people. They have instant credibility with people who have less money than them. A rich person could tell the biggest lie about how they made money or their family history and it wouldn't matter. They have money. That's what matters to people who don't have wealth. Carla had played this card many times before in her life. And she'd played it with Max and Scott. She was worth over six hundred million dollars, which was good, but she had some things to hide.

Chapter 8

BAILEY LOVED GOING to the money field. Hugh scrounged around with a stick, poking at the ground and usually found a few stray one-hundred-dollar bills. Bailey barked, ran around, pulled on Hugh's stick and dug in the ground. It was fun.

For Hugh, determined to find the source of the money, it was maddening. He knew there was a secret to this whole money thing, but what was it? Maybe Max Cooper was right. It could have been a drug dealer or a guy who was serving time waiting to come back for his loot. It made Hugh *very* nervous. Hugh frequently looked over his shoulder, intuitively thinking he was being watched, but this was an abandoned old field that hadn't been used in sixty years and was closed to the public. Still, Hugh looked. This day, a Friday, he found three hundred bucks during his thirty-minute limit, stuffed them into the front pocket of his jeans and headed to the *New Moon.*

Mandy was there, as always. Kathy wasn't.

"Kathy coming?"

"It's Friday," she said, "Fridays are different."

She sipped her coffee out of the thick paper cup that said *New Moon Café* on it. Before she could explain what she meant, a tribe of six folks, including Kathy, showed up carrying a small, insulated soft cooler. "Here they are," Mandy said eagerly to Hugh.

"Hey y'all," Mandy said to the troupe.

"Champagner's 1836!" one of them cheered as they strode into the *New Moon.*

Kathy stopped at Mandy and Hugh's table. "You really ought to join us," she said to Mandy, "you don't have to get a buzz, just have one drink. No one at the paper will care."

"There's a no alcohol rule, Kathy. You know that."

One of the older men piped in, "Are you going kitesurfing this weekend?"

"It's kiteboarding," Mandy said, "how many times do I have to tell you? Kiteboarding. And no, I'm joining y'all at the polo match tomorrow."

Kathy looked at Hugh. "You want some champagne?"

"No thanks."

And then Kathy whispered to Mandy and Hugh, "don't tell the others, but we drink sparkling wine and call it Champagne. You know how we Americans are. Crass pretenders. Champagne only comes from France." She turned and joined her group who entered the café, cooler and cups in hand.

"You know them?" Hugh asked Mandy.

"Oh yeah," she said, "They're quite a group. They have champagne every Friday morning. I wrote a story about them in the "Living" section of the Sunday paper several months ago. They celebrate every Friday morning with some champagne, then go home and get ready for the weekend. The local restaurants let them bring in their champagne on Fridays and have mimosas and breakfast."

"Celebrate what?" Hugh asked.

"They celebrate life. It's what I wrote about in the paper. They decided a few years ago to celebrate life every day they can. On Fridays, they celebrate with champagne. They said when they were younger, they saved champagne for special occasions. Now that they're older they see that every day of good health with good friends is a special occasion. So, they drink champagne every Friday morning. It's called Champagne Friday."

"What does Champagner's 1836 mean?"

"It's the name of their club."

"Club?"

"It's complete bullshit. They said they needed a name, so they made it up. The year 1836 sounds like it was founded long ago—so they've made up stories about the founding mothers and fathers, all fake stuff. Every now and then one of them shouts 1836 and they all cheer. It's hilarious."

"It sounds like they have an alcohol problem."

"Not at all. They're all over fifty-five and have been extremely productive folks."

"I bet they're all Aikenites."

"They're from all over. Some have been here all their lives. Others are horse folks from up north. Do I detect some jealousy?"

"No," he said, picking up his coffee with the authority of a school principal. "I don't drink in the morning."

Mandy wasn't going to let Hugh go on that remark. "Have you ever *tried* champagne in the morning?"

"I'm no drunk. I don't even like champagne."

Mandy leaned into Hugh. "How many bottles of champagne did you and Michelle drink during your life together?"

Hugh put his coffee on the wooden table and looked toward the sky, thinking.

"If you can count them, you haven't had enough. I can tell you haven't enjoyed yourself like you should, Mr. Buncombe," she said, purposely calling him Mr. Buncombe. "You don't know if you like champagne because you haven't tasted it enough to know if you like it. You ought to go in there and join Kathy and the rest of them and taste some champagne and lighten up a little."

Hugh looked at her. He'd only known her two weeks and there she was telling him what to do. And worse for Hugh, he felt a teensy-weensy bit of jealousy about Kathy being with the *Champagner's 1836*. It's a phenomenon that men experience. If a woman talks to a man for a few minutes—if a woman, any *attractive* woman gives a man some one on one—that man, for whatever unknown reason, is slightly jealous when she picks up and leaves with some *other* man. Hugh stupidly felt since he had become coffee buddies with Kathy, a coffee buddy that he didn't even wish to be, Hugh now felt that Kathy owed him some allegiance. How dare she go off with an undeserving, lesser pile of humanity when it was *his* time to be with Kathy?

Hugh still hadn't answered Mandy about needing to lighten up.

"Well," she said, "are you going to go taste champagne? You were invited. You might like those people; they're your age. Go play in the sandbox with those folks and drink something."

A roar came from the *New Moon*: "1836!" Laughter followed.

Hugh stood up. Coffee was finished, and he wasn't about to have Mandy tell him what to do, even if he was young enough to have some fun.

"I'll pass on the drunk Friday routine."

"You shouldn't," she said, as Hugh put Bailey into the back of the truck.

"See you Monday," he waved to her, and then to himself he mumbled in his best curmudgeon style, *Champagne Friday my ass.*

Just as he got into his truck, he received a text message from Maxwell Cooper. *Got a minute?* Hugh dialed Max's office.

"Don't spend that money, Mr. Buncombe. It's federal property. It's not your money. We might ask the government for a reward for finding it, but I don't know how that will turn out."

"Ain't that some shit." They talked for a few minutes, but the message was clear from Max Cooper. It wasn't Hugh's money. Hugh was playing with fire if he spent the cash and it may be that he didn't get to keep any of it.

"I'm gonna keep stashing it away until I find out why it's there." He told Max.

"As long as you know the rules, Mr. Buncombe. As long as you know the rules."

Rules are made to be broken, Hugh said to himself as he drove off.

Chapter 9

QUENTIN CLEVELAND'S HOUSE was a three-bedroom, one story, brick, ranch-style house with a carport. It had two and a half baths, a great room, and an eat-in kitchen. There was a formal dining room, but no one ever ate dinner in there, even when Quentin and Keisha were together.

They'd all been roommates for a week. Jimmy, trying to be nice, looked at Patsy. He sensed she had a case of the nerves.

"I'm sorry about your daughter and you losin' your home and all."

Patsy nodded but said nothing.

"Look," he said, "I lost my house. I figure we can make the best of a bad situation. I got one thing I do real well. I can clean. I can clean anything. Jimmy Nash don't like messes. If I clean, can you help with the cookin'? I'll clean up the dishes, I can vacuum, I can scrub toilets. I wanna be a good roommate."

Patsy stared at Jimmy. He was nice enough looking with sandy colored hair, long arms and legs, and kind eyes. She knew he was trying to be friendly.

"I can cook as good as anybody," she replied, "but my hours at work don't always put me at home in time to cook. I appreciate the offer to help with the cleaning. I'm sure the four of us can figure something out. We have to figure things out, don't we?"

"Yeah, we gotta figure things out," he said, looking down, "I'll do my part, that's all I'm sayin'."

They both looked at the television; there was some show on about a crime scene and a murder that one of the genius cops was going to figure out at the end. Jimmy and Patsy weren't really paying attention to it.

"I know this is Quentin's house," Patsy said to the TV, "but I want to get us all together and figure out money and chores around the house. I don't like living without some ground rules."

"That's what I'm saying, Mrs. Harnett."

"Patsy."

They looked at the TV a few more seconds. One of the cops put drops of something into a petri dish. It turned blue.

"The last time I had roommates, I was in nursing school. It was horrible."

"I never went to college," Jimmy said, "but I've heard stories. I think we can work together. Let's make the best of this."

Patsy didn't respond.

"Hey," he said, "is your husband okay? He doesn't say much."

"He's had a nervous breakdown," she said calmly, "he's having a tough time dealing with the loss of our daughter."

"Oh."

Patsy kept her eyes on the TV show, not really watching.

"Hey look," Jimmy said, "we'll all make the best of this."

"We have to; we're all out of choices. We've got ninety days to move or find money that none of us have."

Chapter 10

PATSY HARNETT AND Quentin Cleveland left the house before seven a.m. Jimmy Nash cleaned up the kitchen and put the coffee cups in the dishwasher. Derek Harnett was up, sitting on the couch watching the *Today* show. Jimmy wanted to get to know his "nervous breakdown" roommate a little better. He also knew that being in the house all day wasn't the cure for a nervous breakdown.

"What you doin' today?" Jimmy asked Derek.

"I don't know; I don't feel like doing much of anything. I might go back to bed in a little while."

"It's eight o'clock in the morning, man. I got something you can help me with, if you want to."

"I don't feel so good."

"Come on, man, I can use some help. All you need to do is ride with me. You don't even have to get out of the car."

Derek Harnett looked at Jimmy. *Maybe,* he thought, *Jimmy can take me to the mini-warehouse where Cleo's bedroom furniture is stored. I can pick up some things from her room and bring them to this new place. Patsy wouldn't let me bring anything.*

"Can you take me someplace if I come with you?" Derek asked.

Jimmy wanted to help.

"Yeah, sure."

Derek sat for a minute looking at the TV. There was a commercial. Jimmy was already moving, making his bed, and putting things away in the bathroom. *I guess I'll go*, Derek thought. *How bad can it be?*

Jimmy didn't know it, but it would be the first time Derek Harnett had left the house without Patsy in five months. He hadn't even gone to the grocery store without her at his side.

Jimmy opened the driver's door to his weathered, faded black Ford Ranger. Derek stood at the door staring at Jimmy.

"Let's go."

Derek remained in the doorway, looking at the sky this time. It was a bright, crisp February morning.

Jimmy started the truck. "Let's go," he repeated from inside the truck, waving at Derek.

Derek looked up again. And then he did it. He walked to the truck, opened the door and got inside. He had barely shut the door when Jimmy backed out of the driveway and mashed the gas pedal sending them off to Jimmy's job.

Chapter 11

To Derek, Jimmy's job seemed like a complete waste of time. At least that's what he thought on the first day. Jimmy rode around to twenty bars, ten restaurants, and three Waffle Houses. He did things that made no sense to Derek, but Derek didn't care; Jimmy was pleasant to be with and seemed to move non-stop. It was good for Derek.

Jimmy had learned how to make a living out of trash. It was a natural progression for him once he lost his job at the plant. He survived by cleaning up after people and collecting things he needed to fix up his granddaddy's old mansion house that was on the edge of town.

The first thing he did was make a deal with the managers of the local restaurants to put the scraps of food into a fifty-five-gallon drum that Jimmy provided. The staff of the bars and restaurants didn't mind the extra trash bin because Jimmy came by every day and picked up the discarded food and cleaned the rest of the trash area. It was easy to like Jimmy because he cleaned better than the staff and made small talk while he did it. And he took the waste with him. He was never late and never missed picking up his "trash."

Then Jimmy went to Waffle Houses. There were three of them in the Aiken area. He'd made a deal with them to pick up their organic trash—the eggshells and old food that had been thrown out. The wait staff separated the organic trash inside the stores and he'd pick it up for twenty dollars a week. Thirty-three customers at twenty dollars a week made him six hundred and sixty dollars a week. The Waffle Houses loved it because its trash bins were less full and they had cut down on trash pick-up from three days a week to two. Jimmy didn't know it, but the Waffle Houses were saving fifty bucks a week on the trash pick-up. Paying him twenty meant they were saving thirty bucks a week per restaurant. It was a good deal for everyone.

Since they loved Jimmy so much, and he was so nice to them, he ate at one of the Waffle Houses every day for free. That way he wasn't eating at the same place every day. And he always tipped the waitresses. He was so easy-going that most of the Waffle House waitresses were very careful about taking care of Jimmy's big drum. And Jimmy figured out how to live on one meal a day, drinking water all day to keep himself from getting too hungry.

Jimmy was never in a bad mood, even though he'd lost everything but his old black Ford Ranger. He never complained about anything; he told other people how good they looked and asked about their families. And he was sincere. In short, Jimmy Nash was a truly nice guy whose circumstances forced him to make a living out of nothing. And he was doing it, happily.

And then there was the Magnolia Café. Lucretia worked there. Jimmy loved seeing her every day. She always spoke to Jimmy and quickly picked up the fact that Jimmy had an assistant.

"Hey Jimmy," Lucretia said, one day after Jimmy had been bringing Derek on his rounds for a few weeks, "is your helper okay?"

Lucretia was a very pretty, young, light-skinned, African-American woman with greenish-brown eyes that were full of sheer goodness. She wore a size six, her rump a nice, small, round delight.

Jimmy was quietly enjoying her enticing, slender-as-a-willow, body. She reminded Jimmy of Halle Berry and he'd made a habit of calling her Lucretia Berry to flirt with her.

"Whataya mean?" Jimmy asked, looking over to where Derek was standing. Derek looked listless.

Jimmy looked at Derek and then at Lucretia. "No, he's not okay." Jimmy said softly. "His daughter died. He's a mess right now."

"Oh."

Jimmy walked over to Derek. "Hey man, we gotta go. Can you help me clean up real quick?"

"Sure."

Derek wiped down the coffee area with a wet cloth. Jimmy pitched in as they finished.

"Let's go, man. We gotta get to the next stop."

Jimmy watched Derek head toward the truck. When he got out of earshot, Jimmy stepped over to Lucretia. "He's a good man. He's just a little broken right now."

Jimmy tossed the organic waste into one of the barrels in the bed of the pickup and got into the truck as Derek sat quietly in the passenger seat.

"Hey Derek," he said, "we got five more stops and then we go get something to eat at the Waffle House. Let's get a salad this afternoon, you want to? Or bacon and eggs? How 'bout some hash browns? Then we'll go to Granddaddy's house."

"Sure, I'll eat whatever they're giving us," Derek said. He didn't care much about food; he'd lost his appetite months ago. But he liked going to Jimmy's granddaddy's house.

After their lunch, and two more stops, Jimmy pulled onto the unpaved entrance to the old homestead. He unlocked the little latch and swung the large metal gate away from his truck. He then pulled the truck a few yards past the gate and re-locked it so he wouldn't have any unexpected visitors. The driveway was more of a lane, unpaved and lined with over twenty live oak trees on each side that opened to a white, four-columned, two-story Southern mansion. It needed work, lots of work. There was a condemned sign on the front door signed by a county code enforcer. There was a no trespassing sign that Jimmy had posted on the massive front porch. The house had seen better days.

Jimmy pulled his truck around to the rear of the house and parked it near a freestanding garage, which leaned a little to the right. It also needed work. Derek got out of the truck and helped Jimmy haul the two barrels of waste over to the side of the garage. With one fluid motion, they picked up each barrel and dumped them onto Jimmy's compost pile that was well defined within a one hundred by one-hundred-foot square border made with cinder blocks. Without Jimmy saying anything, Derek took the barrels back to the truck and strapped them into the bed of the pickup with some tie-down straps. Derek cinched the straps tight.

"You wanna' help shovel some of this garbage with me, Derek?"

"Sure."

The two of them, without speaking, shoveled and tossed the organic trash into an existing mixture of grass clippings, newspapers and chicken manure. The compost steamed slightly in the cool air as the men turned the mixture with large pitchforks. The chicken manure made the smell almost intolerable, but the other natural materials neutralized the odor tremendously.

"That looks good," Jimmy said after a time. They both returned their shovels and pitchforks to the garage and brushed their boots on a large rough-hewn doormat. Then Jimmy used a hose to water the whole mess. It hadn't rained in a while and water was important to allow the compost to cook.

"Let's go sit on the porch."

Derek liked sitting on the veranda. They climbed the five concrete steps up to the back of the big house and sat under the cover of the porch roof in two white rocking chairs that were in perfect condition.

The view from the porch was spectacular. The home sat up and looked over a twenty-five-acre lawn. There were a dozen or so Live Oak trees interspersed here and there, Spanish moss dangling from the branches, and some peach trees near the left side of the property.

A three-board white fence that was in excellent condition bordered the entire estate. Inside the fence were azalea bushes, probably three hundred in number. Some were over eight feet high. At the rear of the property past the fence was a creek that meandered from left to right along the property line. The home was entertained with a concert from nature. Frogs, crickets, cicadas, and a hundred other of God's creatures hummed and called to each other in mid-day rituals.

Past the creek was Hitchcock Woods, a two-thousand-acre slice of heaven where horse riders rode in peace. Walkers, runners, and dog walkers were permitted, but nothing else. No bicycles of any kind, no golf carts, nothing with a motor. Jimmy's granddaddy's house was completely protected from development.

Derek rocked back and forth in his rocking chair.

"When did your grandpa die?" Derek asked.

"Ten years ago. He left the house to me, but I didn't have the money to fix it. I tried paying for my own house, but when I lost my job, I lost that house. I got no money. And now all I got is Granddaddy's home place. I gotta save it. The county says if I don't fix it, they're gonna tear it down. They say it's a nuisance. Now that I got nothing else to lose, I can spend my time and what little money I make on my granddaddy's pride and joy. I ain't gonna lose this. I've lost too much."

Derek continued rocking. He knew something about losing things, too. He didn't say anything for a few minutes. Jimmy looked out over the gorgeous scenery as he thought about the job in front of him.

"Is that a new fence?" Derek asked.

"Yeah, I finished it a few months ago," Jimmy said, "it was the least expensive thing to work on. And it keeps people from just wanderin' around on the property. They were tearin' up my azaleas."

"What are we gonna fix next?" Derek asked.

Jimmy rocked quietly for a moment. It was the first time the word "we" had been used by Derek when Jimmy was included in the "we." Jimmy got up from his rocker and faced the rear of the big home. He looked to his left at Derek who was still rocking.

"We gotta stop the roof from leakin'. I don't know how many holes we gotta patch, but this metal roof is gonna be a bitch to fix. I gotta read about fixin' it. It'll be tough. We gotta get some materials and a big ass ladder. I'll let you be my ladder holder. I ain't lettin' you get on no roof. If I fall off, it's no loss."

"I'll do whatever. I like this place. It's real peaceful here."

"If I show the county I'm workin' on it, maybe they won't tear it down. I gotta do somethin' every single day."

"I'll help," Derek said.

"I know, man, I know."

Jimmy looked at Derek who was still rocking in the chair while he gazed at the scenery. He wasn't any retard. Derek was a good man, a little broken, that's all.

"So, what about the compost pile?" Derek asked.

"When I came out here, the azaleas were in real bad shape," Jimmy said, "I took my granddaddy's formula for fertilizer and brought 'em back to life. Last spring, I put some of that compost in some big plastic bags and sold it at the flea market. Made four thousand dollars sellin' rotten trash. Customers loved it though. I doubled the size of it last summer. I figure I'll make twice as much this year. I got nothing in it but time and gas. The restaurants are payin' me to haul away their scraps. If I keep getting business, I figure I can make a livin' outta this stuff. Bettern' sittin' on my ass."

"The azaleas are amazing," Derek commented.

"They're all organized, man," Jimmy continued, "they start off white here at the house and then go to the soft pink and then the little darker pink toward the creek. As you get to the rear of the property line, those are the real dark pink. Then the purple ones line the left side. You've never seen nothin' so pretty in March and April. When I came out here a few years back, the azaleas were about dead. Look at 'em now. Granddaddy would be proud of those bushes. He loved 'em so much."

Jimmy sat down in the rocker again, and rocked. He and Derek sat in silence as they engaged their own separate peace. Jimmy was determined, from the bottom of his good, hardworking heart, to save that old house he'd inherited, but it too, was in danger of being lost. Jimmy Nash was desperate to save it.

Chapter 12

NOBODY SAID THINGS like "I'll see you tomorrow," when they left each other in the mornings at the *New Moon Café*; most days they sat out front, weather permitting, and had a cup of coffee together. Mandy and Kathy were huge fans of Bailey, the Labrador getting a vigorous petting from the women and treats that Kathy and Mandy either bought at the café or brought in a cloth napkin from home.

The unspoken weekday appointment between Hugh, Mandy and Kathy was something they all enjoyed. Hugh loved hanging out with Mandy Alexander, a beautiful one-hundred-ten-pound package of human dynamite and Kathy, the retired widow who found Hugh to be an entertaining, handsome curmudgeon who, for whatever reasons, didn't like to talk about himself.

It was all very interesting, as they say, with a view from thirty thousand feet. The women didn't know that Hugh was hoarding and hiding money from a suspicious source. And Kathy knew that Mandy lived in and took care of her parent's "cottage," a thirty-room manse while her parents traveled from continent to continent, managing the fifteen hundred hotels they owned around the globe. Hugh didn't care if Mandy lived in a van down by the river. When he asked Mandy where she lived, she told him she rented a garage apartment at one of the cottages; he was satisfied with that answer.

And Hugh, still being married to Michelle in his own mind was wholly unaware that Kathy found him to be the only man since her husband that she was attracted to in *that* kind of way.

Over the next month Hugh and Mandy grew close, like a father and daughter, Mandy being careful not to disclose her wealth and Hugh being cautious about why he never missed his daily trip to the Savannah River Site.

And Kathy and Hugh were dating; at least that's how Kathy saw it, by having coffee three or four days a week at the New Moon Café. Kathy was tender toward Hugh, grabbing his arm while in conversation, touching his hand while making a point. Hugh never noticed those physical notes of affection, though. He was Hugh Buncombe, the steady husband, the now widower of Michelle Buncombe who wouldn't dare think of stepping out on his first and only love, even if she were dead.

Sometimes Kathy talked about her late husband, always in radiant terms, and her champagne friends and others with whom she associated. She frequently asked Hugh to join them in some social settings, but Hugh always said he was busy. He didn't *really* want to be friends with anyone, but he enjoyed the company of Mandy and Kathy more than he realized. And both women, even Kathy, were easy on the eyes. Yes, even Hugh noticed that Kathy was shapely and attractive.

He was a little hesitant to question Kathy about her past—Hugh not wanting to pry, but as to Mandy, he had lots of questions, especially since she had been one of Michelle's favorites. Mandy was almost an open book.

Mandy had spunk, gumption, nerve, independence—whatever you call it—she was one of a few who Michelle had raved about, but Hugh had half listened to those conversations. It was only after he met Mandy at the café that he could put two and two together.

She was *that* Mandy. She'd finished her twelve years of education in the public schools earning academic scholarship offers from a dozen colleges and universities. Instead of following her parents' wishes for her to attend college in South Carolina, or even the Southeast, Mandy heard and followed the beat of a different drummer. While she'd excelled in her academic pursuits, she became an avid kiteboarder.

Mandy's parents owned a not-too-shabby spot on Sullivan's Island where she started surfing the small waves off South Carolina's coast when she was a little girl. The waves became less challenging to her, but the combination of a surfboard, wind, and nylon became the elements, the tools of her trade, as she graduated to kiteboarding. Strapping herself into a harness and controlling a nylon kite with a twenty-knot wind and a small surfboard under her feet became her preferred method of fun. Mandy Alexander didn't simply enjoy it; she became passionate about it, competing in most of the events up and down the east coast while she was in high school. By the time she graduated, she earned the appellation *"Best Female Kite*

Boarder Under 18 from Virginia to South Carolina." in *The Kiteboarder* Magazine. But that wasn't good enough for Mandy Alexander. She'd already felt the warm winds of the east coast and fought challenging waters from Virginia Beach to Miami. So, when it came time to pick a university, with all the scholarship opportunities at her salt-watered feet, she longed to feel the waves and wind of the west coast.

It was simple to her. Pepperdine University in Malibu, California, was known for its excellent journalism curriculum. And besides, the west coast had *real* waves and cooler water. So, ten weeks after finishing high school, to her parent's chagrin, Mandy Alexander packed her things and drove to California hauling a trailer with all her kites and boards. Of course, there is little wind for kiteboarders in Malibu, but an hour drive south on the 405 took Mandy to Long Beach where the wind blew the kite full of air for her to ride.

She wanted to feel the cooler water and to hear the Pacific winds on her kite. Her favorite kite was a patriotic red, white and blue. Her goal was to crush the competition on the left coast. And she did it. She won first place in the inaugural Freestyle competition of the Collegiate Kiteboarding Association. There were three competitions that year and Mandy Alexander blew the other competitors away with her signature move of three 360-degree flips on one wave in a thirty-second time span. She had only been practicing in the Pacific for two months.

Mandy went on to win the Wave Event the next two years. In her senior year at Pepperdine she moved from competing to teaching. Her students, both male and female, won first place trophies in both the Freestyle and Wave Competitions sponsored by the CKA in California. Mandy Alexander was famous in a not-so-famous sport, at least not famous at that time, but she was known in kiteboarding circles as the first Goddess of the sport.

Kiteboarder magazine did countless stories on her accomplishments, attaching video links in the articles to watch Mandy do her thing. There were so many articles about her; she gained the title of "Alexander the Great."

She wasn't just a little better than her fellow competitors. She was light years ahead of the others; her male counterparts frequently discussed her moves as something they wished to perform.

Mandy could have stayed in the sport, but she had other plans and loftier goals than being a commentator on the sidelines of kiteboarding events for the next twenty years. The tensile strength of her kite strings was surpassed only by the pull of her career interests in journalism and writing books. Mandy Alexander, as the clueless Hugh Buncombe learned quickly, was no one's "little girl."

These things came to Hugh in slow pieces and Hugh couldn't help but do a little prying. One day when he sat alone with Mandy having coffee, he decided to push the envelope.

"Can I ask you a personal question?"

"Depends on how personal." Mandy didn't blink.

"Do you have a boyfriend? I mean, you know..."

"I do, Hugh, and that's not too personal. I'm dating Kevin Shaver, a polo player.

We've been dating about six months."

Hugh knew her boyfriend was none of his business, and he was no one's busybody, but he was curious about his now nearly adopted daughter.

"So, is it serious?"

"Is what serious?" she asked, knowing very well what he meant.

"This Kevin guy."

"I want you to meet him," she said. "If I can get him up before eight o'clock, I'll make him come down here."

"Do you live together?"

"Aren't you the curious one," she commented. "No," she said, laughing, "Although there's not much about me that's traditional, I'm not letting anybody move into my house until I'm ready. And I'm sure not moving into his place."

Hugh had already crossed the line and she hadn't slapped him, so he kept going.

"Does he live in a not-so-nice place?"

"Oh my God, no," she said. "His family owns a host of McDonald's franchises, they bought him a four-bedroom house a few miles from the polo field. He wants me to come over there, but I'm happy where I am."

Hugh looked at Mandy. She was a beautiful young woman. Any man, he thought, would be lucky to have her as a wife. He wanted to protect her as any good father would.

"You don't have to worry about me," she said very matter-of-factly, "I've got goals to reach."

Hugh sipped a little more coffee.

"While you're in a mood to answer questions," he asked, "why did you quit kiteboarding? You were probably the best in the country, maybe the world."

"I told you, I've got bigger goals," she said, looking him in the eyes.

"Bigger goals than being the best in the world?"

"Being the best at kiteboarding is awesome, but I'd done that by the time I was twenty-one. I can't keep that physical pace forever. I'd just be an old, wrinkled woman thinking about how things were. That's not how I want my life to be. I've got some business goals. I've got some ideas on philanthropy. I've got some ideas on politics. Kiteboarding has already opened doors for me. I'm scheduled to make a speech at UCLA next month to the Future Women Entrepreneur's group. The only reason I got that invite was because I've moved on. If I'd remained the queen of kiteboarding, I'd only be speaking to surfer dudes and chicks at kiteboarding events. People want to hear from someone who is involved in something more than sports. Even in California." She smiled, thinking her comment about California was cute.

"Don't forget the people in your life, if this Kevin guy is the real deal…"

"You sound like my dad. I want to give Kevin another year to get polo out of his system. When next season is wrapped up, we'll see where it goes. The truth is neither one of us is in a hurry."

"And Kevin wants to live in Aiken, South Carolina?"

"He'll live anywhere there's horses. This is a great horse community. I can accomplish my goals from this little town as easy as anywhere. Look at Darla Moore. She's from Lake City, South Carolina. She's a billionaire who knows how to live away from the hustle and bustle of the big city. I've got my eye on the ball," she said. She rubbed Bailey behind his ears and pulled his head to hers, looking Bailey in the eyes while he tried to lick her face. "Your dad shouldn't worry so much about me," she said.

"I've got nothing else to do, you were one of Michelle's favorite students. She'd be upset if I didn't worry."

Mandy stood up. Coffee time was over. She loved her little talks with old Hugh in the mornings, but she had those dreams to achieve.

"Hey, I gotta go slay a dragon. You oughta think about going to a polo match with the *Champagner's 1836.* You'd fit right in."

"I've got better things to do."

"No you don't."

Mandy grabbed her coffee cup and headed to work as Hugh dug in his pocket to leave a tip on the table. There was a dirty one-hundred-dollar bill he'd found earlier that morning. He *almost* left it, but he tossed two bucks out of his money clip onto the table and secured it with his half-finished coffee.

The next morning of Hugh's new normal, as bizarre as it was—picking up long-lost treasure—took a turn. Digging in center field, about two inches down in the hard dirt, Hugh found a pair of military dog tags. They were still on the stainless-steel chain.

Chapter 13

HE COULDN'T BELIEVE it. Plain as day: Clayton Caswell, blood type B positive. Social security number, Religion: Baptist.

Hugh picked up the tags, rubbed the dirt off and felt a chill go up his spine. Bailey sensed something was wrong, quit his own digging and sniffed the tags as Hugh held them. Bailey whined a little. Even the dog felt something was different.

Hugh quit looking for money that morning and skipped coffee with Mandy and Kathy. He went straight home and googled Clayton Caswell.

"Oh my God," Hugh said to himself as his computer pulled up the name. The story unfolded:

Born in 1920, Clay grew up during the depression. Times were hard, his parents were farmers, and when WWII started, he joined like everybody else. He was well suited to the service; he enjoyed the structure of following orders and keeping things straight. His physicality also made things easier for him. He had a large, athletic frame that served him well. His height, at six feet three, required most people to look up when they spoke to him; his weight, a trim two hundred pounds, made him look like he could whip anyone who got in his way.

Clay was with the First American Army that was part of *Operation Cobra* in July of 1944. At that battle, Clay killed six Nazi soldiers in a firefight at a farmhouse near the town of Caen and saved ten of his own men. Without his quick thinking and willingness to sacrifice his own life for his band of brothers, they wouldn't have made it.

When the war was over, he was awarded the Bronze Star, the Army Achievement Medal, the Distinguished Service Medal, and a Purple Heart.

He could have quit the service and gone home to his family after the war, but his parents had both been killed in a car accident while he was in Germany. Clay had nothing to celebrate when he returned from the war. With his success on the battleground, he was welcome to stay in the service to his country. He became a drill sergeant, teaching new recruits the science and art of combat. He didn't realize it when he returned, partly because he remained in the service, but his combat experience had given him a rough case of what they then called shell shock. Later it would receive an actual diagnosis: Post Traumatic Stress Disorder, but in 1946, people just knew Clay was a little different.

He failed to connect with women, preferring to be alone, a quiet man who showed virtually no emotion. He was a perfect soldier, a man well suited for service to his country. He was a withdrawn person who got along well with his colleagues, but when it came time to find a mate he was incapable of that leap from soldier to suitor. He was content being alone and soldiering. It was what he had been made to do and he was good at it.

Then came Korea.

In Korea, it was known as six-two-five. It was their nine-eleven, the war having started on June 25, 1950 when North Korea invaded Seoul. Clay was ready to go to Korea. He was assigned to the 8th Army. He'd been there six weeks when North Koreans captured him and twenty-six of his fellow men. Over the next seventeen weeks those twenty-seven men, including Clay Caswell, were sent to a prison camp where they were given one meal a day. When they arrived at the camp near Osan, there were already ninety-eight other Americans in captivity. This group of captors had their own brand of torture. When a new prisoner arrived, he was branded, on his back, with the razor-sharp tip of a red-hot bamboo shoot. If the soldier didn't groan or cry out in pain, the branding continued. It was better to scream out in pain, but not knowing the rules, many American soldiers were burned as many as thirty times. Clay Caswell, a drill Sergeant, the model of a man who could tolerate pain, was burned forty times before he made a noise. That was just the beginning.

Their aim was to murder the men in captivity, but to torture them before the killing. One North Korean, a man who, as a child, enjoyed killing cats and dogs, thought it would be a sort of science experiment to see how long a human could live if they took a chicken liver and sewed it into the armpits of captured Americans. The operation was simple. They tied the soldier to a wooden table and cut open his armpit, inserted the chicken liver and sutured the armpit closed. There was no anesthesia. The North Koreans told the Americans that the chicken liver in the armpit would provide some immunity from other diseases.

To keep the men from destroying the suture and pulling the rotting chicken liver from their armpits, an inspection was done every morning to make sure there was no removal of the sutures. If the chicken liver was gone, another one was sewn in immediately.

Because of the lack of food, and the puss-filled infection under the men's arms, many were sent to another facility, a "hospital," where they were supposedly treated and were to be returned. No one ever came back from the hospital.

Although the warden and his guards were doing a good job of killing the Americans slowly, those in command weren't happy with having to feed the prisoners one meal a day of chicken broth and a few pieces of rice. The order came down from somewhere that the Americans should walk to another compound, about thirty miles away, where three hundred more prisoners were being held.

One would think that the thirty-mile trek would start in the morning, but the North Koreans thought it better to make the move in the afternoon, near sunset. Clay Caswell was in the next to last group to be moved, twenty-seven men tied together by ropes around their skinny waists, all in one line. As they stood on the edge of a ravine, they were told to stop. The North Koreans then shot the Americans *rat-a-tat-tat*, the men falling into the ravine on top of each other in a heap of death. Clay Caswell was shot in the back under his left arm, and instinctively fell down, the bullet exiting his body. He had enough sense to play dead; the North Koreans stood over the men and kicked them to see if they groaned. When Clay was kicked, painful as it was, he made no sound. Being late in the day, sun setting, the soldiers of the KPA, moved on. The next day they shot the last group on an edge of another ravine not far away.

Clay Caswell laid still for a full hour before moving, not being sure if there was a Korean standing guard. He heard movement among his dead brothers, another soldier surviving by feigning death. A quiet whisper of sound came across the ravine in English.

"Anyone alive?"

Clay didn't respond, worried that the whisperer was a Korean waiting with rifle in hand. Peering out from under his bleeding left side, Clay spotted Corporal Eddie Granville moving across the bodies, climbing out of the ditch. No Koreans. Clay waited a little longer, knowing there might be a KPA in the woods, guarding. No weapons fired. More silence. Granville cursed in quiet words, lamenting his fallen buddies.

Clay stirred.

"Hey, Eddie," he whispered, "I'm alive."

Two men out of twenty-seven survived. Knowing that the chicken liver under their arms needed to be removed, Eddie and Clay sharpened a half-inch thick branch from an oak tree and cut open each other's underarms to dig out the disease that had been poisoning their bloodstream for weeks. It was a start.

For the next eighteen days, Clay and Eddie walked in stealth, crawled in woods on their elbows, back to U.S. lines. It was a six-mile journey, moving at night, hiding during the day under brush, behind trees, spotting North Koreans on patrol, troops marching past the survivors. They lived on berries, grubs, and worms that they dug out of the mud while making their way back to the front lines of battle.

As they came closer to the fighting, it became more dangerous. Clay and Eddie had both lost over forty pounds, their uniforms on their bodies looking like a flag on a pole with no wind. Survival was important, but like many men who serve in wartime, they considered themselves dead when they got on the airplane to fly to Korea. It helps knowing you're already dead. When they approached the front, Eddie and Clay made a plan. They waited for nightfall.

Finding themselves, by luck, on the edge of the outer lines, they waited on their bellies near the Korean foxhole for the sentry to nod off. Killing the enemy was easy, using his own bayonet against him. They killed the next seven Koreans with the dead sentry's hand grenade. A hundred yards away, thirty or more other Koreans started moving toward the explosion, knowing something was very wrong.

Eddie and Clay called out to the Americans, just two hundred yards away, hollering to give them cover. Shots were fired by Americans and Koreans, bullets flying overhead, a flare being launched in the sky for Clay and Eddie to get to safety. The two of them looked like praying mantises, arms and legs thin as sticks, no energy except adrenaline, running in the bright light, they dove into the protection and security of the American trenches.

Hugh read the story three times, his heart pounding harder each time. Clay Caswell was a war hero. Hugh was holding a war hero's dog tags.

"Is that it?" Hugh asked the computer screen. "What happened to him? How did he die? Maybe he's still alive? How did his dog tags wind up on a baseball field at the Savannah River Site?"

The computer yielded no more. Hugh would have to find it.

Chapter 14

THE NEXT MORNING, Hugh went to Rhodes Field asking himself repeatedly the same questions he'd asked his computer. There were no answers, only more questions.

And there was more money. That day, a Thursday, Hugh found nine hundred dollars. And according to Maxwell Cooper, he couldn't spend a nickel of it. Determined to find the source, though, Hugh talked to Wendell and asked if he could bring a shovel to dig up some old azaleas to plant at his house. Wendell didn't care.

"Just bring me a cuttin'" he said, "I'd love to have some azaleas with some history."

The next day Hugh brought a shovel—a short one—and started digging around the field that seemed to be where the most money was located. He had no luck. As his time limit came close, his phone rang.

"Hello."

"Are you coming for coffee?" she asked.

"I'm on the way," he said.

"I just wanted to make sure you were coming today," she said.

"Yeah," he said, "I'll be there in ten minutes."

Hugh sensed a slight tinge of sadness in Mandy's voice.

As soon as she saw him, she started crying. Her parents had warned her about Kevin, she said. They told her he was nothing but a young, rich polo player who was also playing her. She found out the hard way when she stopped by his house and found him in bed with a young Argentinian woman he met on the polo circuit. When confronted, Kevin admitted he'd been seeing the other woman for the past several months.

Mandy was a mess.

Hugh sat and listened. He told her that she would have to put Kevin behind her and move on. And he listened some more. Cindy came out with a muffin. She didn't know what was going on, but her instincts told her that Mandy needed something to eat. And Mandy ate it, her mouth full of little pieces of muffin, crying and talking to Hugh at the same time. And Hugh kept listening. He didn't have to say much; he knew from being a husband to Michelle that it was better to just keep his mouth shut.

An hour passed with Hugh nodding his head and occasionally touching Mandy's arm in agreement and condolence. And then it hit him from nowhere, like those horses who galloped from one end of the polo field to the other in a few seconds. He felt it first in his cheeks, a warmth, and then his eyes filled with water. He was overcome with emotion for Mandy, a human being other than Michelle. Mandy *really was* like his daughter, and he felt the compassion that all parents feel when their child suffers. It was new to him, this emotion, but he couldn't stop it. He sat there, tears in his eyes feeling the deepest sadness for Mandy. He sat back and wiped his eyes.

"Look what I've done," she said, "now I've got us both crying." She tried laughing, but failed.

Hugh continued to wipe the tears away. He couldn't talk.

Mandy looked at Bailey who was looking at both of them with his own sad eyes.

"Bailey wants to cry too," she said, and then she did manage to laugh.

Hugh looked at Bailey, wiped the bottom of his eyes with three fingers and turned his head to Mandy. "Usually he just licks himself when I tell him something sad. This is a big change for Bailey."

Mandy howled.

The three of them sat there for another hour, Bailey, Mandy and Hugh. They all ate, including Bailey, a bagel with egg and cheese. And Hugh talked in low tones about Michelle and how he was dealing with that loss and he listened some more as Mandy talked about moving on and her passions about the newspaper and kiteboarding. At the end of that hour Bailey would have said these two humans were closer.

Hugh Buncombe changed a little that day. He became a dad, a real live Father. And he was better for it. Michelle would have been proud of that man she married.

And Mandy hugged Hugh before they parted. She hugged him hard, not letting go for more than a few seconds. "Thank you," she whispered in his ear, "you made my day easier."

She'd never done that before, but it would be their new traditional parting. And Hugh hugged her back, like a dad would hug his daughter.

It was ten o'clock in the morning. A few blocks away from the *New Moon* Max Cooper opened his mail. The Order granting Summary Judgment against Cleveland was enclosed. Max finally took the time to look at what Stokes had filed at the hearing in front of Judge Warren. The attachments to the Order didn't look right.

Chapter 15

"SHARON," MAX SAID, "cancel all of my appointments for the rest of the day. I've got stuff to read. Don't interrupt me unless it's a judge." Max walked into his office and sat down at his desk. There were distractions everywhere, files on his desk, phone messages taped to his computer, little notes attached to folders.

He knew he couldn't spread things out in his own office. He stepped down the hall and carefully opened the door to his father's office. It was as though he expected to see his dad sitting at the desk. The room was dark, the curtains drawn closed. He turned on the overhead light and pulled back the drapes, light flooding the room. There wasn't a scrap of paper on the desk. Max picked up the phone and dialed Sara, his paralegal.

"Can you please join me in dad's office?" he asked.

When Sara came into the room, Max was sitting behind the desk, looking up at the ceiling. Sara figured the young man was finally going to deal with Calhoun's loss. She didn't speak.

"Please close the door." Sara complied and stood at the front of the desk. Max was still looking at the ceiling. "The exhibits that Stokes attached to his Motion for Summary Judgment have piqued my interest. Something isn't right. I want all the materials that Ronnie Avery gave me. I haven't taken the time to read this stuff, but I've got a few days to get this done. I need you to help me. Look at websites about foreclosure cases. Find anything on foreclosures, print it and bring it to me. Anything."

Sara was fifty. She'd worked for Calhoun for twenty years; she watched Max grow up, go to college and then law school. She knew Max was still suffering with the loss of his dad and she'd purposely allowed him time on his own. It seemed to her that this was a good thing, Max opening the door to Calhoun's office. Sitting at the desk made it even better.

"I assume you want this starting now?" she asked.

"Yeah," he said, "I don't know what other deadlines we have, but if we can push them out until Monday, please do that. I'm about to make silk out of a sow's ear."

"That's what your dad used to say."

"I know." He looked at his father's desk and back at her. "I know."

"I'll push everything out until Monday. No worries. You can concentrate. I'll get your calls handled and make sure you don't have any distractions." Sara leaned over the desk and looked at Max. "I've got your back, Max Cooper. You do what you need to do, whatever it is. If you need me to come in over the weekend, you let me know."

"Thanks," he said, "right now I need everything that the real estate lawyer sent me. And please look up foreclosure websites. There's gotta be somethin' out there."

It was Thursday at eleven a.m. At one-thirty, Sara brought Max a sandwich from Subway. He didn't eat it. He also didn't hear the staff close the office down.

By three a.m., Max had fallen asleep on the couch in the lobby, his stockinged feet curled under a large towel he found in the break room. When he awoke at 7:30, the sun was shining brightly through the office, cars passing on the street outside. He adjourned back to Calhoun's office. He still hadn't eaten; his stomach churned, begging for food.

Max knew he had to eat and the *New Moon Café* was only a few blocks away. Looking like he'd been on an all-night drunk, he walked, in yesterday's clothing, unshaven, to the little spot on Laurens Street.

And since it was Friday, the *Champagner's 1836* were there, inside, doing their little toasts and hooting it up with each other. Outside the café Hugh Buncombe was with Mandy. It was the second time Max had seen Hugh with her. Hugh and the young woman appeared to be engaged in a deep conversation as Max opened the creaking wooden door to the café.

"Mornin' Mr. Buncombe," Max said, looking quickly over at Mandy and nodding.

"Max! Meet my friend Mandy Alexander," Hugh said, "she works for *The Standard*."

Max let the door go, stepped over to Hugh's table and extended his hand to a less-than-enthusiastic Mandy, who only nodded at Max.

Hugh sensed the unusually cold reception from the normally bubbly Mandy and moved on. "Did you have a long night, Max?"

"I did," Max grinned, "I've got a project I'm working on and fell asleep at the office."

"Tell us about it," Hugh said, motioning for Max to sit down, "can you discuss it?"

Max sat down, pulled his chair to the table. "I can talk about it," Max said, "I'm trying to figure out how to help people in foreclosure. It's not easy."

"Why don't the people just make their payments?" Hugh asked.

"It's more complicated than that," Max said, "the banks frequently don't even own the paper their suing on. It's complicated," he repeated.

"Seems simple to me," Hugh said, "make your payments and you keep your house."

"I've been reading some wire stories about this mess," Mandy added. "It's affecting people you wouldn't normally think would struggle."

"That's right," Max said holding his palms out to Mandy, "it's not as simple as making payments. Some of these banks have sued people who have never had a loan. It's more complicated than you might think."

Mandy said nothing else. She didn't want to get into a whole discussion with a notorious skirt chaser. And Max didn't have time to chat.

"I've gotta go," he said, "there's another few days of reading ahead of me."

He told Hugh and Mandy it was good to see them as his to-go order was brought outside. He stood up, told Mandy it was nice to meet her, and nodded at old Hugh Buncombe.

"See, he's not so bad." Hugh commented.

"Whatever."

As Max walked, he checked messages on his phone. There were several of them; only one got his attention. Scott had written that he wanted Max to meet a new girl he'd been seeing. That was unusual; Scott didn't *date* anyone, he just enjoyed the sexual part of *seeing* someone. Max poked at his phone.

"Seeing who?"

"A girl, a woman, named Susan. She's smart and beautiful, Maxxy."

"When did this start?"

"I tried calling you to come with me, but you were busy. You should think about hanging out with your old friend Scott more often."

"Are you serious about her?"

"I don't know. I just wanted you to meet her, that's all."

"Maybe next week. I've got this thing I'm working on."

"That's what you always say. Still seeing Dharma?"

"Dharma, Reena, yes, all of them."

"Okay. It's your loss."

"I gotta go. I'll call you mid-week." Max was standing in front of his office. It was easier to work than to think about a serious relationship.

Chapter 16

MAX FOCUSED; HE read all day Friday. He ate at noon; Sara brought him a Greek salad from Acropolis Pizza restaurant. He had no idea there was so much to this foreclosure stuff. Original promissory notes. Witnesses on mortgages. Something called an allonge. The banks transferred loan collection to another entity called a Servicer. And those servicers made better money when the loan was in default. Max was like a human sponge, soaking up all the foreclosure law he could read. And, of course, he remembered everything with that memory of his.

When the staff left on Friday, he didn't even know it. They didn't bother to say bye to him, knowing he was in the zone. And they were strangely comforted that Max was in Calhoun's office. It was a first step toward dealing with his father's death.

Max slept on the couch in the lobby for the second night in a row. He was up before dawn, sipping coffee. He'd skipped dinner and breakfast. Whatever hunger pangs he had were quashed by his quest for more knowledge about the foreclosure issues he'd uncovered.

By lunchtime he hadn't eaten in twenty-four hours. He made another trip to the *New Moon Café* where he sat under one of the red umbrellas and ate two roast beef sandwiches. This time, though, he didn't have to make small talk with anyone. He looked like one of those polo ponies that'd been ridden hard and put up wet. Barely speaking to anyone, he walked back to the office.

By mid-afternoon, Max had read the three hundred pages of materials Sara had gathered from the land records at the courthouse, along with countless articles on real estate law. Calhoun's office looked like some tenured professors, stacks of material here, books laid open there, and files piled on top of each other on every available chair. When Max grew tired of Calhoun's office, he sat on the couch in the lobby, his feet on the coffee table. He knew there was a secret in all that stuff, but where? He kept making notes and gaining, little by little, knowledge of the process of mortgage foreclosure in the New World.

He sat up on the couch and separated the copies into piles. The first pile was for mortgages that were sold; the second pile was for loans that were kept by the original mortgage company. A trend developed quickly. The first pile, the ones where the mortgages were sold, were in foreclosure and they all had assignments from the mortgage company to a third party. He made another stack of assignments that were still in the name of the original mortgage company and had not filed for foreclosure. Max wondered: *why would a mortgage company sell the mortgage to another mortgage company right before foreclosure?*

Max got a fresh cup of coffee. He had one of those Keurig coffee makers and he picked out the French Vanilla flavor. He used the same thick paper cup he'd gotten from the *New Moon Café*. Max stirred in all the fixings.

As he stood in the break room blowing on the hot coffee, he looked at his receipt from the *New Moon.* His signature was sloppy, but it was readable. He remembered something about the assignments on those loan documents. There was a common signature on the assignments of those loans. He left his coffee in the break room and went back to the couch.

There in the pile of documents was a signature of Bobby Baine. Bobby was a signing officer of Gocows mortgage. He assigned the loan from Gocows right before the foreclosure. Max looked at the next one. Bobby Baine was the signing officer of GMAC mortgage on another loan. It was signed the same month as the one from Gocows. Max looked at the next one. Bobby Baine, again, this time as a GMAC official. It was signed the same month as the other one from Gocows. Max looked at the next one. Bobby Baine signed as a corporate officer of the Bank of New York two months later.

How did Bobby Baine work for so many mortgage companies in a two-month period? By the time he was done, Max's coffee was cold and Bobby Baine was hot. Bobby was a "signing officer" for eleven mortgage companies during a ninety-day period. Frequently the mortgages showed that Bobby was a vice president. And it got more interesting. Bobby's signature was different on some of the documents. Sometimes his name was completely legible; other documents showed a giant swirl.

What about Quentin Cleveland's file? Max tossed a pile of files from one of the client chairs in Calhoun's office onto the floor under the window. Digging through the pleading file he found an assignment from Bank of America to

Gocows mortgage. The signature on the assignment was that of Mr. Bobby Baine. And who said Bobby was a man? Max Cooper had finally discovered something. And there was more to be found.

Max only had until Monday morning to file a Motion for Reconsideration of Judge Warren's ruling against Quentin Cleveland. Max spent another night at the office, writing and doing more research on the elusive Bobby Baine. By Monday morning the Motion was filed by a tired, but grinning, Max Cooper. Of course, Max called Mr. Quentin Cleveland to discuss the case. Quentin was at work but Max left a message.

They were all at work. Patsy was at the hospital in the operating room. Quentin was at the plant getting in as many hours as he could. And of course, Jimmy and Derek were collecting organic garbage.

Hugh Buncombe, on that beautiful March morning, was at the courthouse doing some research on Clay Caswell. He found some land records with the name Caswell. There it was, a Harold and Martha Caswell owned property in old Ellenton. Hugh printed the deed and headed to the Aiken County Museum where more records were stored.

Who are you Clay Caswell? Who? He mumbled to himself.

Chapter 17

LUCRETIA, THE ATTRACTIVE waitress at the *Magnolia Café*, liked Jimmy Nash. She liked everything about Jimmy, his gentleness, his humility, his crooked-tooth smile, his tall, lanky body, and his spirit. She had waited for her moment to get Jimmy by himself, and after several months of his bizarre work, with his partner having been attached to his hip, she finally got her chance.

Another waitress was on duty with Lucretia on that sun-filled morning when Jimmy and Derek arrived in the faded black pick-up truck. Derek was changing the trash containers when Lucretia seized her chance.

"Jimmy," she said, "have you got a minute you can help me back in the stock room? I've got a big box of plastic bags I need to pull down off the shelf."

Jimmy nodded at Derek as he moved toward the back room where Lucretia stood.

He'd no more gotten into the tight space, a space filled with cardboard boxes, when Lucretia pushed the door closed behind Jimmy.

"Where is the...?" Jimmy started to say, but before he could get another syllable out of his mouth, Lucretia's lips were on his. She grabbed the back of Jimmy's head and pulled it to hers. At first Jimmy pulled back, but there was no stopping Lucretia's lips on his and her hot tongue opening his mouth. Jimmy was not timid as her hands moved from his head to his backside where she pulled his hips to hers. Then she quit, just as fast as she started, and pushed Jimmy back as she looked into his surprised brown eyes.

"I've been wantin' to do that for a while," she said, "you got somethin' about you that's special to me, you know that?"

"I didn't know–" Jimmy stammered.

Lucretia opened the door and walked out in front of Jimmy.

"Thanks, I couldn't get that big box down by myself." She kept on walking and took her place behind the counter. "Have a nice day," she said in a routine voice.

Nature had taken over Jimmy's body in that twenty-five seconds of passion and he hung around the stock room for a minute.

"You ready to go?" Derek said, standing in the aisle.

"Yeah, yeah, I'm ready; we gotta get to the Waffle House over on Pine Log Road."

Jimmy looked back at Lucretia through the glass doors. She smiled a very large, coy grin.

Chapter 18

THE BAILIFF POUNDED his open hand on the wall in Judge Warren's courtroom. "All rise," he said in a stentorian voice.

As comfortable as Max was in a courtroom, his heart raced. He couldn't help it. Quentin Cleveland, seated on Max's right, didn't notice the case of nerves that Max had. Quentin had already put it in his head that he was gonna be okay. Pastor Duplin had preached a sermon about "the Wisdom of Giving It Up to the Lord", and Quentin had done that. He was at peace with whatever was about to happen.

Henry Stokes wasn't at all apprehensive. He had never been seriously challenged before. Foreclosure law was simple. Don't pay, don't stay. Get the bums out. It was easy. Sure, he'd read Max Cooper's Motion for Reconsideration, but so what if Bobby Baine had a string of jobs at the same time? Quentin Cleveland didn't pay. He was a bum who needed to get out. Stokes couldn't lose.

After telling everyone to be seated, Judge Warren sat down, looked at the papers in front of him and opened his left hand to Max Cooper. "This is your Motion, Mr. Cooper. Proceed."

Max explained how Bobby Baine was a signing officer for several corporations at the same time. He referred to the exhibits attached to the Memorandum showing Mr. Baine's signature was vastly different on many filed assignments in the Aiken County Courthouse. Judge Warren seemed bored. Max sensed the judge wasn't grasping the genius of his discovery and went back over the assignment of mortgage in Quentin Cleveland's case.

"You don't need to say things twice, Mr. Cooper," Warren said, "I understood you the first time." Max stopped and stared at the judge. "Yes, Your Honor."

"I'll hear from you Mr. Stokes."

"Your Honor, despite what Mr. Cooper says, there is no law that says Mr. Bobby Baine can't have several jobs at once. What's wrong with working at McDonald's during the day and Burger King at night?"

"But what if McDonald's is in New York and Burger King is in California?" Judge Warren asked quickly.

"McDonald's and Burger Kings are everywhere, Your Honor."

"That's not the question, is it, Mr. Stokes? You used McDonald's and Burger King as an example. I'm asking you if Bobby Baine is authorized to sign for more than one corporation as a signing officer. We're not really talking about frying hamburgers, are we?"

"Your Honor, the bottom line is Mr. Cleveland hasn't paid his mortgage. The property needs to be sold at the next sale. This Motion is frivolous."

Max Cooper wanted to step across the aisle and slap that damn Henry Stokes.

Judge Warren looked over his glasses at Henry. It was the same look he'd given Max when the judge was about to cut his ass.

"Is that all you got, Mr. Stokes? The last time I looked, I was the judge of what is frivolous in my court."

Henry Stokes wasn't accustomed to being talked to like that. He always got what he wanted.

"Your Honor, what I'm saying is that Mr. Bobby Baine can sign for whatever corporation he wants. Filing a Motion for Reconsideration of Your Honor's ruling, after you've ruled on this pointless minor detail, is ridiculous."

Judge Warren got a little red in the face.

"Now you're saying that Mr. Cooper should lose this Motion because I don't have the intellectual integrity to reverse myself. Is that what you're saying?"

Max Cooper began to relax. This was an ass kicking he was going to enjoy. Even Quentin Cleveland saw it coming. Quentin leaned over and whispered in Max's ear, "he's gonna change his mind, isn't he?" Max nodded yes and put his hand on Quentin's arm indicating to keep quiet. The exchange continued.

"No, Your Honor. All I'm saying is the law allows people to work at different places and do different jobs."

"But what about Mr. Baine's signature? Does it bother you that Mr. Baine has seven different signatures as Mr. Cooper points out? One signature looks like it was signed by a third-grade kid just learning to write cursive. Another signature has clear B's and the rest is not clear. Yet another one is completely illegible. What do you say about that Mr. Stokes?"

"Sometimes my signature is different, Judge."

Judge Warren picked up the exhibits provided by Max. "This different?"

"I don't know."

"I'll tell you what I don't know, Mr. Stokes. I don't know if Mr. Bobby Baine is a man. I don't know if "it" even exists. I want to meet the elusive Bobby Baine. I want Mr. Cooper to find this person, man or woman, and take its deposition. I'm going to reverse my prior Order in this matter until a full investigation is held in this matter." Judge Warren looked at Max Cooper.

"Mr. Cooper, I would usually ask you to prepare the order on this matter, but I'm going to do this one. Is that understood?"

Max looked at the judge.

"Yes, Your Honor."

Henry Stokes didn't hang around to watch Max gloat. He put his papers back in the file and walked out of the courtroom. Max thought he saw a small tail tucked between Henry's legs. Quentin sat in silence, his hands together in prayer in front of his face.

Judge Warren hadn't left the bench. He took his time, moving the file around on the bench, adjusting this and that.

Max looked at Quentin, still in prayer. Tears were falling onto his thick fingers. Max tapped him on the shoulder. "Hey, man, we won," he said, "we've got a lot more to do, but this battle was ours today."

"It's God's victory," Quentin said.

"I know, but there's a lot more to do. The devil never sleeps."

Quentin hugged Max. He squeezed him so tight Max felt like the wind was knocked out of him. "The devil don't know my God," he whispered into Max's ear. Max looked at Quentin when he let Max loose. The tears were still fresh on Quentin's cheeks. "You got this, Max. You got this."

Max was so happy he almost floated back to the office. As he opened the door, he spied Sharon standing in the hall. She pointed back toward Max's office. She didn't have to say a word.

"Let me tell you something, you sonofabitch. You put me in this position. You need to fix this. I never should have listened to you. You call the powers that be and get me out of this trap. Do you hear me?" Silence. The phone slammed down on the receiver.

Carla marched past Max carrying her briefcase.

"Anything I can—" Max stammered.

"Not about you. Don't worry about it."

She closed the door to the office and stormed toward her new Lexus SUV.

Things had happened in Carla's life. She didn't need to *bother* Maxwell with those details, but there were reasons why Carla Robeson had mothballed her place in New York and headed home to spend time with her dad. She'd been there three weeks when the accident happened. Carla had plenty to do; she could take care of her dad and keep the Brunswick Cottage in perfect condition. But the cottage wasn't the only thing on her busy mind. One of those things was REVENGE.

Chapter 19

THEY BECAME A family, the four of them. As is usually the case, each person had their own talents, and they figured out who was good at what. Jimmy Nash had a knack for getting bargains everywhere he went. Sometimes he brought home frozen steaks or hamburger meat. Patsy and Quentin were a little fearful of "flea market food," but after a time and no illness, they relaxed.

Quentin liked to cook his meat dishes on Sunday, but they had a "family meeting" and decided that Quentin would cook his meat specialties on Saturday and Patsy would use the leftovers to create casseroles on Sunday. The casseroles were what they ate for the rest of the coming week. Patsy cooked casseroles and large pasta dishes like ziti and froze them with little labels that had the days of the week on the outside of the Reynolds wrap. As the week wore on, the big casseroles thawed and everyone got their share.

Jimmy didn't cook, so he stayed out of the kitchen. The three cooks—Quentin, Patsy and Derek—were happy that Jimmy didn't clog the works. Besides, they depended upon him to clean up, which he did with speed and efficiency. The place looked like no one ever cooked in that kitchen after Jimmy worked his magic. He cleaned up all the dishes, put them in the dishwasher, and unloaded when it was finished. He scrubbed the pots, pans, broilers and the gas grill. Constantly.

At first, the four of them ate separately. Jimmy was always hungry, and he liked eating late in the afternoon when he finished his errands. Derek watched Jimmy eat while they discussed the day's events.

But as they became more accustomed to each other, Quentin gathered his three roommates in the living room and announced that they should all try to eat at the same time. He said they were family and families should eat and pray together. So, after a few months of taking meals whenever they wanted, Quentin set a time for dinner at 6:30 sharp. They all showed up, too. Quentin started the meal with a prayer and not one person touched a bite of food until Quentin was done. One time, Jimmy picked up a roll off the napkin-covered woven basket just as Quentin started the blessing. Quentin cut his eyes at Jimmy and waited for Jimmy to put the roll back, which he did, and then the Voice Of Quentin began with:

"Father, thank you for your many blessings and for helping Jimmy to remember not to take any food until the blessing is finished. In Jesus name we pray, Amen."

And then they ate. At first, they didn't say much at this dinner arrangement staged by Quentin. There was an uncomfortable silence between them all, Jimmy fidgeting in his chair, Patsy saying very little, Derek always quiet. Ugly circumstances were understood. Patsy and Derek lost a child; Jimmy lost his job and was making compost. Quentin lost a wife to the economy and they were thrown together to survive.

But there is a spirit that enters a house when people share food. It is inevitable. Humanity shines best at a dinner table. Ask any school counselor, preacher, psychologist, or social worker about what creates conversation. Food is the answer, and food eaten together by people, whatever their background may be, however harsh their differences, is the ingredient, the Chef's Best Blend to create words spoken between humans. The best way to get to know someone is to eat a meal with them, put your feet under the same table, look into each other's eyes and...talk.

So, Ambrosia, the Greek Goddess of Food, did a little invisible dance around the table, pointed her wand at each one of the tablemates. After several days of looking at each other over their plates, they began to talk. And it was a beautiful thing.

Although they were different races, different educational levels, different everything, they were the same. And there was plenty to talk about. Sports, Patsy's work, Jimmy and Derek's progress on the house. They smartly avoided the three sins of conversation, sex, politics and religion. And there were other things they didn't speak of: Cleo's death and Quentin's ex. Quentin even took down every picture that had Keisha in it.

Since they were all new to each other, they all told stories about growing up. They found out that they all knew people in common and shared stories about those folks and experiences. It turned out the world really is small.

There was little tension in the house. Quentin had been through the emotional turmoil of a divorce and didn't want or need any more drama in his life. Jimmy didn't even know what conflict was. Patsy and Derek had lost little Cleo; they instinctively knew to let the little things remain small. So, they lived together one day at a time knowing there was no reason to make a bad situation worse with arguments about minor issues. Of course, the weeks turned into months, but since their attitude was already fixed on the temporary nature of their existence, they rarely got on each other's nerves. They simply didn't have time for it.

And human nature being what it is, they avoided touching each other for the longest time. It is one thing that humans do well: *not* touching each other. It's a natural phenomenon. Put ten million people on the streets of New York or Tokyo and not one human will touch another one. If they do, they always say "excuse me" or apologize by quickly pulling the offending body part away. It was the same in the home of Quentin Cleveland. At first, they avoided each other, especially Quentin and Patsy. She didn't like being in the kitchen when he was in there. And he didn't like her messing around in "his" kitchen. The dance, the avoidance of being in each other's space at the same time, was awkward, but as time passed, and as they got to know each other, the dance of avoidance became a well-balanced, beautiful waltz. Quentin cooked his meat; Patsy broiled asparagus and stirred vegetables in saucepans while opening and closing cabinets for ingredients, spices, and other necessaries. And as humans do, after they get to know each other, they begin to touch each other. A clap on the back, a touch on the shoulder, a high five every now and then became their new normal. It didn't happen overnight, but it happened. Once they began eating meals together, they became a family.

And then there was church.

Chapter 20

"ARE YOU COMING or not?" Quentin said from the living room, "It doesn't matter what you wear, but don't wear blue jeans."

"I'm comin," Jimmy said, pulling off his blue jeans in a hurry. He sat on the bed, grabbing a navy-blue pair of pants that were one grade above blue jeans. There was a stain on the left front thigh that Jimmy tried covering up by wetting three of his fingers and rubbing them on the spot. It improved, but not much. Jimmy sat back on the bed and put both of his legs in the air. In one swift movement, he was on his feet, stuffing his only shirt with a collar into the slacks.

"If this weren't Sunday, I'd curse you," Quentin said. Jimmy stood before him like a private awaiting inspection from the drill sergeant.

"You need better pants, but let's go." They got into Quentin's car, a green Maxima; Quentin tossed the Bible between himself and Jimmy on the floorboard. "Now there's gonna be some singin' and some hollerin'," he said, "and some people are gonna stare at you 'cause you're white. Don't pay that no mind. You join in when you feel the spirit and holler with us." Jimmy wondered to himself if there were stained glass windows in the church and how they got them cleaned. Jimmy had been raised a Baptist, so he was accustomed to some fire and brimstone, but he wasn't sure about the Ebenezer AME Church. Jimmy could take religion or leave it, but if it would stop Quentin from asking about his faith, he'd go with Quentin to prove he was no heathen.

While Jimmy was thinking about those things, Quentin smiled quietly to himself. He'd been determined to get his new family to go to church with him, but Patsy and Derek had their own church. That was okay, but they never went to church. That meant that Jimmy became the object of Quentin's proselytizing. After six weeks of prodding and then outright telling Jimmy he was going to church with him, Jimmy was in the car with Quentin.

It was a one-story red-brick building, sitting on the corner Hampton and Bamberg Street. It was smaller than Jimmy thought; there were only about twenty pews on each side of the sanctuary. The aisle was about eight feet wide; the pulpit sat on an elevated stage, three wooden steps were on either side of the pulpit. With all the fussing that Quentin did, they were one of the first people to arrive. Quentin had a place he sat every Sunday, on the second pew from the front on the far-right side. Within fifteen minutes the church was packed. The choir filed out of the choir room, about a dozen women and four men dressed in flowing red robes. The singing began right away, the choir swinging and swaying back and forth, the men holding low notes and the women filling in the high ones with a flourish. They praised God, they raised their hymnals in the air as an offering, tossing back their heads with their arms straight in the air and bellowing out praises to Jesus and his followers.

Jimmy became comfortable. The place was spotless, even the stained-glass windows, all eight of them, four to a side. And there was a large, circular glass window behind the pulpit that Jimmy thought looked clean as well. Quentin sang in his low voice, a baritone that sounded like a low hum to Jimmy, but Quentin *was* singing. Jimmy wasn't singing. He was taking in the place, holding the hymnal in one hand and looking over his left shoulder at the congregation. It was brimming with people—tall, fat, skinny, light-skinned, dark skinned men and women of all ages. Armed with as good a sixth sense as anyone else, Jimmy felt people staring at him. *Why me? He thought.* And then, and only then, did he remember that he was the only white person in the church. Maybe this is what it felt like to be the only black person in a sea of white faces. Jimmy started singing the hymns while he turned and smiled at everyone. He smiled that crooked-tooth grin that was so innocent it melted anyone with whom he made eye contact, each person nodding and smiling at him while they were singing.

While the voices were still ringing and singing and bodies were swaying, Jimmy punched Quentin with his right elbow and whispered in his ear, "I like this place. The people seem nice." Quentin looked around at what Jimmy was looking at. Everyone was staring at Quentin and Jimmy, most of them smiling.

"They're just wondering who you are, Jimmy."

"They still seem nice. And this place is so clean."

Quentin looked at Jimmy and shook his head. "You're the cleanest guy I've ever met."

"Everybody says that." The singing stopped and the minister approached the pulpit from Quentin and Jimmy's right side. Announcements were made and two parishioners read some passages from the Bible, one by an old woman and the other by a younger man. They were okay, but Jimmy wanted to hear the preacher. While the passages were being read, Jimmy continued to look over his shoulder, nodding at one person or another.

Just before the preacher began his sermon, Jimmy looked to his left. On the same row, but across the aisle from where he and Quentin were sitting, Jimmy spotted a hand waving to him underneath the top of the pew. It was just a little wave, but it was a wave. There she was, Lucretia, waving at Jimmy, those slender fingers moving back and forth like a pendulum on a metronome. Jimmy smiled another big grin. He really liked this place. Lucretia grinned back and then sat back in her pew. The preacher was gonna lay it out.

The pastor was of medium height, dark skin, and had the body of a fullback. There was no question that Pastor Duplin had played sports when he was younger. He was completely bald, like Quentin. It was hard for Jimmy to figure out how old he was, but he was probably over fifty. The pastor approached the pulpit in his robe and looked over the congregation. He raised his arms into the air.

"I FEEL GOOD!" he shouted. "I feel good, like I *knew* that I would." And he repeated it. "I feel good, like I *knew* that

I would." He stepped back from the pulpit and looked to the heavens. And then he looked out again over the congregation, looking at no one person, but taking the whole of them into his eyes.

"We all know these words, don't we? These are the lyrics of James Brown, The Godfather of Soul, and our own native son from Aiken County who, God rest his soulful heart, has gone on to our maker. James Brown didn't get much credit for being a man of God, but he was. He danced and sang and brought people together in his music, his songs, AND YES, in his lyrics. What's wrong with that?" he shouted. "What is wrong with that? Nothing is wrong with it. What is wrong with feeling good? What is wrong with feeling the spirit of the Lord and sharing that spirit in song, in your life, in your RELATIONSHIPS with your fellow man? Nothing is wrong with it. We too often think of Jesus as being a person who didn't feel good, who didn't want us to feel good about ourselves. That notion is false. JESUS wants you to feel good, to feel like you should, and to share that good feeling with your family, with your co-workers, with everyone you meet. It's time, my brothers and sisters, to feel good about Jesus like you knew that you would." And then Pastor Duplin opened his Bible. The pages were worn, and Jimmy noticed about a hundred little sticky notes of different colors attached to some of the pages. The pastor turned to the exact page he wanted.

"Let's look at what the word of God says about feeling good. Galatians chapter five, verse 22: 'But the fruit of the spirit is love, joy, peace, longsuffering, gentleness, goodness, faith.' And verse 25: 'If we live in the spirit, let us also walk in the spirit.'

"Love, joy, peace, says the word of God. And he wants us to live and walk in the spirit. That is what God, what JESUS wants you to do. Feel good, like you knew that you would, and share your good feelings about the Lord with others. And dance if you want, dance the way Jesus wanted you to dance. Dance like James Brown to show your spirit, your love of your fellow man." Pastor Duplin stepped back again from the pulpit, his Bible still open in his large palm. And then he stepped forward again, flipping the pages to exactly where he wanted to be.

"Let's look at Psalm 139:14: 'You are fearfully and wonderfully made.' The Lord made you wonderfully. He made you in his spirit in a wonderful way, and you should go out into this world, this earthly place, and let others know about your faith, about how Jesus makes you feel good."

And then Pastor Duplin moved to the side of the pulpit, near the choir. He looked at the choir members and then to the congregation. "James Brown was The Hardest-Working-Man in Show Business. That was one of his trademark sayings. And we all know there was One Man, JESUS, who was and is THE HARDEST WORKING MAN … EVER!" And then Pastor Duplin talked some more about feeling good and feeling the spirit and he shouted some more at the congregation and Jimmy heard a woman's voice in the back of the church shout AMEN. And then another male voice shouted AMEN. And then it seemed like the whole place was shouting. And the choir stood up and Pastor Duplin stepped back again with the Bible in his hand and cried out at the top of his lungs, "I FEEL GOOD ABOUT JESUS."

The place went crazy—the choir singing, the congregation swaying back and forth and Jimmy couldn't help but raise his arms in the air with Quentin and sway back and forth with him and all the others in the second row. Jimmy didn't feel out of place. Everything was so clean and the people seemed so nice and even the hollering didn't bother Jimmy Nash.

When it was all over, Jimmy looked toward Lucretia. She was still there. Jimmy was anxious for everything to end so he could talk to that skinny girl who'd kissed him only two days before.

"You know her?" Quentin asked in a hoarse whisper.

"Yeah, she works at the Magnolia Café. She's real nice to me."

"Oh," Quentin replied with surprise in his voice.

Not everyone wanted to meet Jimmy, but everyone wanted to know who he was, some folks pulled Quentin aside and questioned him innocently about his white friend. Others looked askance at both Quentin and Jimmy, reserving judgment until Wednesday when there would be fewer people around.

Jimmy didn't think about the fact that he was something of a topic of conversation. He shook hands with the minister at the back door, Pastor Duplin telling him how welcome he was and Jimmy telling him how he enjoyed the service and how clean the church was. Jimmy's presence was different enough, so it didn't seem too odd, even to Pastor Duplin, that Jimmy was impressed about the cleanliness. And then Jimmy almost bounced down the four steps to look for Lucretia. She stood next to a very pretty older woman, also rather thin. She was Lucretia's mother, Fristella.

Lucretia found Jimmy about the same time he found her, Lucretia pulling on the arm of her mother as she walked toward Jimmy.

"Hey, Jimmy," she said, "this is my momma. Momma, this is Jimmy, the man I told you about."

Fristella looked at Jimmy with friendly eyes. At first, she extended her hand, but then withdrew it and put out her arms, just a little. It was as though her elbows were tied to her sides. Jimmy didn't even notice the half-open arms. He grabbed her with both of his bony arms, pulled her head to his and hugged her.

"You have a very nice daughter," he said, "Lucretia looks out for me on my job."

"Oh," she said, "what kind of work do you do?" She was like any other mother. She hoped he would say he was a multimillionaire shop owner, or the worldwide CEO of anything. Instead, Jimmy told her exactly what every mother feared.

"I pick up trash. I make fertilizer out of it and sell it at the flea market." Jimmy smiled that big crooked tooth smile at her and looked at Lucretia. "I like cleaning up messes."

"He sure does, Momma, he picks up old coffee grounds and cleans up at the café. We always look forward to seeing Jimmy and his friend." Lucretia looked at her mother who was still staring at Jimmy. Her eyes went from his shoes, to the top of his head and back to his shoes.

"That's nice," she said, "Lucretia, let's go talk to Pastor Duplin. I want to see what he needs us to do about the pot-luck supper tonight." Fristella tugged on Lucretia's arm.

"I'll come in a minute, Momma," she said, standing by Jimmy. "I'll be there in a minute." Fristella didn't want to appear unfriendly to Lucretia's friend, so she ambled slowly in the direction of the busy minister.

"How do you know Quentin Cleveland?" Lucretia asked.

"I live with him," Jimmy said, "He asked me to come to church. If I'd known you were here, I'd have come sooner."

Lucretia smiled.

"I don't live with my momma," Lucretia said, "I come to church with her every Sunday, though. Why don't you come by my house this afternoon? I make the best chocolate chip cookies in the whole world." Lucretia knew her momma didn't approve of Jimmy, especially him being a garbage man and all, but Lucretia knew there was something more about Jimmy than picking up organic waste. And of course, Fristella couldn't exactly tell Lucretia whom to date or not date. Lucretia was a grown woman. The date was made. Before sundown, Jimmy and Lucretia ate Lucretia's homemade chocolate chip cookies while sitting on top of a picnic table at Hopeland Gardens.

They shared stories. Jimmy told Lucretia about his grand-father's house and Lucretia confessed that she was considered the black sheep in her family. She smiled as she said "black sheep" because she, it turned out, was the daughter of a white man. Fristella had an affair with a white businessman while she was still married. Once Lucretia was born, her live-in father was damn sure Lucretia wasn't his and the marriage was over. Fristella never remarried.

Poor Lucretia never got to know her real father. Lucretia's two brothers, very dark-skinned like their mom and dad, tolerated her, but didn't accept her as a full sister. Lucretia told this story and smiled the whole time. She'd accepted her place in life and didn't look back. Her kind, gentle ways and her generous soul captured the clean Jimmy's heart. They had a spectacular afternoon kissing and enjoying cookies. And that was all they did. Jimmy had the natural pangs of desire, but the afternoon together was all they both wanted for the time being. Companionship, at its core, was what they shared. It was perfect, not to be spoiled by anything other than touching each other's gentle lips.

The previous day, a gloriously warm Saturday afternoon in April, Hugh Buncombe's research at the historical museum paid off. He found an article about Clay Caswell, war hero, and native son of Aiken. In 1954, a Congressional investigation was made about the atrocities in the Korean Conflict. Clay Caswell and Eddie Granville testified before the Senate Subcommittee on Korean War Atrocities, along with a host of other survivors. Clay and Eddie's story of war crimes by the North Koreans wasn't unusual. When the Report was finished, there were over 1,800 documented cases of murderous brutality, all in violation of the Geneva Conventions.

During World War II, the Germans murdered less than two hundred American prisoners of war. In Korea, out of seven thousand POWs, only three thousand eight hundred survived, the others being brutally murdered. There was the Hill 303 Massacre, the Sunchon Tunnel Massacre, the Taejon Massacre, the Bamboo Spear Case, the Naedae Murders, the Chaplain-Medic Massacre and other Marches, such as the Seoul-Pyongyang Death March. It is still not known exactly how many soldiers were killed, tortured, maimed, starved, poisoned or walked to death. Some of the soldiers survived and testified before Congress; others chose to stay at home and return to "normal."

After Korea, just like after World War II, the Veterans Administration didn't have a well-defined policy of diagnosing or treating soldiers for what they called "shell shock." Most of those men were put back in their communities, homes, or with their loved ones, with a pat on the back and best wishes. It was not unusual.

In the article, Hugh found a picture of Clay Caswell sitting at a table at the Senate hearing, microphone in front of him. Hugh studied the picture, copied it and enlarged it. Clay's face was drawn, his eyes hollow, like there was a kind of blindness in both eyes.

"Who are you?!" Hugh screamed at the blown-up photo. "Why are your dog tags in my hand?!"

Hugh would have to wait.

Chapter 21

"MAXXY, I REALLY want you to meet Susan. Instead of you telling me you're too busy, Susan and I are taking you to dinner on Saturday. We're going to *Melia's*."

Max was stuck. He had talked to Scott a few times in the past couple of weeks, but he hadn't seen Scott since Scott started dating Susan. The routine of Scott and Max chasing the women on Saturday night had been put on hold.

"What time?" Max asked in a bored voice.

Before Max arrived for dinner, he called Scott to let him know that he had a late date planned with Reena, the beautiful Hindu girl, later that evening. Scott didn't pay any attention to Max's time constraints; he had his own agenda.

It turned out that Susan was a delight. She was smart, entertaining, gorgeous, and *loved* art. She and Scott had kept the conversation so lively at dinner that Max lost track of time and was thirty minutes late for his rendezvous with Reena.

Before Max left, Susan excused herself for a moment. Scott informed Max that he was going to ask Susan to marry him.

Max felt like a parent, an uninformed father who didn't know his son was in love.

"You just met her."

"I know, isn't she great?"

"But you just met her," he repeated. "How about the Widow? How many other women are you seeing?"

"None, Maxxy. I quit 'em all. Sometimes you know when you've found the right one. I'm done with the chase." Max looked off behind Scott's shoulder. There was a painting, a beautiful scene of a man and woman holding hands, walking on a lane, and a horse behind them on a long rein. Those people were in love, that's what the message was. And they loved horses. *Oh, come, on*, Max thought, *that kind of love only exists on the canvas.*

Susan returned to the table. Max graciously excused himself and headed to Reena's house where she was waiting, patiently waiting, with nothing on but a sleek black negligee.

Max was happier with that kind of love.

Chapter 22

"HUGH," MANDY SAID walking out of the Half Moon Café on Friday morning with two cups of coffee, one for Hugh and one for herself, "you know you've asked me like a hundred times about kiteboarding."

"I know," Hugh said, not knowing where this was headed, "I've never seen it before."

"That's what *I* thought," she said, "Hugh has never seen kiteboarding. And since I don't have a boyfriend anymore, and since I need some company, and since the wind is blowing in Charleston, and since there is a little event on Sullivan's island this weekend, *you*, Mr. Hugh Buncombe, are coming with me to Charleston for the weekend."

Hugh had one thought. What if someone else wandered over there and found his honey hole? That would ruin everything.

"I can't go; I've got yard work to do."

"That's ridiculous," Mandy said, turning to Bailey, "has your dad ever showed you the beach, Bailey? Has he?" she asked, with Bailey standing up receiving a good scratch on the top of his head. "I didn't think so. So, you want to go to the beach?" she continued talking to Bailey who seemed receptive to anything, his tail wagging in agreement.

Kathy walked up with two more members of *Champagner's 1836*, both women, one carrying two bottles of champagne, the other carrying a plastic water bottle full of orange juice.

"Did I hear you say beach?" Kathy said, "we're going to the beach today. This is the weekend of the wine and food festival in Charleston. The men left early this morning. We're leaving in a few hours."

"Hugh is going with me," Mandy said, "there's a kiteboarding competition tomorrow afternoon on Sullivan's. And Bailey wants to see the beach."

All three Champagne women jumped at the chance. "We would love to see you do kitebeaching stuff."

"Kiteboarding."

"Whatever you call it, we'll come."

Plans were made, all the women getting cell phone numbers and chatting about where and when to meet while Hugh shifted uncomfortably in the wooden seat knowing he couldn't go away for a weekend. He'd never left his money alone before. He had so much digging to do. It was impossible!

Two hours later, they were watching Bailey hop into the crew cab of Hugh's truck with two of Mandy's favorite kiteboards strapped down in the bed. Having a surrogate daughter, especially one like Mandy, was problematic.

Chapter 23

SULLIVAN'S ISLAND GETS a lot of author's ink for good reason. It is old-style, no condominiums, no high-rises and it's "comfortably shabby." Only three miles long, and about a mile wide, Sullivan's Island is a special place on earth. The local government won't let people purchase a house if they're going to rent it; it can only be rented if it was "grandfathered" as four decades ago.

Hugh paid little attention to where they were going, taking Mandy's directions with a left here and a right there, and there they were. It wasn't what Hugh thought. He assumed it was a small cottage off the beach that probably needed a lot of work. He couldn't have been more wrong.

Mandy's little "bungalow" was first row, on the beach, but it was so protected by dunes and sea oats, the house couldn't be seen from the water. It was a wooden, two-story home containing five thousand square feet of heart-pine floors, some covered with hundred-year old Persian rugs, others with the new beach-style hemp; some other floors left to their barren exquisite beauty, burnished in satin polyurethane every two years whether it needed it or not. There were six bedrooms, five and a half baths. The kitchen was completely modernized. On the right-hand side, as Hugh entered, was an open floor plan that had a thousand square feet of space.

The house sat at the tip of the island. From the road, Middle Street, the house could barely be seen, but the acre and a half lot had at least a dozen hundred-year-old Live Oaks that seemed to hover over the home like a canopied halo. From the driveway, made with concrete and crushed oyster shells, the white painted wooden home looked like it might be a little small. There were twelve steps up to the landing from the driveway, and as Hugh stood on the landing at the "front door" which was the roadside door, (really the back door) he noticed the wrap-around porch spread out like one at a resort hotel, with eight-foot tall Wavy Leaf Ligustrum surrounding the property.

As Hugh entered the living area, he was amazed at the expanse of it; there were three couches, all with comfortable chairs surrounding them. A sixty-five-inch flat screen TV was on the far-left wall. He looked to his right at the massive kitchen with granite countertops and stainless-steel appliances and implements that would make any chef envious. He walked through the great room toward three large casements, three circular glass windows that stretched from the floor to a height of ten feet. They were like giant portholes, each taller than he was, drawing his eyes to the sea. At night, he learned later, there were electric screens that lowered from inside the casements to make the room cozy and either bright or dim. One of the large circular windows had sliding glass doors that opened to the broad Brazilian-hardwood deck that could entertain an entire wedding reception.

Hugh dropped his little night bag onto one of the couches as he approached the center circular window in the massive room. Breath left his body. There was the ocean; he hadn't seen it in fifteen years. He and Michelle always spent their vacation time in the mountains. He sighed again.

"That's a beautiful sight," he said, talking to himself.

Bailey was wandering around, tail wagging, smelling everything in sight as Mandy came in behind them. There were some kiteboarders on the water, their kites twenty feet off the water with the boarders flitting to and fro.

"You want to try kiteboarding, Hugh?" she asked.

Hugh ignored the question.

"Mandy, this is no weekend bungalow. This is a first-row palace on one of the world's most renowned beaches. I mean—"

He stopped short, knowing that he was treading on territory that was none of his business. It had never occurred to him until that moment that Mandy was from money, real money. The realization hit him as though he'd been duped. He was a man, that's all, a man that didn't listen—like most men who are too involved in themselves to listen to what is being said. All the signs were there—the education at Pepperdine, the weekend competitions up and down the East Coast, Mandy's parents were "gone away" on some "assignment" or "business," the polo matches, the garage apartment at a cottage. And she worked at the newspaper that paid next to nothing. Mandy talked about a political career and philanthropy? Maybe that was one thing she liked about him. Hugh didn't have any airs to put on; he was a nice man whose very nice wife had died and Mandy sort of adopted him as her dad since her real dad was so busy all the time. Mandy knew exactly where the conversation was headed. She quickly changed the subject.

"I can teach you kiteboarding this weekend if you want."

"No way in hell I'm getting out there. I'll watch you, though. And Bailey will have a helluva time on the beach."

"I've got about a dozen tennis balls around here somewhere," she said, "we'll wear 'im out."

The potentially uncomfortable moment behind them, Mandy pointed at the kitchen. "And we've got beer. I know you want a Coors Light." She strolled across the room, opened the stainless steel, side-by-side refrigerator, and pulled out two silver bullets, setting one on the counter and opening the other for herself.

"Drink this while you help me unload. Bailey can help too." She headed down the stairs, back to the driveway where she and Hugh, with Bailey's help, unloaded her kiteboards and their various parts and put them into one of the five garages, three of which had no cars. There were other "toys" in one garage, two jet skis, and in another, a golf cart.

After showing Hugh his room on the second floor, a room with a king-sized bed, his own bathroom, and a forty-eight-inch flat screen which came up with the remote out of the foot of the bed, Hugh and Bailey went outside to the back deck. Hugh got another beer.

He was completely at home. He was away, his money forgotten, and he relaxed. He installed himself on the back deck in a thick-padded love seat that rocked on a glider underneath. He sat there, moving back and forth, looking at the water, the sun sparkling off it, while Mandy was busy under the house, organizing her kiteboards and tossing balls to Bailey, who was running to and from the beach carrying one ball after another to Mandy.

It was still bright outside, only about three in the afternoon, the sun behind the house headed on its transit toward the Ravenel Bridge, a few miles from Sullivan's Island. Shade had come to the back deck and Hugh was very comfortable. There's something about the ocean and beer, or wine, or a good drink of liquor. They go together. Even if a person is not a big drinker, there's something about salt water, the smell of the sea, the pelicans flying in formation along the shore, the sand stretching to the water line, the tide moving that line a little at a time, there's *something* about it that makes humans thirsty.

Hugh got another beer.

Ten minutes passed while he drank, closing his eyes occasionally, listening to the waves in the distance and the gulls cawing and carrying on about their own dramas with others in the air. He opened his eyes and noticed Mandy, board tucked under her arm, headed toward the water. Bailey was beside her, barking and running into the water and then back onto the beach. Mandy positioned the board just so and within ten seconds she was out of the surf and into the air while Bailey sat on the beach. Even Bailey was amazed. There she was, sailing, gliding on the water with her feet tucked into little slips on the board, lifting the entire board out of the water, skyward. Just as quickly as she left the water, she was back on top, moving along the surface at what looked like a hundred miles an hour and then she was airborne again. Bailey didn't move for a few minutes. Hugh stood up at the rail and watched his surrogate daughter sail, as they say, with the greatest of ease. And for no reason at all he felt tears well up in his eyes. He didn't know why. He was overwhelmed. There was life, staring him in the face, a life with nature, with people he had come to know and care about—with sunlight and a beach. And the child he'd never had, a woman with values, a woman with her eyes on the prize, a woman who he was proud to call his friend. It was the best he'd felt since Michelle died.

He wiped his eyes, gathered his composure, and got another beer.

Kiteboarding practice, as Mandy called it later, was like something Hugh had never seen before. There were twenty or thirty of those folks on the water, doing flips and turns, playing with and taming the wind as though it were a tool, not a force of nature. Miraculously, the group of kiteboarders didn't smash into each other. Instead they gracefully kept their distance, independently owning an area of the beach seemingly reserved for each person. After a time, Bailey grew tired of running up and down the beach chasing Mandy and he joined Hugh on the deck. As soon as Bailey made a few turns and found the place he liked, he lay on his side, sat up and licked himself as he always did.

About the time Mandy came up the stairs to the deck to join Hugh and Bailey, her wetsuit still zipped to her neck, she spotted the women letting themselves in the front door. They were carrying champagne.

"You made it!" Mandy hollered, waving them out to the deck.

The beer had kicked in. Hugh stood up, waving them in as well.

"Champagne Friday!" he said, holding up his empty beer can. "I'll have a glass."

Chapter 24

THERE WERE THREE women; Kathy, Lynn, and Dorothy; the females of *Champagner's 1836*. Kathy was carrying the bottle, Lynn and Dorothy each holding a red solo cup with the bubbly. They all greeted each other with little hugs, even Dorothy and Lynn hugging on Hugh. They'd all been nodding at each other for several weeks, and Kathy, it turned out, had told Lynn and Dorothy about how she and Hugh had been having coffee with Mandy. She'd confessed to liking Hugh in a way that wasn't platonic. Of course, Hugh didn't know anything about those conversations, and he certainly wouldn't have considered being alone with a woman for thirty minutes a "date."

At this point in time, though, Hugh had had three or four beers and he was one happy camper. So were Kathy and Lynn.

"Tell me about the drive," Mandy said while pulling champagne flutes down from the glass-fronted cabinet filled with wine glasses of all kinds.

"Kathy and Lynn were obnoxious by the time we got to Mount Pleasant," Dorothy said. "They made me stop at Publix on the pretense that they had to pee, and then they bought six more bottles of Domaine Carneros. They don't need to drink anything but coffee for a few hours."

"Not a word of that is true," Kathy said, "there was no pretense about having to use the ladies room, and, we do need something else to drink." Kathy looked at Hugh who was now holding an empty flute in one hand and his mostly empty Coors Light can in the other. She put her arm around him and batted her eyes in the most exaggerated way, and in the deepest southern accent she could, she asked, "Rhett, would you be a dear and get our cooler out of the car? I can't lift that heavy thing."

"See what I mean?" Dorothy said.

"Of course, Scarlett," Hugh said, recognizing her reference to *Gone With the Wind*, and in his own deep-voiced Clark Gable impersonation, he said "I'll be right back with your beverages." And turning to Lynn and Dorothy, he bowed and said, "And to you my dear ladies, I'll pop the cork without spilling a drop." They all burst into laughter as Hugh pranced, not walked, to the front door.

When Hugh returned, he popped the cork with flair and everyone got a glass, Hugh quickly downing his beer. A little toast was made to their safe travel, another toast to Friday, and another one to good friends. Mandy, still in her wetsuit, excused herself to get dressed while the rest of the group went out to the back deck where Bailey greeted them all with a tail that seemed to wag him.

They stood at the rail, looking at the ocean with a host of kiteboarders doing their thing on the water. The ladies included Hugh in their conversation, treating him like an old friend, commenting on the beauty of Mandy's beach house, the décor of the home and the special nature of Sullivan's

Island. Hugh was completely at home. Maybe it was the beer and champagne, maybe it was the ocean, maybe it was that he forgot about his digging for cash, maybe it was all those things, but he felt at *home*.

Kathy asked Hugh to open another bottle of champagne. When he returned to the deck, full bottle in hand, he topped off some glasses, and with Mandy now dressed, they asked her to show them how the kiteboard worked. Everyone went down the back steps while Mandy pulled out her board, without the kite and its strings.

"Let's go to the beach," she said, still toting the board, "I'll show you what those boarders are doing."

They were genuinely interested, each asking questions about the sport, how she got into it, the seeming impossibility of it all, the coordination it must take, the strength that they themselves didn't have, while Mandy eagerly responded. Hugh was still holding the mostly-full bottle of champagne.

"Hugh, let's walk down toward Fort Moultrie," Kathy said. Hugh, being a man, didn't think about who wasn't invited. Kathy and Hugh, bottle of champagne in hand, started their walk, stopping every now and then to sip and then to pour. The two of them sauntered down the beach, close to the water, chatting like old friends. Bailey couldn't resist following, Hugh and Kathy occasionally throwing the tennis ball down the beach or into the water.

The others noticed that they weren't invited on the walk. Mandy looked at the two walkers and back to her older friends.

"I've been telling you how special he is," she said, "he's a very good man. He's become like a dad to me."

"And Kathy likes him," Dorothy said.

Lynn, who'd had more to drink than the other two, said in a slightly slurred voice, "They both need to get laid."

"You are cut off," Dorothy said, "that's enough for you."

Mandy, still watching Hugh and Kathy, quietly turned to Lynn and Dorothy.

"Lynn's right," she said.

A burst of laughter filled the air.

When Hugh and Kathy returned from their little walk, the crew had adjourned back to the kitchen and the great open room.

"What time do the men finish golf?" Mandy asked.

"They're probably done by now," Lynn said, "I'll bet they're at Morgan Creek having a beer. Bob loves that place. They said they'd call."

"If y'all don't have dinner plans, why don't we go to Poe's or High Thyme," Mandy said, "we can take the golf cart and the men are only a ten-minute drive away. That way we won't get caught up in the Charleston traffic on Friday."

With some cell phone conversations, plans were confirmed to meet at High Thyme for cocktails and dinner.

High Thyme was located on the only busy street on Sullivan's Island. Charming art shops surrounded several restaurants on the street; every shop and every restaurant was a former residence. The houses were quaint—with wooden floors and single pane windows—most of the little places needed a coat of paint. High Thyme was across the street from Poe's, the eponymous restaurant named in honor of Edgar Allan Poe who lived on Sullivan's Island for a short time a hundred and fifty years earlier. The street epitomized charm. High Thyme had a reputation for the best white-table cloth restaurant on Sullivan's—its fare of freshly-caught fish and excellent tenderloin, not to mention great service made customers very happy to return over and over again.

Mandy drove the six-person-golf cart to meet the rest of the crowd, Hugh riding shotgun. Dorothy had caught up with her champagne-drinking friends. Mandy was the only sober one by the time they all arrived, the golfing men also having had several adult beverages.

The men, Bob and Steve, had met Hugh at several Champagne Friday mornings and they treated him like he was an old fraternity brother. More cocktails were consumed at the bar, the women getting the Champagne spritzer with a splash of vodka and pomegranate.

It was loud, dozens of people in the restaurant, others standing around outside, plastic cups in hand, drinking on the sidewalk. Despite little signs that prohibited that activity, the cops of Sullivan's Island ignored the rules while the tourists were in town. High Thyme was a very busy place and Hugh felt at ease.

After a time, they got a table for seven that was outside on the deck. Mandy made sure that Hugh sat between herself and Kathy, the others not noticing. More drinks were served, and dinner ordered. The men again included Hugh into their conversation. Bob and Steve invited Hugh to play golf with them, an invitation that he accepted only because he had been drinking. Of course, Hugh told them that he was going to watch

Mandy compete on the beach the next day, but he would play golf in Aiken when they returned. It was unlike Hugh to be so willing to do anything with people, but there he was, acting like he enjoyed human contact. It was true, Hugh did like other humans; he just didn't welcome them like a salesman. He chose his contact with others very carefully, but with Michelle gone, he'd limited it to Mandy and a few old co-workers that he didn't call very often. His newfound friendships were something Hugh secretly cherished.

More drinks were served during dinner. Mandy imbibed little. She was competing on Saturday afternoon, and she didn't want anything to ruin her chances, the competitor in her still strong.

And then it happened. The check arrived. It was so simple. They all could have thrown cash on the table. They could have done some basic division and figured it. But Hugh Buncombe had had too much to drink. He had five one-hundred-dollar bills in his front pants pocket that he had retrieved earlier in the day before he and Mandy left on their journey. In a stupid and magnanimous moment, he pulled out three of those bills to take care of the whole tab. The others protested, but once again, Hugh was so kind, explaining that he didn't get out very often, that he enjoyed Champagne Friday, that he wanted to treat the whole troop. The others yielded to his generosity. Hugh tossed out those bills, old bills that were out of circulation, into the little leatherette case from the server. When the waitress picked it up, she noticed the old bills and made a comment about not having seen those before. Hugh told her that he'd gotten those out of his private stock as a joke, and she left the table.

But she checked with the manager, who confirmed that one-hundred-dollar bills used to look that way and that it was okay. And of course, in today's world, everything is video recorded. Everything.

If a little winged angel had been floating around Hugh's shoulder, if a protective guardian had been hovering nearby, they both would have screamed at Hugh, grabbed the cash and stuffed it back into his front pocket. Use your credit card, they would have said. But there was no such protector, no light-footed elf to stop the happy Hugh. The cash was now in the stream of commerce; the same cash that had been missing for over forty years. Richmond, Virginia, one of the places where money was re-circulated, was about to get very excited about those three bills.

Chapter 25

IF MANDY HADN'T been recently released from a serious relationship, if she didn't consider Hugh Buncombe a friend and a father figure, she wouldn't have been hanging around a stack of folks who were old enough to be her parents. But she liked, she truly enjoyed, the *Champagner's 1836*. Hell, they were fun.

While Mandy had plenty of friends her own age, her split with Kevin and her relationship with Hugh and the Champagner's made it easy for her to associate with the older crowd. Mandy invited them all to her house for an after-dinner drink.

As if anyone needed another drink.

The *Champagner's 1836*, including Kathy, had their own place to stay, but Mandy's house was closer than their house on the Isle of Palms. Mandy's house was only a three-minute golf-cart ride from High Thyme. It was dark when they arrived; Mandy closed the electric blinds on the massive circular windows on the rear of the house. Drinks were made, liquor added to the menu of beverages. Bourbon on the rocks, Scotch and water, some Chardonnay and Pinot Grigio for the women. Mandy couldn't resist her own Margarita recipe, deciding to have a few drinks regardless of the competition the following afternoon. Bob, Steve and Hugh made drinks while Mandy showed the house to the ladies and turned the satellite radio to a classic rock station, music she figured would please her over-aged friends. Tastefully disguised, speakers were everywhere, including the back deck.

Although the music wasn't too loud, the next-door neighbors heard it. There were six of them; three young married couples, in their mid-thirties. It was their weekend away from Atlanta, their children all with babysitters at home for the weekend. And the owner of their home, a person Mandy's parents' age, had allowed the house to be used that weekend by the oldest sibling and his band of married friends. They were a younger version of *Champagner's 1836*, and were soon listening to fabricated stories about old, passed away, members and the health benefits of lots of champagne.

Mandy greeted the oldest sibling and his wife, a couple she'd known for years, having attended their wedding in Atlanta. Although she didn't know the other four, it didn't matter. Liquor, once again, the friend lubricant, made introductions unnecessary, everyone as happy as they could be to hang out and sing along with old music. They were all welcome, each toting some adult beverage. More liquor was pulled out of the cabinets. The music was turned up, still classic rock.

Before long, some chairs were moved to make way for dancing. The music was turned up again, everyone singing some of the anthems like *Satisfaction* and *Dirty Deeds Done Dirt Cheap*. Even Hugh sang along, if you called it singing. It was more like yelling, but there were thirteen voices, none of which could have made the most desperately needed voices for a church choir.

More liquor, more beers, more dancing, led Hugh to take a break; he sat down on a three cushion couch in the living room. The music was still blaring; he sat there by himself, rocking and humming along to *Sweet Home Alabama.*

Hugh continued singing and without warning, stood up on top of the coffee table and shouted: *Champagner's 1836*!

Everyone cheered. Hugh was an automatic member—as if there was any committee or membership board.

Kathy grabbed Hugh by the hand, a champagne flute in her hand and whispered, "let's take a walk."

Hugh rarely drank too much, but he was so happy, so relaxed, he thought he should have a bubbly to go on the walk. "Hey," he said to Kathy, "You want something else to drink? I'm getting a bottle of 1836."

"I'd love another glass of that," she said, handing Hugh a mostly empty glass.

When Hugh came to the deck with a plastic stemware, Kathy was standing with her back to Hugh at the rail of the deck. It was a very clear night; Kathy was looking up at the moon, just about two o'clock in the sky, as a mariner would say, its light shimmering on the calm water.

"Let's head toward the lighthouse," she said, "Bailey probably needs to pee."

Hugh didn't say anything; he obeyed, unleashed Bailey and grabbed a stray tennis ball still on the deck from the afternoon. They walked on the beach, chatting again about one thing or another, about the people from Atlanta, about the music, about Mandy. Bailey continued to chase the ball that was thrown by Hugh or Kathy, Bailey sometimes purposely bringing the ball to her hand instead of Hugh's. They were out of earshot of the music from Mandy's deck, their voices growing quieter in their conversation. They had reached the same turning-around point as they had in the afternoon, and humans being creatures of habit, even newly-formed habits, they stopped to turn. Kathy threw the ball as best she could as they both watched Bailey go on his chase. And then, just as Bailey got to the ball, Kathy did it.

She turned Hugh with her body as though turning back toward Mandy's house and stood in Hugh's way. With one smooth movement, one that only a woman knows how to do, she put her arms around Hugh's neck and kissed him. That's right. She kissed him on the mouth the way a lover kisses someone, not a peck on the lips, but a real kiss. Hugh responded like a lover. And then he stopped himself and pulled away.

"Kathy, what the hell are you—?

"I think I'm kissing you," she said, "and I think you just kissed me back."

"But I'm a married man," he stammered, "I'm a married man."

"You're not a married man," she said, "you're a widower and I'm a widow."

"Even more reason why you shouldn't be kissing me. You're married."

Knowing that was a ridiculous comment, Hugh said no more, but suddenly sober, walked toward Mandy's house with Bailey stuffing the ball into his hand. Kathy walked right next to Hugh, saying nothing. She understood his faithfulness—that was part of what attracted her to him—but she also wanted, in her own way, to let Hugh know she was interested in something more than a coffee buddy. She was very content to leave it alone for a time. Hugh didn't speak another word for the five-minute walk back to the house. It wasn't that he was rude; he was simply quiet. Kathy became the ball thrower, Hugh being too deep in thought to pay Bailey any mind. When they arrived at the back deck, Hugh put Bailey back in the garage while Kathy went up the stairs to the party that was finally winding down. It was midnight.

The music was still on, everyone was still there, but it was closing time, the young folks volunteering to take the Champagne People to Poe's where they could get a late-night cab to the Isle of Palms. Kathy found her way to Mandy.

"You got a second?" she asked Mandy, pulling her toward the dining room where no one was standing.

"Of course," Mandy said, walking to the head of the table.

"I think I pissed off Hugh," she said with a slight slur.

"How?"

"I kissed him."

"No you din int," she said.

"I did."

"And?"

"He kissed me back and then told me he was married." Kathy shrugged. "I reminded him he was a widower."

Mandy hugged Kathy.

"Good for you," she said.

In the next few minutes everyone filtered out. Hugh had put Bailey in the garage and he went straight to bed, barely saying good night to anyone. Alcohol put him to sleep, but he awoke in the middle of the night, thirsty. He got some water from the bathroom and went back to bed. He couldn't sleep. He thought about Michelle. He thought about his new life, about Mandy, about Bailey, and he thought about Kathy. She had been like a feather under his nose when he was asleep. She'd been tickling him little by little, waking him up one swipe at a time, ever so slightly. In his sleep-state he moved the feather away, but there it was again, touching his nose, aggravating him a little more. Finally, that vellicating feather had, in the form of a kiss, made him wide-awake to the thought that there was life after Michelle.

And he felt tremendous guilt.

He *couldn't* care for another person. He had promised Michelle his fidelity. But Michelle was gone. It wasn't right for him to feel life after Michelle, but there it was, life, a renewed sense of being, challenging his belief that his life had been all but over.

Chapter 26

IT WAS 6 a.m. Hugh quietly went downstairs, got some more water and retrieved Bailey from the garage. He walked on the beach with his dog, in the dark, tossing the same tennis ball that Kathy had been throwing, until the sun came up. Bailey was worn out; Hugh didn't even notice.

The sun just bright enough to read by daylight, Mandy stood at the rail of the back deck with a Styrofoam cup filled with coffee in her hand. She noticed Hugh, head down, deep in thought, as he walked on the little path from the beach to the house.

"Hey Bailey, has your dad given you any food?"

Bailey, tired as he was, bolted up the steps to see Mandy, tail smacking against the rail, his head accepting both of Mandy's hands. "Has your dad been thinking about Kathy?"

Hugh arrived at the top step to the deck.

"Has your dad been wondering what to do if a girl kisses him?"

"What the hell?" Hugh said.

"I saw it on channel seven," she said, "it's all over the newspapers. Good looking man kissed by woman on beach at Sullivan's Island."

Even Hugh couldn't resist smiling.

"She told you, huh?"

"Women talk and tell the truth. Men make up stuff."

"Good God."

"Let's go to the Seabiscuit," she said. "It's five minutes away on the Isle of Palms. They've got a fantastic breakfast menu and a deck where we can eat outside with Bailey. He told me he wanted a bagel with egg and bacon."

Hugh didn't even shower. Ten minutes later they were on the front deck of the Seabiscuit having coffee. They ordered breakfast for three, Bailey happily leashed to Hugh's chair.

This time it was a daughter-father talk. That's different from a father-daughter discussion. Their relationship had grown into one where Hugh completely trusted Mandy with his feelings. Who else could he talk to about things of the heart? A therapist? Not Hugh Buncombe. An old guy-friend? No way. And he sure couldn't talk to Bailey. Every time he did that, Bailey licked himself.

Mandy looked at Hugh across the table. He had the look of a child about to be scolded for something he'd done wrong.

"Mr. Buncombe," she began, "you know the reason I started drinking coffee with you in the mornings was because of my affection for your wife. You don't have to tell me how wonderful she was. I know it from first-hand experience. But the reason I *kept* having our coffee together was because I became fond of *you.* You're a good, decent man, Hugh. You deserve all that life should give—all that life offers you from *this* point forward. And your life is not over. You need to consider moving on. Sure, you can continue to grieve in your own way, but you must keep on living, too. Seize life, even in its seemingly autumn days, for all that it's worth." She paused and pulled her shoulder-length hair back behind her head. She looked Hugh square in his quiet eyes.

"There's a certain freedom in choosing to live life to its fullest, Hugh. Choose life. Take a deep breath, grieve, and choose life."

Hugh looked at Mandy without speaking.

The food arrived. Mandy tore a bagel into bite size pieces and fed Bailey one bite at a time while Hugh watched, still silent. Bailey seemed very happy with his bagel. Mandy then took a bite of her own sandwich.

With her mouth mostly full, she looked at Hugh again.

"You know," she said, "there's a great sense of connecting with nature when I'm on that kiteboard. There's the wind, the water and the board. And then there's me. I'm the only human element connecting those things. And there's a tremendous feeling of freedom when I'm out there, just me trying to control things that are really beyond my control if it weren't for my humanness, my ability to hold those natural elements in check. And sometimes, when I'm in the zone, as they say, and there is such a thing, Hugh—sometimes I just let the wind pull me. I choose that freedom that exists with the wind. And that's when it's the most fun—letting the wind pull me—it is a force of nature, a true force of nature. And we humans make choices, choices that are tied to nature—like our inability to stop death.

But we can choose the force of nature that is life. Try it, it's exhilarating."

Hugh looked at her, still silent. They ate for a few minutes, Mandy saying nothing, occasionally looking at Hugh, waiting for him to say something. He was deep in thought. Mandy swallowed a big chunk of sandwich, and she leaned into Hugh at the table.

"You know what?" she said, "When I have that feeling, that exhilarating feeling of being tied to nature—that's when I win." And she sat back in her plastic seat and looked up, away from Hugh. "That's when I win," she repeated.

"You are wise beyond your years," he commented.

"I'm your good friend telling you to live your life, Hugh. I may be young, but I've got some wisdom in these youthful bones. My parents have always called me an old soul."

Hugh leaned in to Mandy.

"I know this is none of my business," he said, "I've never asked you any personal questions about things"—Hugh stopped, and then got right to his point—"about money," he said, "but who *are* your parents? I mean, they've been gone away on business for six months, and I never thought about it, but, this house here on Sullivan's Island, the polo … "

Mandy stopped Hugh, she sat back in her green plastic chair, pulling her hair this time into a ponytail with a rubber band.

"My grandfather was a hotelier, my parents, both of them, have been very successful in real estate development. They own my grandfather's cottage in town. That's where I'm living.

My parents own fifteen hundred hotels around the world. My family has a net worth of more than a billion dollars. And it grows every day. I have a trust fund that supplies me with more income than I can possibly spend. The truth is, though, Hugh, I don't care about all that money. It's nice not to worry about money, but I don't want to waste my time on earth just enjoying myself. I've got things I want to do and my parents have encouraged me to do the newspaper job to hone my skills as a writer. "

"And you hang around with me," he said in a questioning tone, "I mean, I—

"You didn't make your judgment of me because of my background," she said, choosing the word background instead of money, "you liked me because I knew your wife. I must be careful whom I call my friend, Hugh. And you are my friend because you like me for who I am, not what I have." She looked at Bailey. "And the other truth is, you have Bailey. He loves me because I feed him human food." Bailey stood up and welcomed her hands on his back, Mandy scratching him vigorously.

The money talk was behind them. The severity of her wealth disclosed, Mandy was done with it. And Hugh knew it. Mandy was the third generation of a family whose wealth was over a billion dollars, money that was sheltered in places that Hugh couldn't imagine, and Mandy had to be very careful about who she considered her friends. And she knew that Hugh didn't want anything from her except her friendship. She had chosen her friend very wisely. Hugh and Mandy could move on with their very special relationship with no further discussion about how rich she was.

Mandy continued with her lesson to Hugh.

"I'm telling you Hugh," she said, "you need to think about living life. You need to let go. Grow your hair; get a tattoo." She leaned in again to Hugh. "Love someone. It's okay to love someone."

"Tattoos suck."

"Don't pretend you didn't hear me," she said, "live life to its fullest. It's what Michelle would want you to do. Love to the best of your ability." And then she thumped him on his chest with her little fist, like she was knocking on a door. "I know there's a big ole' heart in there, Hugh." She stopped for a minute and looked into the sky, above the bright blue umbrella that was shading their white plastic table.

You need to work *with* nature, Hugh," she continued, "don't fight natural things." She stopped again. "It's one of the reasons I'm good at kiteboarding. I've learned to make the wind my friend; I don't fight the wind like a lot of other competitors do. It was a trick I learned early on. When you come out today, don't watch me; watch my *kite.* I let the kite pull me and I become one with the wind. When I do that, I win. Watch my kite, Hugh; don't watch me. When I let nature do her thing, it is a very freeing experience."

Hugh sat back in his chair while Mandy, like an enchantress to the spellbound, like a muse to her subject, went silent. It was time for Hugh to think about what she'd said. Mandy untethered Bailey from Hugh's chair and told him she was going to show Bailey around the Isle of Palms. Hugh sat there in that green plastic chair like one of Michelle's schoolchildren who had been placed on a time-out stool in the corner. Mandy hadn't cast a spell on Hugh; she'd simply told the truth, a truth he didn't want to hear.

Before she left on her little walk with Bailey, she came back to Hugh and whispered into his ear, "besides, you're probably a little horny. Some sex would do you good." And then she left. Hugh was silent for another few seconds.

And then, because he was so deep in thought, because he forgot where he was, and was impulsive as he was when he blurted out to Max Cooper about his not being a drug dealer, he shouted at Mandy who was walking on the road in front of the Seabiscuit. "I am not horny!"

And then he remembered there were twenty or so diners staring at him.

And it got worse. Looking at them, and pointing toward Mandy, he said, "She's not my sex therapist, she's just a friend."

Mandy smiled a huge grin and kept walking.

Realizing he'd painted himself into a corner of embarrassment, he threw a couple of twenties on the table and marched toward Mandy and Bailey who were still in sight.

Hugh Buncombe had a lot to think about.

And those three one-hundred-dollar bills were marching toward Richmond. Hugh, poor Hugh, was thinking about his widower status. He should have been planning an exit strategy.

Chapter 27

THE CURRENT AT Breach Inlet is deadly. It's where the Isle of Palms and Sullivan's Island are separated; for hundreds of years the current has swirled, curled, and swept away the unsuspecting visitor. Signs are posted in three-foot letters: Dangerous Currents, Do Not Swim.

The competition was a half-mile away from the current in safe waters, but the competition was set close enough to currents to allow the boarders to use it to its full potential. And kiteboarding competitions are always in the afternoon. The wind doesn't blow in the mornings like it does in the afternoon. The venue for the competition was at Breach Inlet, a little over two miles from Mandy's house. She had been there hundreds of times; it was literally like competing in her own back yard. At three o'clock the beach was crowded with kiteboarders and their colorful equipment dotted here and there on the broad beach. The ocean was making low tide; inside of two hours the beach would be even bigger, the waves seemingly pushing out to sea. With the wind blowing at fifteen knots, the boarders were excited. There would be enough wind for them to show off their skills.

Kiteboarding isn't exactly the NFL. There aren't thousands of fans, but some dedicated followers and friends of the competitors were sitting on towels, beach chairs, or milling about the beach. Mandy had her own set of fans—the *Champagner's 1836* were there and Mandy's next-door neighbors, all supporting Mandy with well wishes.

An air horn blew announcing the start of the competition.

Hugh stood near the sand dunes, away from everyone else, holding Bailey on the leash. The Champagners brought some beach chairs, Kathy and the others all sitting in a small group. It didn't surprise Hugh to see little red Solo cups in their hands. Bob spotted Hugh and waved him toward the rest of the crowd and Hugh held his finger up letting him know he would join them in a minute. Hugh had no intentions of going over to them, though. Instead, he wandered over to the judging area in hopes of learning how it was scored and hoping to get the inside scoop of what the judges thought about Mandy.

Seven other women, all younger than Mandy, had already had their turn. They were all very good, turning forward and backward rolls, executing moves that pleased the judges. Before Mandy entered the water, she whistled at Hugh with two fingers in her mouth and pointed toward the sky. Hugh knew what that meant. He nodded back to her. Her kite, a red, white and blue one, filled with air as Mandy jumped onto her board. She was off in an instant, the wind pulling her sail high into the sun-filled sky, her board leaving the water with her feet attached. Hugh watched, amazed at her dexterity. She looked like a trapeze artist, twisting, turning, looping the kite, doing forward rolls and backward rolls with ease. That was the warm-up. She then started a series of 720 spins turning two complete rotations while in the air. Hugh was like a proud papa, clapping on the sidelines near the judges, but standing away from the rest of the crowd. And then he remembered to watch the kite, not Mandy. The wind was pulling the kite up into the air; it seemed like a hundred feet off the water. Suddenly, once again with Hugh watching only the kite as an object, a line following the kite, he noticed the wind shift at a higher altitude away from the beach. And there was that object again, seemingly in pursuit of the wind. Still watching the kite, Hugh noticed that it shifted again, pushing out to sea. Mandy was ten, maybe twenty feet off the water letting the wind pull her dangerously like a little rag doll attached to a string. She did two complete 1080s without tangling one of her lines on the kite and landed on the water like a waterfowl lands on a still lake, barely making a splash. The crowd went crazy, clapping, arms in the air, congratulating Mandy's performance. The judges nodded to each other; Hugh struggled to listen, but it didn't matter. No one else in the competition had done a 1080, much less two of them. Within thirty seconds, Mandy was back near the shoreline, coming at the beach like she was out of control—Hugh was sure she was going to pound herself into the sand or worse, but then with a thin flick of her wrist she was airborne again, another fifteen feet off the water heading south, skimming along the shoreline like one of those pelicans scanning the thin water for a meal. The crowd went crazy again as Mandy executed another 1080 and landed, once again, atop the water without a splash.

Mandy turned back to deeper water for a few seconds and then with another quick turn of her wrists she headed again toward the shallow water. This time the judges looked at each other, knowing that coming too close to the beach carried the potential for a serious accident—crashing into the sand at fifteen knots could result in broken bones—or death. Hugh sensed that something dangerous was happening and he couldn't help but turn his attention to Mandy instead of the kite. If she was going to be hurt, or worse, he wanted to be there. Mandy approached the beach at incredible speed, the board in less than a foot of water, a small wave yielding its last bit of water to the sand. Mandy was suddenly in six inches of water; Hugh started running toward the beach with Bailey in tow. One of the judges grabbed the other by the elbow, knowing that a disaster was occurring before their eyes. Hugh had run several feet toward the beach when she did it—she tugged the kite with the dexterity of a surgeon—she was airborne, fifteen feet off the water, headed out to sea, away from danger. Hugh kept his eyes focused on Mandy. There was no smile, no childish sense of seeking approval. She was in a zone that Hugh didn't imagine a person could achieve. She was teasing death and moving on. Hugh put his hands on his knees, this time looking up at the kite. The kite pulled her out to sea again, with Mandy back on the water, holding steady. Hugh had never seen such a display of skill and courage. He turned toward the judges. They were shaking their heads in disbelief, speaking in tones of approval.

Mandy was right. She let the wind do the work. She wasn't in charge, nature was. And like she said, that's when she won—when she didn't try to control it. Hugh sat down on the beach as Mandy finished her set.

The other competitors in Mandy's category didn't come close to her achievement. An hour later she accepted a plaque from Stuart Shuck—a judge who had seen her perform many times. The plaque was like so many of the others she'd earned—a little line that said, "First Place" with the date and name of the competition. As Mandy stood on the beach with her fellow competitors and judges, she was humble and nonchalant, chatting with them all. Hugh blew up with pride inside, but he left her alone to enjoy the victory with her kiteboarding family.

Standing away from the crowd, he thought about what she'd said about nature, about having a big ole heart. He wasn't sure about his heart, but he felt nature in his gut, pulling him toward more life.

Mandy's neighbors and the Champagners broke Hugh's reverie. Like the current at Breach Inlet, they approached Hugh and swallowed him up. Bob handed Hugh a red Solo cup full of beer, the others toasted Hugh and held their cups toward Mandy who didn't even notice them. They were all good buddies now, the evening before having greased the wheels of friendship.

Hugh looked at the water; above the horizon stood a South Carolina crescent moon, barely visible in the bright sunshine. But the moon was there, like a maiden in the wings—patiently waiting for the sun to bow out—yielding the limelight. Hugh looked over Bob's shoulder. Kathy was also standing like a maiden in waiting, a little shy, anxiously desiring the sun to finish the day, hoping that she could have her own private limelight with the man she'd kissed the night before. She tipped her red Solo cup toward him with a blushing smile; Hugh reciprocated, tipping his fresh cup toward Kathy. The current of time, healing Hugh little by little, had pulled him like the undertow at Breach Inlet toward the lovely widow with whom he'd decided he might share that "big ole heart."

Mandy approached her older friends who showered her with hugs and a congratulatory cup of Domaine Carneros. After the clinking of several toasts with their plastic cups, Mandy found her way to Hugh. Before he could speak, she grabbed his forearm and pulled his ear to her mouth.

"Ask her to dinner. The worst thing that can happen is she says no. I'll bet my little trophy she says yes." Hugh stood back as she released his arm.

"Did you hear me?"

"I'm going to ask her to dinner, just the two of us, right now."

"That's my boy."

Of course, but of course, Mandy was right about her prediction. Kathy said yes. There was *everything* romantic about a cloudless sky, a star-filled night and a crescent moon that glimmered on the ocean at Sullivan's Island. Dinner was excellent. Hugh moved a little closer to moving on with his life after Michelle.

If he just hadn't spent that damn money.

Chapter 28

DHARMA WAS FORTY and divorced. She had a friend who worked at the *Aiken Standard* who had tattle-tailed to Mandy about Dharma and Max. Dharma was very attractive; she was blonde, thin, had lovely alabaster skin and a very cute figure. Her eyes were more than romantic; they were lustful, longing light-blue eyes. There they were, in Dharma's living room, one dim lamp with a twenty-five-watt bulb providing romantic light on the accent table next to the couch. Both still standing, Dharma handed Max a Heineken and poured herself a red wine in a stemless glass. Looking at each other in the mostly dark room, Dharma leaned in to Max. She graciously, generously kissed him and pulled on his belt. At first Max responded like he always did, a soft touch on the breast, a tug on Dharma's ass and a deep kiss. But then something happened. He didn't feel up to the task. He had done this sexual play many, many times. He knew in his heart that this relationship was not going to lead anywhere but where it had been: the bedroom. Dharma expected more. She deserved more. And she was nice. As for him, Max wasn't ready to commit to a long-term relationship. She was in his harem, his seraglio on the booty call list, but that was it. And it wasn't fair to her.

Max, smart but horny Maxwell Cooper, did the improbable. He turned down sex.

He knew that true love *did* exist, this thing, this special connection between a man and a woman. He'd never seen that in his parents; his mother died when he was eleven, and his father never, ever brought another woman around Max. But as Max's libido turned into high gear, his brain told him he wasn't feeling the big spark that he should feel. Sure, he felt the lust, but he had been feeling that for the past ten years without feeling much else. So, he stopped it.

"What's wrong?"

"I just can't keep this up. It's not fair to you."

"You're dumping me. You are *dumping* me! After all I've done—the sacrifices I've made to be with you?"

Max looked at the floor and then to Dharma. "I just need time to think. My dad's death, my office, my life ..."

"Don't do this Max. Don't do this to me."

"I've just got to take some time and think."

"Go think. But know this, Max. I've put time in this relationship. You owe me more than this."

"I know."

Maxwell Cooper headed home, shirttail out.

Thirty minutes later he was in his bed, arms folded behind his head, staring at the ceiling, wondering what the hell was wrong with him.

Max hadn't paid much attention to Carla's comings and goings. He was busy with the frantic pace of the firm since his father died and didn't have time to keep up with the very responsible Carla. On Sunday, though, after his abrupt rejection of sex with Dharma, he found himself wandering around his office and stepped into the space where Carla's computer was set up. The area was always kept clean. Carla took every piece of paper with her that she brought in on those days she worked.

Max couldn't help but notice a copy of the Wall Street Journal on the table of her workstation. It was the previous Friday's edition. There on the front page was a picture of a man in a suit. The caption under it said: *Lousteau In Better Days.*

Someone had circled the picture with a yellow highlighter and even better, they had drawn horns on the man in the picture and given him a mustache that resembled the one like Hitler wore. On the side of the picture an arrow had been drawn. At the end of the arrow were the words: "A Picture of an Asshole." It was in Carla's handwriting. Max looked at the picture and giggled. *Carla doesn't like that dude*, he said to himself.

Max spent the rest of the day working. He never gave Carla another thought. He should have.

Chapter 29

"HEY DEREK," JIMMY hollered, "Turn on the water."

Derek was upstairs in the master bedroom of the old home place. He turned the cold- water faucet on.

"Nothing coming out. I don't hear anything running either," Derek hollered back.

"Turn it off, turn it off. I hear water runnin' down here."

Jimmy put his ear up to the downstairs wall near the kitchen. There was a spraying sound that subsided, then changed to a dripping sound.

"I figured as much," he said to himself, and then to Derek as he came into the vacant space. "There's a drip. We got a busted pipe."

The place was looking better; once the roof was repaired, the county had allowed Jimmy to remove the yellow condemnation tape. Getting the water turned on was another movement in the right direction, as Jimmy paid the old bill out of his micro business. Jimmy looked at the cavernous, empty kitchen. There wasn't one appliance in the place and the old porcelain sink was cracked and rusted. The original wooden floor had a nasty cheap vinyl laid over it that was worn through and peeling.

"I could hire a plumber, but that'll cost an arm and a leg. I gotta figure this thing out. These are plaster walls and the plumbing is old copper that has gotten thin over time. I don't know what to do. This job is so durn big."

Late spring had arrived in full force; Jimmy and Derek had planned on getting started on some inside work to stay out of the sun. The plumbing was the first inside challenge. A leak made it that much tougher.

"Well, you know what my granddaddy would say?" Jimmy said, "He would always ask me how do you eat an elephant? The first few times he asked me that, I didn't know what the hell he was talking about. I told 'im I didn't know how you ate an elephant. My granddaddy looked at me with a big smile on his face and put his hand on my shoulder. I wasn't but about ten years old. He said Jimmy, you eat an elephant one bite at a time."

Derek smiled. Jimmy loved talking about his grandfather.

"That's what we gotta do, Derek. We gotta eat this elephant one bite at a time. I think we come in here tomorrow with some sledge hammers and start tearing out this plaster. It'll take us a few months, but we gotta strip this place down to the structure and tear out the plumbin' and the electrical. We'll eat this elephant one bite at a time."

They walked outside to the porch and rocked in the chairs. It calmed both of them to sit for a few minutes; the view overlooking the estate was awe inspiring, the trees fully green, and birds feeding and chirping, squirrels hopping about. It was Derek's favorite time of day, sitting on the porch in that white rocking chair, thinking about nothing. Many times, after their morning of errands and churning compost, Derek fell asleep for a few minutes. Sometimes they talked, but mostly they sat and looked out at the vast acreage. It was a lot easier than looking behind them where the work seemed endless. The sun was beginning to creep over the roof and slowly pull the shade away from them; without speaking they both got up and headed to Jimmy's pickup truck that was parked near the compost pile.

"Sledgehammers tomorrow, Derek. Sledgehammers."

"Sounds good to me," Derek replied.

There was only one problem with their plan. They forgot to turn the water main off in the front yard. The dripping water inside and under the house would make another mess, even harder to fix.

Chapter 30

JIMMY AND DEREK carried their borrowed sledgehammers into the big house. Derek was a little nervous about tearing out walls, but Jimmy assured him the house wouldn't come tumbling down on them; it was built to last eighty years ago and the structure was still solid. As they approached the kitchen, Jimmy noticed a puddle of water on top of the cracked, yellow vinyl.

"Oh no," he said, "Look at that water."

The water was seeping behind the counter, behind the rusted porcelain sink, underneath the cabinet below the sink and onto the floor. The water wasn't deep, but it was a definite puddle. Jimmy followed the trail of water to a low spot in the kitchen where it was dripping through the floor to the crawl space under the house. Jimmy cursed as Derek stood by, the heavy sledgehammer on the floor, the handle balanced on the palm of his hand.

"I forgot to turn the water main off, Derek. I can't believe I did that. I knew it was leakin'. I just forgot. Damn it!" Jimmy fell to his knees and then sat down on the floor away from the water. He put his head in his hands and said nothing. Neither of them spoke for a time.

"You know what I think?" Derek asked, breaking the silence.

"What, Derek, whataya think," Jimmy said, his face still in his hands.

Derek put his hand on Jimmy's shoulder. "I think we got a wet elephant. Your granddaddy was always askin' about how to eat an elephant. Maybe it's easier to eat a wet elephant."

Jimmy didn't say anything for a few seconds. Then he looked up at Derek, poor damn Derek, who'd lost a child and suffered plenty. Jimmy understood. This was a mere bump in the road compared to what Derek was going through.

"Hell, Derek, you're right. Maybe it is easier to eat a wet elephant. You just gotta put stuff in the right light. A wet elephant is probably softer." And then Jimmy sprang to his feet, clapped Derek on the back and looked him in the eyes. "It's not so bad we got this problem. I just gotta get busy and not sit on my ass. I'll go out and turn off the water. That's the first thing I gotta do. Then I'll get under the house to see how bad it is. We can't let this little thing get us down, now can we?"

"No, Jimmy, we can't let this get us down. It ain't worth it."

Jimmy pulled a big wrench out of his truck and turned off the water main. Derek watched as Jimmy walked around the back of the house, about twenty feet from the back porch where there was a small access door, about two feet high by three feet wide. The house was built less than three feet off the crawl space. It was tight, but Jimmy didn't hesitate as he turned the latch to open the rotten wooden door. He crawled on his belly on the soft, sandy soil toward the kitchen. It was musty and dark, but since there were cracks in the floor all through the house, a little light made it easier to see. Jimmy didn't even think about the spiders that had spun webs; he pulled those down with his bare hands as he crawled ever closer to the water source. All he wanted to do was see how much damage there was to the bottom of the old place.

As he got closer to the kitchen, he heard a hissing sound. He thought it was the water. It wasn't. An Eastern cottonmouth water moccasin, desperate for water and protection from the sun, had found a place to call home under Jimmy's granddaddy's house. The hissing sound was the last thing Jimmy heard before the fanged strike struck the meat on his right forearm.

"Derek!" Jimmy screamed, "Derek, I got bit by a snake. I got bit. Damn, man, I got bit!"

Derek, for some reason, looked at his hands. There was nothing in them. He shoved his hands in his pockets for a split second. There was no knife. He didn't even carry one. He didn't know what he was thinking. Panic struck. It was Derek's time. He would either do something to save his friend or let him die under the house. Doing nothing was not an option.

Chapter 31

Cottonmouth snakes, or water moccasins, are pit vipers. A dark snake, it matches the color of dark water in streams and ponds. Pit vipers earn their name because they have a small dip, or pit on either side of their head, between the eyes and nostril. They don't grow to be much more than four feet in South Carolina, but their venom is deadly to humans. They love water; when the water source dries up, they find another place for it. They love to be in cool places, especially during the day; they usually hunt at night. If bothered, or if they feel threatened, they will make a little hissing sound in defense. If they feel further threatened or encroached upon, they deliver the venom. The inside of their large mouth, when opened, is white, like cotton. Their name makes sense.

Jimmy didn't know what kind of snake struck him, but he did notice its dark color as it slithered away from him under the big house. It would have been better if Jimmy had the less deadly venom of an Eastern diamondback rattler, but as Jimmy's luck had been in so many things, he got the poison of one of the most dangerous snakes to be found in the state.

Derek stood in the kitchen; Jimmy lay writhing on the dirt three feet below him. Derek had no weapons, no gun, no knife, no nothin'. After looking at his empty hands, and pausing for a few seconds, he came alive. He knew he had no time to waste. His friend, this good man, the kindest-hearted, cleanest man in the world, Jimmy Nash, was going to die.

In a matter of seconds Derek was standing at the access door. He knew he had no time, but with his mind in a whirl, he did the strangest thing. He took off his shirt. Now bare-chested, he dove under the house and crawled like a soldier on his elbows and knees, as though he were sliding under barbed wire on a battlefield, toward his best friend. Jimmy was still aware of his surroundings, but in his own panic, he lay on his back, not moving, holding his forearm.

"Don't move Jimmy," Derek hollered, "I gotcha."

Jimmy obeyed. Derek grabbed Jimmy by the ankles and began pulling him, two feet at a time, with his back to the opening, toward the access door.

"Damn, man, I got bit. I got bit," Jimmy repeated.

"What color was the snake, Jimmy?" Derek asked, still pulling him toward the door.

"I don't know, man. I don't know."

"Was it dark, was it golden, was it striped? I gotta know."

"It was dark. It wasn't striped. Damn man, I got bit." Still under the house a mere six feet from the access door, Jimmy brought his poisoned arm toward his mouth. "I'll suck out the poison."

Derek stopped pulling for a second, grabbing Jimmy's arm, jerking it away from his mouth. "You don't suck poison. It makes it worse, damn it. That shit is only for the movies. Don't suck. We got no time to play here."

Derek kept pulling Jimmy's body toward the door.

"I need your keys and cell phone, Jimmy. Where are they?"

There was a two-row brick foundation that he had to pull him over to get him out into the clear; Derek was careful not to scrape Jimmy's back or bang his head on the bricks as he got him out into the bright sunshine. "Where's your keys and cell phone?" Derek repeated.

Jimmy didn't respond.

"Where's your keys and cell phone?" Derek asked for a third time.

"In the truck," Jimmy slurred.

Jimmy's body began to shake, partly from panic, mainly from the venom that was now coursing its way through Jimmy's thin body. His forearm, in less than five minutes was already a third larger than normal. Because of the panic and the venom, he couldn't get up. He tried getting to his knees, but he rolled over on his stomach.

Derek, still bare-chested, in dark khaki shorts and gray tennis shoes, picked Jimmy up under his arms and dragged him to the Ford Ranger pickup and stuffed him, shoe-horn style, into the passenger seat. The keys and cell phone were on the center console in the plastic tray, just as Jimmy had said.

Derek, poor hapless, hopeless Derek, hadn't driven a car in nine months. Until he became Jimmy's friend, all he'd done was sleep and take his medication. He didn't even want to drive. It was easier to stay home or ride with Patsy or Jimmy.

Derek grabbed the keys and tried to start the little truck. It wouldn't start. Looking down, Derek realized this was a stick drive. He pushed in the clutch with his left foot. The truck started. He'd driven a straight drive when he learned to drive, but that was seventeen years ago. He pushed the stick into third gear thinking it was first gear. The truck lurched forward as he let the clutch fly off his left foot. The truck stalled. Derek cursed, looking at Jimmy whose mouth was foaming white fluid. He was going to die soon.

Derek recalled something he learned from his old high school football coach. *"Slow down,"* he remembered the coach saying. *"Take a deep breath. Focus. Take another deep breath. Focus."* Derek breathed, and breathed again. He looked at the gearshift, noticing it was tilted slightly to the right. "It's in third gear," he said to himself. He breathed again. "I've got to put it in first gear and ease the clutch." The truck running, he did just that. The truck moved forward. He was on his way, this time pulling the shifter back into second gear smoothly.

Derek didn't own a cell phone anymore. It was one of the luxuries he lived without since he and Patsy had lost everything. Now in third gear and traveling nearly forty miles an hour, he pulled the shifter into fourth and dialed 911from Jimmy's phone.

"I'm on Whiskey Road," he said, "I've got a friend who got bit by a snake, probably a water moccasin. I need an ambulance to meet me on the way to the hospital. The ambulance needs to be carrying the anti-venom Crofab. Do not hesitate. Get the ambulance moving NOW!"

"Where are you now?" the 911 responder asked.

"I just told you, I'm on Whiskey Road moving east toward Woodvine Road. I'll meet the ambulance at Pine Log Road. If the ambulance can't get there, I will go to the hospital, but they need to have Crofab ready when I arrive."

"How do you spell that?"

"C-R-O-F-A-B. Ask someone at the hospital; they'll know what it is. Put me on hold and call the hospital. Let me know if I need to meet the ambulance or take him all the way to the hospital. This a matter of life or death!" Derek put the phone on speaker and threw it into the console. He looked at Jimmy, mouth still foaming.

"You're not gonna die, Jimmy," he said, touching his left, good forearm, "you're not gonna die. I've lost Cleo, but we ain't losin' you, you hear?" Of course, Jimmy didn't hear anything, but if there was a spirit, a god, a deliverer of good things, it was in that faded Ford Ranger screaming down the road, flashers on, passing cars on the right-hand side, throwing dirt and gravel everywhere.

"You're not gonna, die, Jimmy, you're not gonna die. I've lost too much; I ain't losing you."

"Sir, are you there?" the phone speaker asked.

"Yeah, I'm here. Where do you want me to go? Tell me quick."

"The ambulance is going to meet you at Pine Log, at the corner of Whiskey and Pine Log, at the Waffle House. Do you know where that is?" Of course, Derek knew. He ate there on Wednesdays.

"Yeah, I know exactly where it is. Have they got the serum? There's no reason to meet me without the Crofab."

"They have it, sir, they have it. What is your ETA?"

"I'll be there in seven minutes, not ten. Get the ambulance there. Tell them I'm in a black Ford Ranger. We can't lose my friend."

Derek moved the truck easily from fourth to third gear when he needed acceleration, honking the horn, screaming at slow drivers as if they could hear him, all the time encouraging Jimmy to hang on to life. "I can't lose you, I've lost too much," he kept repeating, the tears in his eyes blurring his vision.

Six minutes later he was at the Waffle House. The ambulance was there, in the parking lot, yellow lights spinning, and a female attendant guiding traffic away from the entrance to the diner. It was easy to spot Derek. The flashers on, Derek honking the horn, he cruised to the rear of the ambulance while the two EMS employees pulled the unconscious Jimmy out of the truck onto the gurney. They gave him a shot of Crofab and started an intravenous tube within seconds. Off they went.

Two Waffle House waitresses, Jimmy and Derek's good friends, stood in the parking lot watching the whole episode unfold.

"What's happened to Jimmy?" Brenda hollered, her little Waffle House hat slightly askew on her head, her apron, scattered, smothered and covered with the work of the trade.

Derek didn't look up, but shouted back, "Snake bite!" With that, the still shirtless Derek hopped into the truck and followed the ambulance, his flashers still rhythmically clicking.

No one knew it yet, but Jimmy, in addition to being allergic to fire ants, was terribly allergic to snake venom. His throat was already closing.

Chapter 32

MANDY RARELY ATE at the Waffle House. She preferred the little boutique diners with special sandwiches and an atmosphere that was more inspiring than the florescent lit, yellow painted, double-wide trailer look of the Waffle House. On this day, however, she was to meet Paul Streeter, a man who built wrought-iron gates for those rich folks who could afford such things. Paul Streeter *loved* the Waffle House. He was especially fond of the hash browns. Paul Streeter was late. He'd not arrived at the appointed time and Mandy was filling the gap by checking her email on her I-phone.

Mandy couldn't help but hear the aggravating siren when the ambulance arrived, and she noticed the drama as it played out in the parking lot with a shirtless man running about and another man, obviously injured, being loaded onto a folding, rolling bed with an oxygen mask.

In a bigger city, a reporter might inquire about the injury, but wouldn't be interested unless the injured person was a celebrity or there was a twisted love triangle that would sell newspapers. But this was Aiken and Mandy had a nose for a good story in a small town. When she learned it was a snakebite and recognized Jimmy's truck, she quickly told her waitress to tell Paul Streeter, the wrought-iron gate artist, that she would call him later. She was off to the hospital.

When Derek arrived at the hospital, a few minutes behind the ambulance, he parked in a no parking zone, took the keys and left the flashers on. He ran into the emergency room, shirt off, looking for anyone with news.

"Where's the guy who was in the ambulance?" he barked at a man in hospital gear walking just inside the automatic-opening double-glass doors.

"I don't know," he said, looking toward the four-foot high emergency desk where a woman with nurses' hat stood, looking down the hall. She knew, Derek could tell.

"They just took him to surgery," the woman said, "he's in good hands, sir," she continued, looking at Derek with comfort in her eyes.

"Why does he need surgery?" Derek asked, "He needs anti venom, he was snake bit, not injured."

"They performed an emergency tracheotomy in the ambulance, sir. They needed to finish the surgery properly. Are you the man who called the ambulance?"

"Tracheotomy?"

"Are you the man who called the ambulance?" she repeated.

"Yeah, I called the ambulance," Derek said, looking for, and finding a seat, a plastic chair with metal legs near the nurse's station. He sat down and put his head in his hands. He was shaking, adrenaline still moving through his body.

"You need to stay here, sir, the doctor will probably want to talk to you. Are you that man's family?"

Derek didn't hesitate. "Yeah," he said, "he's my brother."

The nurse, a plump woman in her fifties, with mostly gray hair and pale white skin, took the few short steps to where Derek sat. She put her cold hand on his bare shoulder. "You need something, sir? You want some water?"

Nurses know not to say things like 'he's going to be fine', but they are trained to say things like 'he's in good hands, now', and she repeated that a few times while she got Derek a little four-ounce paper cup full of water out of the five-gallon upside-down jug which stood nearby.

Derek was still shaking, sipping water with both hands from the tiny cup when Mandy arrived. She recognized Derek. He was the only person in the emergency area with his shirt off. Within a few minutes, she gained the nurses' confidence, showing the powers-that-be her press credentials and nodding toward the unsuspecting Derek. He was too lost in his own thoughts to notice her; he was in his own world, re-playing the events of the past hour in his head, wondering what he could have done to save Jimmy.

"I saw you at the Waffle House," she said, putting her feet in Derek's vision.

"Yeah, I was at the Waffle House," Derek said, not really knowing what she meant. "I got him to the Waffle House."

"Hi," she said, "I'm Mandy. I'm with the *Aiken Standard.* Can I talk to you for a minute?"

Before Derek could answer, before he could get a word out of his mouth, Doctor Fleetwood strode down the broad hallway, his surgeon's mask off his face, under his chin. He was a short man, in his sixties, wrinkles around his eyes and a friendly face.

"Is this the man who saved that man's life?" he asked, pointing at Derek. "I want to shake your hand, young man. You saved that man's life."

"Is he ok?" Derek asked, putting his meek hand out to the waiting, strong hand of the good physician. "Is he gonna be alright?"

"At least he won't die from suffocation, my friend. I don't know why you called to have the ambulance meet you, but he would have died without that. We performed an emergency tracheotomy. He wouldn't have lived. You saved his life." Doctor Fleetwood was still gripping Derek's hand. Derek gained strength and gripped back.

"He's gonna live?"

"Because of you, yes."

Patsy arrived on the scene. News travels fast in small places, and it didn't take long for someone who knew Patsy to notice Derek in the emergency room. Mandy and Patsy stood by, watching Derek receive the best news he'd heard in nine months. He'd saved a human life, something he couldn't do for his little girl, but he'd saved his best friend.

Mandy and Patsy exchanged glances, Patsy noticed Mandy's press badge and instantly understood Mandy's reason for being there. They smiled at each other. Patsy leaned over to Mandy's ear and whispered, "that's my husband; I work here."

More hospital workers arrived in the big emergency area as Doctor Fleetwood explained to Derek how Jimmy's throat was closed and how he would have died and how the anti-venom should save him and on and on about Jimmy's health and how

Derek saved him. It was a scene for the movies, Derek beginning to puff out his bare chest with his wife standing by his side looking at him with longing eyes.

Mandy took pictures with her iPhone with Dr. Fleetwood, Patsy, Derek, and the ambulance drivers. She made notes and got phone numbers and names as quickly as she could for a story that would appear on the front page of the paper the next day.

Before the happy crowd was dispersed, another young nurse commented from the back, "who's the hottie with no shirt?"

"He's my husband," Patsy shouted back with a huge smile on her face, "keep your hands off."

In thirty minutes, twice the time of the profound fifteen minutes of fame, the scene ended, Doctor Fleetwood patting Derek on the back, continuing to repeat how "this man saved another man's life today" over and over, again.

Before Derek left the hospital, he was allowed to see Jimmy, sedated, but awake. Doctor Fleetwood assured Derek and Patsy that Jimmy was out of danger and that their roommate would be home in a few days.

Patsy walked Derek back to the emergency room area before she headed back to her station. She was still beaming from ear to ear, her arm around Derek's waist.

"I was wondering," she said, "why *are* you not wearing a shirt?"

Derek looked at her and then at his bare upper half. "I don't know. I don't know why I don't have a shirt on." And he didn't know.

This much *was* known. When Derek Harnett crawled into Jimmy's truck, flashers still flashing, and headed toward home, *their* home, Jimmy, Quentin and Patsy's home, the world seemed different. The grass around the hospital grounds seemed greener; the trees looked healthier; the birds chirped louder, the sky was bluer and the clouds looked puffier. The opaque filter that had been over Derek's eyes for nine months cleared, and the world, in the span of several hours, looked better than it had in a very long time.

The lid of depression, the feeling of hopelessness, the utter and complete despair Derek felt since Cleo's senseless, unexplainable death ended the day he saved Jimmy's life. Although Jimmy had been pulling Derek out of that black hole one day at a time, one afternoon at a time while rocking in a white rocking chair on the back porch of Granddaddy's house, the fog in Derek's life lifted when he helped someone else. Patsy knew it was happening little by little, and she also sensed that her Derek, the Derek she married ten years earlier, was *back* that afternoon in the emergency room.

Before Derek drove home, he made one stop. He went to the Magnolia Café and gave Lucretia the news about Jimmy. There were no secrets between Derek and Jimmy; Derek understood Lucretia and Jimmy were more than friends, especially in the past several weeks. With a quick explanation to her boss, Lucretia was on her way to the hospital.

Within two hours of the whole incident, Lucretia parked herself at Jimmy's bedside. She told the nurses he was her brother. Jimmy, it turned out, poor Jimmy who had no living family, suddenly had a brother named Derek and an African-American sister named Lucretia who kept passionately kissing his hands and his cheeks.

No one cared about the rules when it came to Jimmy Nash. He was an accidental celebrity and the hospital wasn't about to turn away anyone who cared about him. Lucretia was welcome. The hospital fell in love with all of those folks. The fact that Patsy worked there made it even more charming.

Chapter 33

THE HEADLINE ROARED: *MAN'S QUICK-THINKING SAVES FRIEND FROM CERTAIN DEATH.* Mandy had hung around the hospital and got her story. There was always a bad news story to write, but Mandy knew a good news snakebite story would sell more newspapers than any story about a robbery. Under the headline was a grand picture of Derek and Patsy Harnett with Doctor Fleetwood, the ambulance drivers and the hospital staff all standing in the emergency room. Mandy got all her facts right. She'd interviewed the ambulance drivers, Doctor Fleetwood, the emergency room staff, and the 911operator–complete with a tape transcript. She interviewed Derek, of course, this time with his shirt on, standing outside Quentin Cleveland's house. It turned out that Derek worked at a zoo when he was a teenager and knew all about snakebite anti-venom. It was part of his training to work there and he never forgot it. And everyone knows that a story about a man who loves animals sells newspapers.

As Mandy peeled back the onion of this story, she saw the layers of what was going on. Over the next several weeks, the story got deeper and deeper, all true of course, about the hodgepodge of people in financial and emotional ruin moving in together. The stories came out about Quentin Cleveland's factory going to half weeks; about Jimmy picking up organic garbage and creating compost for the farmers in the new push for "from farm to table." Patsy and Derek were interviewed about losing their darling Cleo. Derek sat by Patsy, holding her hand, his face stoic, as she told Mandy about Derek's slow but certain return from the abyss.

Mandy interviewed Jimmy. She found out about Jimmy's granddaddy's house. A picture of the manse made the front page. Then she learned about Lucretia and Jimmy. When Lucretia and Jimmy's photo made the front page, Lucretia's mother, Fristella, welcomed the garbage man with the open arms of acceptance.

Quentin's minister was interviewed; the whole congregation had fallen for the endearing Jimmy Nash. And he was easy to love, this compost-making man with a drive to save his grandfather's home from the county wrecking ball.

The sisters of the church brought food to Quentin's house as though Jimmy was an invalid. Although Jimmy was back at work, completely healed, trays of macaroni and cheese, bowls of collard greens and tins of freshly fried chicken seemed to appear magically every day for three weeks. Jimmy no longer sat with Quentin; he sat in the pew with Lucretia and Fristella. Jimmy couldn't help but look at the little chapel every week wondering how they got the stained glass so clean. It was just his thing.

The phone at the *Aiken Standard* rang off the hook, people wanting to know more about those deserving folks. The stories even softened the heart of the old curmudgeon Hugh Buncombe. And he was happy that his adopted daughter Mandy got one helluva story.

There are machines in Richmond, Virginia that look for counterfeit bills. Those same machines search for other errors. When Hugh Buncombe's bills from High Thyme came through, a little beep sounded on the machine and halted everything.

"Hey Justin," the man said holding one of the bills. "This bill's got a different code on it—says call the Bureau."

"Call 'em."

An investigation was launched, not by Richmond, but directly from the Bureau of Engraving and Printing.

Chapter 34

ALTHOUGH HUGH WAS now dating Kathy, coffee was no different. The three of them met most mornings after Hugh dug in the ground and scored a little bonus. With the story about the snake-bit man and the upcoming foreclosure, Mandy interviewed Quentin Cleveland. He told her about his experience in court with Maxwell Cooper. He let her know that attorney Cooper had essentially taken on the case *pro bono* and had won a critical motion because of the assignment of the mortgage that was supposedly signed by Bobby Baine. Patsy and Derek also had high praise for the young lawyer. With the reading audience wanting more, Mandy called Max Cooper. Her opinion of him as a whore-dog shifted slightly with the knowledge of the good work he had done without compensation for the four refugees.

Max told Mandy he would meet her after work for coffee at The Willcox where she could do her interview. Trading cell phone numbers, they made sure of the time, and later in the afternoon, she sent a text confirming it was still a go. The Willcox was no flophouse; built in the late nineteenth century, the hotel had accommodated such guests as Winston Churchill, Harold Vanderbilt, Elizabeth Arden, and others.

Max loved the place and enjoyed Diane's company, the bartender who watched Max pass the time with many a female. Max met Mandy in the lobby, Mandy dressed in her work outfit, Max still in his suit from court. Max suggested a seat at the bar. They both ordered coffee. Max answered Mandy's questions handily without any fanfare. There was no hint of his coming on to her, no smiling, no checking her out with lecherous eyes. Women can sense those things, and Max wasn't simply on his best behavior; he was on his *new* behavior. The interview lasted all of fifteen minutes, Mandy efficiently making notes. Max told her about Bobby Baine's questionable signature on Quentin's assignment of mortgage and Judge Warren's ruling. He discussed the frustration in losing Patsy and Derek's case and his growing interest for helping people in foreclosure. Max didn't embellish anything and the passion for helping his clients was obvious. There was no personal conversation between these two good-looking young people; when there were no more questions, Max looked around as though he were bored, ready to go home. Still seated, he fumbled in his jacket pocket for his phone.

Mandy couldn't help but get in one dig.

"Gotta call Dharma?" she asked.

Max stopped. "What about Dharma?"

"This is a small town. I have friends who know about your arrangement with Dharma."

"That's odd. If your friends cared to keep up with Dharma, they would know that I am not seeing her anymore." Max's face stiffened, like when he was dealing with Henry Stokes.

"I have had, in writers' terms, an epiphany, a revelation, a tergiversation. I have ended all relationships and am enjoying celibacy." He stood up, Mandy still seated.

He looked at Mandy again and curled up his mouth. "If this interview was for the purpose of embarrassing me, or embarrassing my former lovers, you can consider this entire meeting off the record. I insist on approving whatever you print."

"I was only asking … " she said to herself, as Max was already out of the hotel.

Mandy didn't chase after him. Instead, she sent a text: "I'll send the proposed copy." There was no apology. She was only slightly impressed with him; her opinion rose on the scale from skirt chaser to *former* skirt chaser.

Max didn't respond to her text.

Chapter 35

A WEEK AFTER her article about Max, Patsy called Mandy and gave her more big news about the status of the case.

Judge Warren had scheduled the trial at which it would be decided whether Quentin's house would be lost to the auctioneer's gavel. Mandy let the public know about the hearing with a small headline in the Metro Section of the paper: *Foreclosure Trial Scheduled on Cleveland Home; Snakebite Victim and Family May Be Homeless.*

The article explained that Quentin had saved almost enough money to reinstate the loan; that were it not for attorney's fees and other charges, he could save the place. Mandy also wrote about Max's theory that Gocows had been assigned the loan through the suspicious signature of Bobby Baine and that Judge Warren would be hearing the case on Monday at 10:00. The article also said that the court proceeding was public, inviting all of Aiken to watch the trial.

Henry Stokes was from Charleston, some hundred and seventy miles away, and had no idea of what had been going on in Aiken for the past several weeks and the celebrity status of Quentin Cleveland, Patsy, Derek, and the snake-bitten

Jimmy Nash. When Stokes arrived in the courtroom with his one and only witness from Gocows mortgage, there were over one hundred spectators ready to watch the action.

Max Cooper had a trick up his sleeve. He'd named Bobby Baine as his witness the same week they'd won the Motion to Reconsider. Henry Stokes knew that Bobby Baine was not living in South Carolina; Stokes was sure that Max couldn't find Bobby. Max drew on his dad's wisdom. Old Calhoun told Max a hundred times: "Put a subpoena on someone with a check for travel expenses. You never know, their dumb ass may show up." Gocow's signing facility was in Alpharetta Georgia, some one hundred fifty miles from Aiken, but when Bobby Baine got the big old blue subpoena from Maxwell Cooper with a respectful letter and a check for three hundred dollars, he cashed the check and showed up. And Bobby Baine had left the "signing facility" for a better job that paid more than the nine dollars an hour he had been receiving as a signatory officer of a dozen banks. He was happy to show up for the generous Max. He was dressed in a pair of khaki slacks and a white button-down shirt in the front row. Bobby looked to be in his mid-thirties. Max had sent a copy of the subpoena, per the rules, to Stokes. Henry knew that Max had no jurisdiction in Georgia; Stokes hadn't given a thought to Bobby Baine showing up.

When Stokes walked into the courtroom, he noticed the pews were full, but he figured Judge Warren had some other contested matters to hear after the simple foreclosure case of *Gocows vs. Cleveland.* Of course, there were no other cases to be heard. Mandy was there, iPad in hand, in the third row.

Henry Stokes was ready with his Gocows witness, still unaware that Max had found the mysterious Bobby Baine. In Stokes's mind, it was simple. Quentin Cleveland was six months behind on his payments when the suit was filed; he now owed for a year. The bank was entitled to get the house. Henry Stokes and Max Cooper only nodded at each other from their large, dark, oak counsel tables that sat in front of Judge Warren's bench. Max was aware of the full courtroom, knowing there was nothing else pending but this serious case. He knew this was an important case. He'd been around courtrooms all his life, full courtrooms with his father, many, many times. Max Cooper had been groomed for bigger moments than this, and he was ready with his trial notebook and Bobby Baine, seated on the front row behind counsel table.

Quentin Cleveland was there, dressed in a navy-blue suit, a white shirt with blue stripes and a yellow and blue tie. He looked as much like a lawyer as Max who was wearing a dark gray suit with a red and blue tie. Quentin, his baldhead shining, was ready, face forward, holding his well-worn, black leather Bible, the one he carried to church every Sunday. He knew he didn't need any more than that.

Even Judge Warren was a little surprised at the number of spectators when he entered the courtroom. Knowing there was nothing else on his morning calendar, he understood the town of Aiken was interested in the case involving the hometown celebs.

There was no fanfare, no opening statements, or other formalities like in a jury trial. Judge Warren told Henry to call his first witness.

"I call Jonathan Halifax, Your Honor."

Halifax was accustomed to testifying. He flew around the country for the bank, when needed, to testify in case some borrower had the audacity to answer a foreclosure lawsuit. He was ready with his numbers, the facts and figures about the note and mortgage, the missed payments, late fees, attorney's fees and costs. It wasn't rocket science.

Stokes, still thinking the spectators were there for other cases, moved his questions along quickly. A copy of the note, a certified copy of the mortgage, default date, last payment date, amount due with fees and costs, it was like a well-rehearsed song and dance routine, Stokes asked the questions and Halifax answered them almost before the end of the query. Max didn't object to anything that came from the canned testimony between Stokes and Jonathan Halifax.

Then it was Max's turn.

"How did Gocows come into possession of the note?

"I don't understand the question."

"Did Gocows originate this loan?"

"What do you mean by originate?"

Judge Warren wasn't in the mood for the word games. "You know what he means by originate. Answer the question."

Without acknowledging Judge Warren, Jonathan Halifax looked at Max.

"Gocows bought the loan from a prior owner."

"Who was the prior owner from whom Gocows bought the loan?"

"It's in the discovery that Mr. Stokes provided. You can look it up."

"I'm asking you, Mr. Halifax. You're the witness. Tell me: From whom did Gocows buy Mr. Cleveland's loan?"

Jonathan Halifax stared straight ahead. He was accustomed to the back and forth with lawyers who didn't know how to try a lawsuit and took a special pride in frustrating them.

"The plaintiff Gocows bought the loan from Bank of America. It's in the discovery."

"Does Gocows have the original mortgage?"

"You should know the rules, Mr. Cooper. Bank of America is a national bank. We don't have to bring the original to court under article three of the uniform commercial code." Halifax was so pleased with his legal answer he cracked a little smile at Max Cooper.

"So, the only assignment of the mortgage is the one that is recorded here in Aiken County, is that right?"

"I don't understand the question."

Judge Warren fidgeted in his seat, Halifax noticing it out of the corner of his eye. "You understand the question, Mr. Halifax. Answer the question."

Max repeated it: "It's a simple question. Is there any other assignment of this loan from Bank of America to Gocows other than the assignment that is recorded in the Aiken County courthouse?"

"Let me see the assignment."

Max had the assignment in his hand, a pre-marked copy of the one signed by Bobby Baine, and showed it to Halifax.

"That's the only assignment."

"I'd like to enter this into evidence your honor."

"Any objection, Mr. Stokes?"

"None, your honor."

"Alright, Mr. Halifax, if this is the only assignment of the loan, and the original mortgage is no different than the copy that is in evidence, the way that Gocows received possession and ownership of this loan was by the vice president of Bank of America, a person known as Bobby Baine, isn't that right?"

"That's right, Mr. Cooper. Just like Gocows said in the discovery we provided."

"And Mr. Bobby Baine was an authorized vice president of Bank of America, right?"

"I just answered that, Mr. Cooper."

"And you would agree with me, wouldn't you, Mr. Halifax, that if Bobby Baine wasn't a vice president of Bank of America, the assignment would be invalid, wouldn't it?"

"Objection. Calls for a legal conclusion of a lay witness."

Before Judge Warren could rule on the objection, Jonathan Halifax wanted to show Max Cooper a thing or two. "We've been hearing about the legitimacy of Bobby Baine's signature for some time from you Mr. Cooper," he said, "There is a list of vice presidents with signatory authority on page 407 of the discovery that Gocows sent to you. Bobby Baine is on that list. He is a vice president of Bank of America and he assigned the loan. We don't need to prove anything else. Mr. Cleveland didn't pay. Gocows owns the loan. The foreclosure should proceed."

"One more question."

"If Bobby Baine was a vice president of Bank of America but the signature on the assignment was not his signature, wouldn't you agree with me that the assignment would be invalid?"

"Objection. Calls for a legal conclusion."

"Sustained, Mr. Cooper. Move on."

Although Halifax was a trained witness he couldn't help but answer the question despite the sustained objection. He looked at Max Cooper with his eyebrows raised in pure certainty: "We've looked into the signature issue, Mr. Cooper. It's his signature. We've verified it on hundreds of assignments."

"Thank you, Mr. Halifax. No more questions." Max sat down.

Judge Warren addressed Henry. "Any more witnesses, Mr. Stokes?"

"No, your honor."

Halifax stepped down from the witness stand and pulled his chair up next to Henry Stokes. A big grin broke across his face, a grin of self-satisfaction, and the grin of victory.

"Mr. Cooper, call your first witness."

"Your Honor, I call Bobby Baine."

Chapter 36

IT'S WHAT LAWYERS call the Perry Mason moment. Those moments occurred every week on a legal TV show in the 1950s and 1960s, but in real courtrooms, in real life, those moments are as rare as, well, finding cash bubbling out of the dirt in a ghost town in the middle of nowhere. Those Perry Mason moments happen once, maybe twice, in a forty-year career. And it was time for Max Cooper to have his first one. Those in attendance stirred and whispered to each other as Bobby Baine walked to the witness stand, right hand raised, ready to be sworn.

Stokes leaped to his feet. "I object, Your Honor,"

"On what basis Mr. Stokes?"

"Your Honor, Mr. Cooper didn't tell me that Mr. Baine was here. He should have told me."

"Mr. Cooper, was Mr. Baine on your witness list?"

"Yes, Your Honor, and I also included a copy of the subpoena to Mr. Stokes per the rules."

"But Your Honor, Mr. Baine lives in Georgia. Mr. Cooper doesn't have jurisdiction to bring Mr. Baine here."

"That may be correct, Mr. Stokes, if Mr. Baine hadn't wanted to be here, but he's here. Objection overruled. Mr. Cooper, you may proceed."

"But Your Honor ..."

"Sit down, Mr. Stokes. You can ask Mr. Baine some questions when Mr. Cooper is finished."

Bobby testified for almost an hour. He said that he had been unemployed; he was formerly a truck driver, but when shipping goods slowed down, he lost his job. He answered an ad in the paper that promised nine dollars an hour to work as a notary. He was authorized to notarize in Georgia and applied. The next thing he knew, he was in a one-story brick building in Alpharetta, Georgia with seven other notaries, signing documents. The odd thing was, he said, he didn't notarize anything. He just signed as a vice president of corporations. The people who hired him disappeared quickly, but documents came into the little building every morning via FedEx, thousands of assignments of mortgages that required signatures. After a few days of signing his name to documents, he asked the boss why he was signing as a vice president of Bank of America. And why he was also a vice president of GMAC, CitiMortgage, J.P. Morgan Chase, Wells Fargo, New Century, and many others. He was told it was not his concern.

He testified that he was never a vice president of any of those banks, that he never went to any corporate meetings, he never met anyone from any of the banks for whom he was signing, and he never received a paycheck from any bank. He also testified that when he got tired of signing his name, the big boss told him that he could authorize other employees to sign for him. He thought that was a grand idea because his wrist hurt. So, he allowed other employees to sign for him. And he got a raise because he became a supervisor of signatories, he said. But after about six months, the documents slowed down and Bobby was terminated. He applied for unemployment benefits but was denied because the banks alleged he wasn't a full-time employee.

When Bobby was asked about his signature on Quentin Cleveland's assignment, he said that it wasn't his signature.

When Bobby first started testifying, Henry Stokes made notes, furiously writing on a long legal pad. After a few minutes, he put his pen down and shook his head. When Max was finished with Bobby Baine, Henry Stokes asked for Bobby's driver's license that Bobby showed him. The signature on the driver's license was different than the signature on the assignment he supposedly signed. Stokes asked a few other questions and sat down.

Judge Warren was *very* interested in Mr. Bobby Baine's testimony. Several times during the testimony he sat back in his chair with his hands behind his head and looked up at the ceiling. He knew this Perry Mason moment could affect foreclosures all over America even though it was happening in his courtroom in the small county of Aiken, South Carolina.

After Bobby returned to his seat, Judge Warren looked at Max.

"Do you have any other witnesses, Mr. Cooper?"

"No, your Honor, but I do have a motion."

Judge Warren knew there would be a motion. "What might your motion be Mr. Cooper?"

"Your honor, I move to dismiss this case. I can recite the reasons, but I won't state the obvious. I believe the court has seen the lack of evidence to prove the bank is the proper party holding the note and mortgage."

Judge Warren looked at Henry Stokes. "Mr. Stokes?"

"I would like time to find the appropriate evidence."

"That request is denied. This foreclosure is dismissed with prejudice."

And then it started. It was as though some folks in the courtroom didn't know what just happened. Sitting in the courtroom was the Pastor Duplin along with three Trustees from Ebenezer AME Church. Pastor Duplin stood up.

"Your honor, I am the pastor at Ebenezer AME Church. I want the court to know that our church has raised one thousand dollars to give to Quentin Cleveland. We will pay those funds immediately."

Before Judge Warren could speak, ten more Aikenites stood up. "Your Honor, the employees at Betsy's On The Corner have put some funds together. We have seven hundred and eighteen dollars to contribute to save Mr. Cleveland's house."

"The New Moon Café has six hundred dollars, Your Honor."

The Rotary Club and seventeen nurses from the hospital had pitched in. The Waffle House waitresses had money.

When it was over, ten thousand dollars was pledged, more than enough to reinstate the loan.

Quentin Cleveland had turned his chair around, watching the generosity of friends and strangers. As the citizens kept standing up with their promises of money, Quentin gripped his Bible, looking upward toward the providential domains, tears forming in his eyes. A village had shown up, a town had demonstrated its generosity and thrown its bounty to help one of their own. And Max Cooper, still on his feet, his hand on Quentin's shoulder, felt his lip quiver. Mandy typed vigorously on her iPad. She noticed Max Cooper's moment of emotion, making a mental note of it.

As the donors looked around at each other, none knowing that others had the same idea, all proud of their individual offers to save the home of Quentin Cleveland and his band of roommates, no one seemed to have listened to what had just happened in the courtroom. Bobby Baine had testified that his signature was a forgery; the whole signing operation in Alpharetta, Georgia was nothing but a fraud and banks had conspired to make something legal that was quite illegal. Max Cooper and Henry Stokes sure knew there was a card on Judge Warren's bench that was begging to be seen.

"For the fine citizens of this community," he said in a firm voice, "this court is impressed with your generosity. The court has dismissed the foreclosure. Mr. Cleveland is no longer in debt to the bank. If these kind people want to pay the bank something to make sure it never comes back, well, that's up to Mr. Stokes and Mr. Cooper." The judge looked at the two lawyers and put his hands up in the air. He was going to let the lawyers figure out how to settle the matter with a little money so there wouldn't be an appeal.

The audience looked around at each other.

The judge wasn't finished. "One more matter," he continued, "This court is very concerned about what appears to be false documentation. I want to see counsel in chambers for further discussion. The court will deal with that regardless of what financial efforts are made by you. This court thanks every person here. It is a pleasure to be a judge in this town. The court stands adjourned."

And then, "Counsel. Chambers. Now." He exited the courtroom behind his black judge's chair.

Smart judges know when to go in chambers. They know, with their robes off, maybe their feet up on the small ottoman under the desk, they can chat with the lawyers without spectators dissecting every syllable of the conversation.

While the courtroom was at ease, the whole crowd got together and planned a covered dish supper at the church for that evening. Social media took over—Facebook, Instagram, and Twitter—and in the quick space of two hours the whole town knew about the impromptu dinner.

Back in the privacy of his office, he announced that he was going to call the prosecutors' offices and report the bank for having participated in, and known about, a forgery. Henry Stokes had lost the shine off his vainglory. He sat silently while Judge Warren made his pronouncements in cold stilted phrases, each sentence ringing with more and more anger. Judge Warren never took his robe off, a symbol that these three men, despite the usual ease of his chambers, were still in Judge Warren's charge.

"Counsel," he said, "I will write the order in this matter. There will be no mention of any investigation." And then turning to Max: "There will be no mention of any investigation in any media." Max said he understood. When Judge Warren was finished, he stood up, took off his robe and told Henry and Max they were dismissed.

Henry slinked out of chambers, his shoulders low; he shuffled back to the courtroom. This case had blown up and his face said it all, wrinkled forehead, down-turned mouth, hollow eyes.

Max watched Henry slither out of chambers, a nice moment for Max to gloat, but he didn't. Old Calhoun had told him many times to avoid that outward display of victory. He turned to Judge Warren. Before Max could squeeze out one utterance, Judge Warren put up his hand.

"You're dismissed, counselor. I'll contact the authorities."

It was over. Judge Warren didn't want to have any conversation with, or any boyish congratulations to, Max. Sometimes it's better to leave things unsaid. With his head high, unlike Henry Stokes, Max stepped into the empty courtroom and quietly gathered his trial notebook and snapped the pages into the three-ring binder with a note of finality.

Chapter 37

IT WAS SLIGHTLY before one when Max left the courthouse, a gorgeous day filled with sunshine. Mandy was leaning against Max's car.

"You kicked some major ass in there today."

"I can't talk about it. I have no comments for any newspaper articles."

"I'm not going to ask anything for the record. I was going to ask you to lunch, completely off the record. I owe you an apology."

"I'm not answering questions about my ex-girlfriends or my celibacy."

"I said I owe you an apology. I don't beg."

Max's face softened a little. "I'll eat. Where?"

"Betsy's Corner. It's all I can afford."

Five minutes later they sat at a table near the door, Max saying nothing, playing with the thin paper napkin, waiting on their sandwiches. Mandy knew she would have to start any conversation.

"Everything is off the record, you understand?"

"Can I trust you on that? I can't talk about this case to the media."

"You can trust me. It's part of our ethics. If you tell me it's off the record, I can't write about it. Understood?"

Max nodded.

"I was wondering though," she said, "what if Bobby Baine hadn't shown up today? What would you have done?"

"I don't know. Litigation has risks. The other truth is Quentin Cleveland has saved all but about one thousand dollars to reinstate the loan all by himself. I think Judge Warren would have entertained a motion to allow Quentin some time to get the money together. I had some confidence, though, that Bobby Baine was gonna show up."

"Why?"

"His wife called me. She works for a guy in Atlanta who owns horses. That guy wants a new saddle. She wanted to know if I knew a good place to buy saddles in Aiken."

"You're kidding."

Max smiled. "No shit."

"So, if Aiken wasn't a horse town, if some guy in Atlanta didn't a need saddle, if Bobby Baine's wife didn't work for that guy, this case has a different result."

"Maybe. Got lucky. And good people showed up."

"It's a great town."

"Quentin and his roommates aren't just lucky; they are fortunate that one of them got bit by a snake. It's pretty funny, isn't it? Snake bit usually has the opposite meaning." Max smiled a big grin.

"I can't write any of this stuff, can I?"

"You promised."

Mandy chose to change the subject. "You know, you have quite a reputation around town as an excellent lawyer who is also a player. How long can you keep both of those reputations?"

"You said this was an apology lunch. Is this the beginning of the apology?"

"Yeah, it is. I'm sorry for what happened at The Willcox. But I am curious about, well, you said, *celibate*."

Max smiled again. Mandy did apologize, he said to himself.

"I just grew up. About thirty days ago, I quit all women. It's been interesting. I have a lot more time on my hands. I've taken up knitting."

Mandy smiled. "Baby booties?"

"Baby hats. They're easier." He smiled back.

"So, you know how to purl?"

"What's that?"

She laughed. "You're obviously not knitting."

This Mandy girl wasn't only beautiful; she was very smart.

"Seriously. I'm curious. I've learned that men don't change their spots very easily."

Max looked at Mandy. She was nice enough and it was good to talk to someone, especially after his big courtroom victory. Why not tell the truth to someone?

"To be honest, my best friend told me he was getting married. And, long story short, that is something I think that I want. I want more to my life than short relationships and I'm tired of hurting people. I'd like to share life's successes and failures with someone; it's an empty life if you just enjoy it by yourself. Growing up isn't always easy."

Max stopped and looked at Mandy. She didn't respond, quietly waiting for more. A lesser woman, a woman wanting to be heard, would have interrupted, would have given comment. Not Mandy. She knew to wait.

"And…?"

"What do you mean, 'and'…?"

"And how's it been?"

Max hadn't talked with anyone, not even Scott, about his sudden decision to quit all relationships, and he sure wasn't ready to discuss his thoughts, but something inside him wanted to talk about it, and here was a beautiful woman, about his age, a person he barely trusted ten minutes earlier, probing him with questions that he could answer as a man not trying to be charming. It was different; he could answer honestly.

"It's been pretty cool. I'm learning some things about myself." Max stopped and looked at Mandy. It was time to stop talking about him. "Enough about me. Tell me, have you always wanted to write for the paper? Most newspaper people want to write books. I bet you want to write a book."

Mandy also had a choice to make. She could play off the question like she frequently did, but with Max being so candid; she decided to share a little bit about herself.

"I do. I want to write a novel. I want my first novel to be as good as Toni Morrison, George Eliot, Edith Wharton, Virginia Woolf, and Donna Tartt. Something of substance, not a romance novel."

"That's terrific. Tell me more." Max sat back in his seat, waiting for her to talk about herself. Her opinion of him having changed, she chose, at that moment, to talk.

The lunch lasted two hours. They both shared thoughts and ideas with each other that they rarely discussed with others. But with Max's newfound monastic attitude, why not share? He wasn't hitting on her. As for Mandy, she was approachable. She was as open as she could be, telling the truth about her view of the world, her politics, and her goals. She avoided, with the expertise of a magician, any discussion of her family's wealth. Max Cooper got the same line that was handed to Hugh Buncombe. Mandy was a hard-working girl whose parents were in Atlanta working on some rental houses. That was her only deception, one she'd learned was in her own best interest when it came to any relationship with another human, regardless of who it was. The other truth was that Max Cooper would not have cared about her wealth.

After the lengthy lunch date, they parted, shaking hands, with the understanding that they would see each other at the covered-dish supper at the church.

Max worked the rest of the day. Mandy wrote her column about the trial, the version that told about the generosity of the community, not the one about the potential for an investigation into the signature of Bobby Baine.

She also called Hugh and Kathy and got voicemail from both.

The day wasn't finished. At 4:30, Max got a call from Henry Stokes. The bank had agreed to payment in full from the funds that Quentin Cleveland had been putting aside. No money would be needed from the community. The only stipulation was that the agreement would be confidential. Cleveland

and Max couldn't reveal the agreement. Phone calls were made back and forth. By 5:30 it was done. Quentin Cleveland was no longer a debtor on his house. Max had to keep his mouth shut. That part was easy.

Quentin Cleveland was one happy trooper at the potluck supper at the church. He told the community of good souls, at Ebenezer AME Church that no money would be needed, that the lawyers were working on things. He didn't reveal anything else. To the people there, it didn't matter. They had seen what happened in court. More than a hundred and fifty people filled the annex building with dishes of barbeque, chicken, pork tenderloin, squash, cucumbers and tomatoes. Pastor Duplin gave a beautiful blessing. It lasted almost three minutes; Jimmy Nash, arm in arm with Lucretia, kept opening one eye looking at Quentin, who stood like a marble statue, eyes closed, his hands tight-fisted at his side.

And the other roommates were there; Derek and Patsy held hands, smiling at everything and everyone. The home had been saved, the instant stars were happy. Their lives, in many respects, were never to be the same.

And Max, uncomfortable in the hero role, kept telling everyone that "it takes a village," or words to that effect. Mandy mingled, but stayed near Max.

Max, in a moment of passing Mandy, as they made nice with the crowd, asked Mandy to join him for a drink at The Willcox Hotel bar. She nodded yes and moved on. By eight o'clock, the function wound down; Pastor Duplin gave a benediction, and the party broke up.

Max and Mandy drove separately and met at The Willcox.

As they seated themselves at the bar, Diane brought Max a Heineken and took Mandy's order.

Diane leaned back ready to watch Max work his magic with a new girl.

"Tell me about your dad," Mandy asked. It was the biggest taboo topic she could have touched.

Max looked at Diane who smiled. She knew Max would avoid *that* question.

"My dad was a great guy," he said. That was usually where he stopped. But this time he continued. "My dad was my idol. My mom died when I was eleven and my dad raised me without any help from anyone. He sacrificed marrying again; he sacrificed fun, he sacrificed everything for me. He taught me the value of hard work, of honesty, of treating others like you'd like to be treated. My dad was the best father ever. I can't say enough good things about my dad. When he died, something inside me exploded and I'm doing my best to learn to live with that huge gaping hole in my heart."

Max sat back and took a sip of his drink, then excused himself to the restroom.

Diane knew a boundary had been crossed. She looked at Mandy. "Who *are* you?" Diane asked.

"What do you mean?"

"In the past year, Max has never talked about his dad. I've known that young man for years. He never tells anybody about his dad. He only says his dad was a great guy. And tonight, out of nowhere, he talks to you? It's unbelievable. Consider yourself the first person he's allowed to hear about his feelings in the past year. Max is a closed book on many topics. Anything about his dad is forbidden. Wow."

Mandy kept looking at Diane, saying nothing.

"Max is a very good person. A *very* good person."

The human phenomenon between women is: trust another woman. Don't trust a man telling a woman about how good a guy is—trust a woman, or a kid, or a person you've never met, but *never* another man. When Diane, a person who knew Max, told Mandy that Max was a good guy, it was a well-received endorsement.

Max returned to his seat. He was quiet.

"Hey Max, would you like to get coffee in the morning at the *New Moon*? I get coffee there almost every day with Hugh Buncombe."

"Yeah, I saw you with Hugh the other day. I'll get some coffee. What time?"

"We meet about eight. Hugh has a woman friend now, a widow named Kathy. She'll probably join us. We solve all the problems of western civilization, and then I go to work. Hugh hangs out with Kathy and Bailey. You remember Bailey, right?"

"The black Lab, sure."

It was done. Max and Mandy waved goodbye to each other in the parking lot, with a promise to see each other for coffee in the morning. There was no hug, no peck on the cheek, nothing. Max was comfortable in his role as a monk and Mandy wasn't about to push any of those buttons.

All in all, it had been quite a day. Max saved a home and started what would be an avalanche of litigation. Quentin Cleveland and his roommates were going to be safe. Maxwell Cooper slept well that night, beginning to make progress in dealing with his father's death. As he dozed off in the comfort of his king-sized bed, he had no idea what was about to happen.

Chapter 38

THE COFFEE CROWD had grown from Hugh sitting with Bailey in the chilly air of January, reading a history book about the villages previously existing on the land of the Savannah River Site, to three more adults crowded around the small wooden table under the red Cheerwine umbrella. It was toward the end of May, almost too hot to sit outside, as Max joined Hugh, Kathy, and Mandy.

They all knew about the courtroom victory the day before; Hugh and Kathy congratulated Max and asked the required twenty questions. Mandy watched, saying nothing, impressed with Max's humility. They moved on, Hugh and Kathy asking Mandy about future articles forthcoming from what appeared to be a reality show of entertainment in what could have been a tragic loss of Quentin Cleveland's home.

Kathy, a woman sensitive to another's feelings, knew something was up when Mandy invited Max to coffee. For Kathy, the little meeting in the morning between Max and Mandy was like watching herself with Hugh months earlier. Mandy asked questions and touched Max on his arm when he responded. Hugh and Max, being men, didn't notice any of the things that were happening. But something was going on.

This little activity went on for two weeks, a good time had between the four of them each morning. By the time Hugh got to the *New Moon,* he already had his secret stash of cash; then he discussed the issues of the day—the economy, sports, and politics. Max was new to the game and listened more than he spoke. At the beginning of the third week of their coffee meeting, the two veterans, Kathy and Hugh, stood up. It was time to leave. Max, learning the routine, grabbed his paper coffee cup, said his goodbyes, and headed toward his office.

Kathy and Hugh walked away, Mandy waited at the table. Max was only a few steps away when Mandy spoke.

"Got another minute?"

"Sure."

"Whataya doing for dinner?"

"I was going to do some knitting tonight."

Mandy laughed. "How about *Melia's*? We'll go Dutch."

"Ok."

"I'll meet you there at seven."

When Max arrived a few minutes before seven, Mandy was already seated. It was clear that she was in charge of the evening. She wore a black skirt and a fitted white blouse, the outfit accenting the lines of her figure, the flat tummy, her slender athletic arms, and her rather voluptuous breasts. Max, suddenly aware that he was underdressed, realized he was wearing what he had on at the morning coffee.

"Wow," he said as he joined her, "you look fantastic." He looked down at his shoes and back at Mandy. "I'm sorry. I didn't think..."

"Why the apology? I expected you to be wearing a monk's robe with one of those ropes used as a belt. This is a pleasant surprise."

Max laughed.

They enjoyed dinner for two hours, quietly eating, discussing everything from their taste in wine to the last book they read. Max asked probing, not piercing questions; Mandy responded honestly, humbly telling him of her athletic achievements and her life goals of writing.

Mandy wanted to hear more about Calhoun Cooper and Max answered honestly, a few times stopping to sip his red wine, taking a break. It was emotional for him; Mandy sensed it, knowing he was baring his soul. It wasn't all so serious though. They shared their thoughts about things from popular music to reality TV.

Mandy was sizing him up, checking him out, Max *mostly* clueless. He was more like a man riding in a raft—just going where the river steered him.

They ordered dessert. Max got the key lime pie; Mandy ordered the "Death By Chocolate," an obscenely large piece of cake. Still chatting amiably, Mandy had eaten half her cake when she reached across the table, took Max's fork from the side of his plate, not asking for permission, and daintily took a bite of his key lime pie. She smiled and put Max's fork back on his plate.

There is a hint, a signal in the dating world: when the female takes a bite of dessert with the *man's* fork, there is more going on than the formality of a first date. That was the moment that Max became fully awake, jolted into realizing this was a date.

They paid, Mandy insisting that she pay for half as she'd promised.

They'd both taken their own cars. It was nine-thirty, summer almost at full tilt, a scrim of light still in the evening sky. As they stood at her car, the four-door Land Rover, Max sensed that this night wasn't the one where he asked her to have a nightcap at his house. He wanted to, but he didn't want to be *that* guy, so as they stood next to her car, he extended his hand for the evening parting.

Mandy, leaning against her car, pulled Max's hand to her side, slid the other hand behind his back, looked up, eyes wide open, and kissed him. As their lips met, Mandy's arms loosened, falling to her sides, as she was completely relaxed, head tilted up as Max put one arm around her back and drew her to him. It was a long, deep kiss.

When their lips parted, Max looked into Mandy's eyes and tried speaking. "I never…I mean…I hope…I didn't see that coming."

"Good night, Max," she said. "I'll see you in the morning for coffee."

Mandy got into her car, not looking around for Max. She closed the door and sat for a full minute, head on the steering wheel.

As for Max, he reached his Tahoe, climbed in, and also sat staring at nothing.

They both, separately, apart, out loud, said this: "Oh my God!"

Chapter 39

THEY BOTH KNEW. They knew there was something different, something better that had happened. It was the ease with which they enjoyed each other's company, the feeling of companionship, and the fact that neither of them had to force conversation. And then there was the *kiss*. That was the final sign. They both knew.

Coffee went as usual. Hugh and Kathy had no idea that Mandy and Max had had a real date the night before. Bailey ate a muffin under the table supplied to him by Mandy. After licking his chops, getting every morsel of the muffin, he licked himself. It was his routine.

Hugh had already been to Rhodes Field, picked up his money, and had dug around right field as long as he could. Kathy talked about the heat, how the horses around town were being trained in the mornings, not in the afternoon.

Max and Mandy said little to each other, joining in the conversation with their senior friends.

There was a break. Hugh shook his cup, stirring the remainder of the medium roast while Bailey licked himself.

Mandy said, "You know, Max, my parents have a little place at Sullivan's. The wind is supposed to be perfect in the afternoon this weekend. You wanna go to Sullivan's with me and learn some kiteboarding?"

Hugh and Kathy looked at each other with their heads tilted like Bailey's. They looked at Max. Before Max could answer, Hugh and Kathy almost shouted: "You should go to Sullivan's!"

Max was nonplussed. "I guess I'll go. I don't know anything about kiteboarding."

"You will not be disappointed," Hugh said.

"No, you won't," Kathy chimed in. And then she asked, "Just the two of you?"

"Yeah, I figure we can find things to do."

"I'm sure that won't be a problem," Hugh said, "there's the beach, the wind, good restaurants, beer, champagne. It won't be hard to find something to do."

"Y'all will have a good time," Kathy added.

Did they ever. Max cleared his schedule for Friday. They left Aiken before noon; Mandy drove. They chatted like old friends for those three hours, laughing, telling stories about their parents, about growing up. They talked about their work, Mandy discussing how fun it was to interview so many different people and Max talking about how every piece of litigation is a story, a miniature book with a beginning, middle, and end. It was so easy for both.

When they arrived at the "little place" Max was quiet.

"Throw your bag over there," she said, pointing to the foyer, as she went to the refrigerator. Max looked out of those windows, the same ones where Hugh was transfixed by the whole scene, the beach, the water, the waves, and the birds flying along the small breaking surf.

"Good lord, it's beautiful."

"Yeah, we've enjoyed it," she said like a person who says they enjoy a good nap. "I thought we'd open a bottle of champagne. It is Friday." The cork was already popped; she had two flutes poured and approached Max. "Want to sit out on the deck? There are some kiteboarders out there. It's cool to watch."

Max stood at the rail, mesmerized by the scene.

"I'll be right back," she said, leaving him alone on the deck.

Max, like Hugh, hadn't been to the beach in several years. A few minutes passed; Max watched the kiteboarders in the short distance, riding the wind and waves.

"You know what goes well with champagne?" she asked. Max turned around.

"Cheese." Mandy had a tray of cheese and crackers. She set the tray and her champagne flute down on the little coffee table in front of them. She stood in front of Max, her back to the house, and kissed him. It was their second kiss, just as moving, just as powerful as the first. She didn't sit down, they didn't rip each other's clothes off like in the movies; they kissed. They kissed a very passionate kiss, that's all. And then she whispered in his ear, "do you think we can wait until after dinner?"

"No," he said into her ear, "we can't."

And they did not.

Chapter 40

MANDY TOOK MAX by the hand and guided him to her bedroom. Her shoes already off, she laid on her back on top of the covers, feet off the side of the bed. Max joined from the side, still dressed, shoes off. Mandy wore a blouse with five buttons. As they kissed again, Max, carefully, slowly unbuttoned the top button of her blouse—and then the second and third button. Mandy wasn't wearing a bra. She'd discarded it before she put the cheese and crackers on the tray.

"Oh," he murmured to her as he looked into her eyes.

"I took it off a few minutes ago," she whispered back. "I didn't want to waste time."

Max knew what to do, making his way with his mouth from her lips to her neck, kissing, sucking, ever so tenderly, her neck, and moving to her breasts, nipples firm and erect.

And then they ripped each other's clothes off just like the movies.

The first time they made love that afternoon, it lasted all of seven minutes, better than anything they had ever known. They lay together, knowing that it was magical, saying nothing.

Mandy cuddled under Max's arm, stroking his chest.

Max rolled to his side, facing Mandy, and put his hand to the right side of her face, pulling her to him.

"You are one beautiful woman. I don't think I've ever..."

"Be quiet..." Mandy turned her face upward and exhaled, a big breath out like one of those yoga-class exhales.

They knew, they both knew that they had just had the best sex they'd ever had. It was better, in Mandy's mind, to simply enjoy it. She didn't want to hear his lines.

A few minutes passed; both lovers at peace. Max rolled to his right side, and ever so tenderly, kissed the corner of her mouth. She responded at first with a simple touch of her tongue to his, and then a full-blown kiss, rolling on top of Max, lips, tongues, faces in a wet mess. It was round two.

It was thirty minutes of sheer excitement, tenderness, rousing, arousing, energized sex between two people obviously falling, already fallen, as deep as they could fall, in love.

At the break, after round two, Mandy sat up on the side of the bed.

"We can't keep this up," she said. "We need food. Let's order pizza. We can pick it up from Luke and Ollie's."

"I don't know where that is, but as long as it's not an hour away..."

"Ten minutes. I'll call. Trust me on the pizza."

Daylight was fading by the time they got back, the huge pizza filled the car with the aromas of onions, pepperoni, cheese and tomato sauce.

Mandy opened another bottle of bubbles. They sat out on the back deck, ate the entire large pizza and finished more champagne. It was hot outside, mid-June in South Carolina, brutally humid. The moon came up, nearly full, a hump-backed, gibbous-shaped moon. Mandy and Max barely noticed it. They were engaged in conversation, Max showing his sense of humor. Mandy told tales about growing up, the funny stories, the family traditions at Thanksgiving and Christmas.

By ten o'clock they were worn out. Mandy stood up in front of Max and tugged on his hand.

"I'm tired," she said.

"Exhausted."

They weren't too tired for round three…or four. They finally got some rest, a little after two a.m.

The next day, Saturday, Mandy showed Max her world-class skill at kiteboarding. They made an afternoon of it, Mandy requiring that Max get on the board, strapped in, kite in hand, and feel the wind carry him over the waves. Max fell, tripped, splashed, and did face plants twenty, thirty, countless times until he got the hang of it enough to enjoy a three-minute ride.

When he finally got it, Mandy stood on the beach and clapped both hands in front of her like a mom watching her little boy hit his first baseball.

Max made his way back to the shallow water and stood in the surf, maybe a foot deep.

"That was awesome!" he screamed.

Mandy, happy he finally got it, responded, "If we're going to date, you have to think that's awesome. I'm so happy."

"Do we have to have sex, or can we just stay out here?"

"We have to do both."

"Ok. Only if you insist. But it's a tough choice. I've never done anything like that."

And then, with the kite floating in the water, carrying the board under his arm, he approached her.

"I've never felt like this before. I mean...about any woman. This is different, Mandy. I'm feeling something..."

He put the board on the sand and kissed her, a big saltwater smack. Mandy hugged him, her arms around his neck. "I know," she said. "It's mutual."

"That's what I get? It's mutual?"

"I'll put it this way, Max. I've *never, ever* invited a man to this house I've *never, ever*, had sex in that bed," she said pointing to the house. "But I've been hurt before, and if you are insincere, if you are making statements that aren't true, I will hunt you down, find you, and cut off some very important body parts with a big knife that I carry with me at all times." And, then, she smiled.

Late that night, Max took her face in the palms of his hands, looked her in the eyes and told her he meant what he said.

"I know," she said. And she kissed him.

It was the fastest, they didn't expect it, they didn't see it coming—couldn't happen to them—romance. But it was the real thing. They both knew it. But Mandy had that money problem, that very singular problem of having *too much* money. She had to be careful how she approached the issue, Max not knowing the extent of her wealth. But all problems have a solution: sometimes time is the answer, sometimes thought and action, sometimes faith, sometimes serendipity, sometimes providential divination.

The next two weeks would provide the answer.

Chapter 41

HUGH ARRIVED AT Rhodes Field by seven o'clock. The sun had been up since six; the grass in the outfield was almost dry when he started digging, singing the lyrics to John Fogerty's *Centerfield.*

He'd already gathered his money and stuffed into his front jeans pocket as always. Hugh had done so much digging, Centerfield looked like families of groundhogs had been making homes, having parties underground, serving large portions of groundhog food and doing other groundhog activities, whatever those are—but it was Hugh's digging that made the outfield pockmarked. This day, a Tuesday, the earth seemed easier to penetrate as he dug around the other holes he'd dug. Hugh checked his watch. He had two minutes left on his timer. The shovel shaft got shorter, digging into the sand. With thirty seconds to go on his watch there was a scraping sound, *metal on wood.* There was no question; no doubt, it was the tip of the shovel hitting something besides rock. Hugh stopped. He was out of time. His heart raced; he knew he couldn't stay, but he'd hit the mother lode. Wendell would come looking for him, or worse, the authorities would stop him from coming on the property at all. Bailey sensed there was something different, Hugh moving quickly, Bailey smelling Hugh's adrenaline wafting from his pores. Bailey barked as Hugh walked around the barrier near the guard gate.

"Bailey see a deer this morning?"

"I think he saw a ghost. He's been crapping at a new place. He's picky, you know."

"Gotta love a dog, man, gotta love a dog."

Hugh walked on by. Sometimes he made small talk with Wendell, but not today. His body was so tense, so taut, he didn't want to give any hint to Wendell that something had happened in the barren village of old Ellenton. Hugh pulled down the tailgate of the truck and Bailey hopped in, as always, barking at nothing. Everything was different, though. Hugh knew he needed to make some plans. He called Kathy and told her he had some errands to run. He called Mandy and said he wouldn't be at the *New Moon* for coffee.

Hugh didn't sleep that night.

Chapter 42

HUGH ARRIVED A little earlier than usual at the gate, carrying a shovel and a small hatchet. He had a relationship with Wendell, a legitimate friendliness that he'd established over the past six months. With only a thirty-minute time limit, Hugh slung dirt out of centerfield like a cartoon character burrowing his way to China, sand going this way and that, Bailey jumping all over the place, barking at the new game Hugh was playing.

In the first ten minutes of his digging, the ground seemed to give way, suddenly making it easier to sling the sand out of the hole. Hugh dug faster, hurling the dark sand out of the cavity. The lines in his face hardened as he flung the full shovel again and again. With perspiration dripping down the sides of his body under his shirt, he felt like his heart would explode. Then, after six months of picking up money, a half-a-year of thinking of little else, his shovel tip found the wooden crate. He had fifteen minutes left. He got on his hands and knees, four feet into the hole, and started tossing the dirt out with his bare hands. The crate was mostly disintegrated, but it still had some shape to it. Burlap bags were stuffed inside the crate, many of them split, ripped and torn. Money poured out of the bags.

"Oh my god!" Hugh said to himself and to Bailey, who was standing above him, barking.

"I've never seen so much money in my life."

There was the money, so much money, so damn much money, almost smiling at Hugh for being found, being freed from its underground coffer.

And there was a manila envelope. It had been sealed tight, tape across the clasp, long ago dried out, allowing Hugh to open it quickly.

"Oh my God, Bailey, there's a letter!"

Part Two

Chapter 43

YEARS BEFORE CARLA'S dad was injured in that terrible accident, Carla worked on Wall Street. She did her own trading and sat on many Boards of Directors. One of those boards was Awendaw Financial. The CEO of Awendaw was a man named Ralph Lousteau. Mr. Lousteau had asked Carla to sit on the board because of her excellent reputation and savvy knowledge of the market. It was more than just another Board to Carla; she enjoyed the terrific movements that Awendaw was making on the Street.

And Ralph Lousteau was *the man*. Journalists and business writers came from all over the globe to learn how Awendaw had gone from a minor league payday lender to the number two mortgage company in America. Lousteau had been featured on magazine covers, rang the bell on Wall Street, and had been interviewed a few dozen times by the stock analysts on TV. Lousteau had achieved a kind of sick rock star status and surrounded himself with fawning toadies who blushed when they were in his presence. His personal wealth had grown to six billion dollars.

Lousteau wanted to start a new branch of Awendaw and asked Carla to take the Chief Operating Officer position. The new company was NOVA Bev Lending. Usually, not much happens fast when a new company is started. But if you have money and power, those things don't take much time. Within thirty days of the idea, NOVA Bev Lending was formed and operating with Carla Robeson in charge. NOVA Bev was named with a completely different name than Awendaw for a reason. Lousteau wanted to make sure he could be given credit for successfully creating a "new kind of company" which stood on its own, if it was successful. If it weren't a big hit, Lousteau would keep his distance from that bastard child.

Because Lousteau's star was shining so brightly, he believed his own press releases. He didn't need any guidance in the regulation of the new company and told Robeson what to do and how to do it. Robeson complied, at first willingly, but after about six months, she approached Lousteau about the legality of some of the deals that were being made. Lousteau dismissed those warnings and told her to disregard whatever thoughts she had about the trivial details of the law. Robeson sent an email to Lousteau about her concerns. Lousteau read the email and deleted it.

NOVA Bev's numbers were terrific. New, smaller loans were made under the guise that the borrower was "improving" their property. Most of the loans were between twenty-five and fifty thousand dollars. The interest rate was higher than the first mortgage because there was more risk. The interesting *illegal* part of it was that NOVA Bev charged ten "points" or "discounts" up front. That meant the borrower was paying an effective interest rate of seventeen percent, but that wasn't disclosed on the federal form. Violating federal lending laws is a big deal.

Carla requested a one-on-one meeting with Lousteau to warn him of the possible problems with federal law in the event something, somewhere, went wrong. A lunch was scheduled.

Chapter 44

THERE ARE VERY ostentatious, very pretentious, very ornate dining rooms at The Holland Club, a members-only private enterprise located on 55th East Street in Manhattan. Lousteau and Robeson were both members, but the staff and management knew that Lousteau was the one to be treated like royalty. And he was. When he blessed The Holland with his presence, when the elevator doors opened and his shining, overblown face was seen by the greeters, everyone scattered about to make sure every need of Mr. Lousteau was met. He peacocked in a gray pinstriped suit with a soft purple tie. The hostess ushered him into the private dining room where Carla Robeson had been patiently waiting for twenty minutes because Lousteau had been meeting with his biographer.

Lousteau had grown accustomed to having the wait staff pull out his chair while he prepared himself to sit, which they did as though presenting the throne to their king. Once seated, he sat motionless for a moment while another waiter snapped open the black-cloth napkin with great flare and placed it on Mr. Lousteau's lap. Lousteau mustered the energy to pull his own chair up to the table and tugged at his sleeves under his suit coat revealing radiant lapis cufflinks. After all that pomp and circumstance, Lousteau looked at the fiftyish, tall, skinny waiter with a black-dyed comb over.

"I'll have an espresso," Lousteau said, "and bring me an order of the mussels in the garlic butter sauce for an appetizer."

Carla Robeson had already finished one glass of iced tea. She watched as another waiter poured water for her and Lousteau and, from a separate silver goblet, more iced tea was poured into her glass.

Lousteau did not engage in conversation until he ordered his lunch. He examined the menu with great care and asked the comb-over waiter several questions about whether the beef was grain fed and its origin. He finally ordered the filet mignon, but he wanted it in a mustard aioli sauce, which wasn't on the menu. The waiter said, "no problem" several times and then trotted off to satisfy the king. Robeson ordered the chicken. Once all of this was accomplished, Lousteau turned his attention to his lunch mate.

"What's wrong, Carla?" Lousteau asked, "You said there was a problem we needed to discuss?"

"I wanted to get your undivided attention for thirty minutes, Ralph. NOVA Bev is making plenty of money, our default rates are low, but I've received two troubling letters. The attorney general from Minnesota wants to review our pre-loan disclosure materials. We got the same letter from Arizona. We don't have some required documents in our pre-loan disclosure package. The legal team from Awendaw says don't worry about it, but I am worried about it. These loans are being sold to Wall Street as securities. If NOVA Bev has violated federal law, those securities can be considered as fraudulent. It's a big deal."

"You've got to learn to trust the legal team I've assembled, Carla. This isn't a question for me; it's for the lawyers. Besides, Awendaw can *buy* the states of Minnesota and Arizona if it wants. Quit being such a worrywart. You've got to be more confident in your team of professionals." When he finished, he felt satisfied. This was the second time he had varnished that tale in the space of one hour. His biographer had written down every word of it only thirty minutes earlier. Carla Robeson had heard it all before and knew it was bullshit. She looked Ralph in the eyes.

"Ralph, I've contacted some outside attorneys who substantiate the fact that we need pre-loan disclosures. We've trusted the Awendaw legal team but they are wrong. These loans are Section 28 loans. They require different disclosures. NOVA Bev has violated federal law. We need to fix this."

At first Lousteau turned slightly pink. He had a garlic-butter-sauce mussel in the corner of his mouth and he left it there, buried in his back molars, as his color changed from pink to a full-blown red. He looked at Carla Robeson and took a deep breath as he began his apoplectic rant.

"You don't go behind my back, Carla," he began, "you don't question my authority. You do what I say and follow my orders. I don't give one happy shit what *your lawyers* say. I've been in this business for twenty-five years and know my way around regulations and little things like government requirements. You follow *my* rules, Carla. This is *my* company and we will do it *my* way. Don't ever go behind my back again." Lousteau tried to swallow the mussel that got caught in his throat for a second, but he managed to gag it up and spit into his napkin, as his face changed from deep red to purple.

Robeson's face didn't change. She didn't reach the upper echelon of Lousteau's companies by being a spineless yes woman.

"You put me in charge. I'm telling you there are problems. We can't *buy* Arizona and Minnesota. I think we need to review this with another set of eyes. It could result in some devastating consequences."

Lousteau's color had returned to a deep pink. He set the mussel-filled napkin on the table and stood up.

"I've got your back, Carla. I've always got your back. I'll get my lawyers to look at this again, but don't ever go behind mine. You've got to trust Ralph Lousteau. Ralph Lousteau didn't get to be a billionaire by worrying about regulations. You get around them Carla. You get around 'em. And when you can't, you change the law. I've got your back, Carla."

The meeting, the lunch, the private talk, was finished. Ralph walked out of the ornate dining room, coughing as he went.

Ralph Lousteau had only recently begun to refer to himself in third person. It was something he picked up from his biographer, a question about how 'Mr. Lousteau handled a situation in his life.' Lousteau liked the way it sounded when the biographer referred to him as some sort of deity, and Lousteau continued the pattern of referring to himself as Mr. Lousteau or Ralph Lousteau. It made him seem even more important.

Chapter 45

THERE'S AN ANCIENT rule that's been followed for thousands of years. When a ship is in trouble, when a ship's mast or tower is the last part above the water line, there is the Captain. He is the last person to leave a sinking ship. It's a well-known true tale about one of the chief officers on the Titanic who jumped on a lifeboat filled with women and children. He survived that horror, but he was shunned the rest of his life. And he wasn't even the Captain. The Captain of the Titanic and most of his officers *did* go down with the ship.

Many business leaders find creative ways of blaming subordinates for their errors. And so it was for Ralph Lousteau. He chose the cowardly path of blaming Carla Robeson for what was wrong with NOVA Bev Lending. Although Mr. Lousteau had been warned, and although Carla did everything she could to protect herself and the company, when the prosecutors came around with their subpoenas as calling cards, Ralph Lousteau was nowhere to be found. In fact, he signed an affidavit that stated, in detail, that he tried to stop Carla from violating the law, but Carla was unstoppable. And since big money always wins, since America loves a hero, especially one who is self-made and promoted by the media, it was easy to put a big red dot on Carla's back. She knew she'd been had and that her freedom was much more important than trying to convince the government and the press that it was all Lousteau's insatiable greed and outright disregard for laws and authority that caused NOVA Bev to do stupid, unlawful things.

Chapter 46

RALPH LOUSTEAU WATCHED the bus roll over Carla, never once taking any responsibility. NOVA Bev was new in the market and he'd distanced himself ever so gingerly from it that he didn't need to salvage his reputation. He moved on, as they say, to other important matters as Carla Robeson faced the government with no one at her side.

Carla Robeson, a person whose worst prior crime was speeding on the interstate, was suddenly made aware of her very limited options. She could plead guilty and still walk around. She could keep her freedom, or she could force the government to prosecute her fully with a trial. If a jury found her guilty, she would get up to fifteen years in the crossbar hotel. Carla Robeson's body itched and broke out into big red hives on her arms and back as she struggled with her decision. Like so many others before her, and certainly innumerable souls to follow her limited path of options, she chose to have her freedom instead of fighting. It made her vomit, which she did every day for a week before she went to court with her lawyers. She'd already paid those dudes a quarter of a million dollars to "keep her out of jail" and she felt like she could have better spent that money slinging dice in Las Vegas or gotten advice from a palm reader in a mobile home along a dirt road in Kansas.

The deal was cut.

Carla wouldn't do any time and she would retain the profits from Awendaw, but not from NOVA Bev Lending. Her abundant trust fund was untouched by the Feds. In the whirlwind of ninety days, NOVA Bev was closed and Carla Robeson signed an agreement with the Securities and Exchange Commission. Carla got to keep her money, which was a gracious plenty. And she got her freedom. So, NOVA Bev was a blip on the radar screen of time with no real injury to anyone except the federal government who "caught it in time."

All Carla heard from her lawyers was that she would keep her freedom and her money. At the time, that was all she cared about. What she learned later, in the fine print of the agreement, though, was that she couldn't trade stocks or bonds for five years. It was a devastating blow to Carla. She loved trading stocks, following the nuances of the market every day and figuring out what was hot and what went cold.

Sure, she could do some consulting, but the phone never rang; no one wanted an old washed-up crook like Carla Robeson around to help. To make it worse, she couldn't trade a nickel's worth of stocks.

Part Three

Chapter 47

HUGH HAD READ the three-page letter from Clay Caswell so many times since he had dug it up that he could quote it from memory, like when he was in the seventh grade and had to recite the Gettysburg Address. But this letter was not a famous president speaking in erudite terms. It was Clay Caswell screaming:

"If you are from Korea, go to hell. I hope you burn in hell. And I hope you all eat maggots. If you are an American, take this money and buy weapons. Kill all Koreans in Congress."

Hugh tucked the letter into a new manila folder and kept it in the top drawer of his dresser. Clay Caswell, Hugh learned from the epistle, had a second career after doing twenty-three years in the army. Since he was so well-respected and admired, one of his superiors took it upon himself to make sure that Clay Caswell was rewarded with good employment upon his retirement from the United States Army. He was recommended for a job at the Bureau of Engraving and Printing in the security department. With his service record, Clay was employed with hardly an interview. Clay Caswell was the man who could keep America's money safe. It was a made-to-order job for a person who required and thrived on protocol. So, it was that Sergeant Caswell left the Army on a Friday and went to work in a quieter career as Mr. Caswell the next Monday on 14th Street in Washington D.C., where money is printed. He never even had to move from his apartment.

The security department alone had one hundred and twenty-seven employees by the late1960s, and by 1969, Clay Caswell was the number-four man in that division of the Bureau.

The sixties were tough on the United States of America; things changed so fast Clay couldn't keep up.

Clay was not the kind of guy who could go to the VFW and drink beer with the rest of those grizzled vets; his war-time experiences kept him an unmarried homebody. He talked to his fellow workers about the sad state of America, but in the mid to late 60s there were so many differing opinions, he learned quickly to keep his thoughts to himself. He found his own nirvana with the work he did at the bureau. And his life was made full by, of all things, a cat.

In 1968, while Washington D.C. looked like a city under siege, Clay found a little white kitten with a light orange marking on his back that looked like the continent of Europe. The poor feline was surviving on scraps of food tossed out by a café down the street from his apartment. The tiny, meowing fellow survived on the goodness of the café owner until Clay could no longer resist the starving cat winding around Clay's ankles every day, tail up, begging for food and attention. Once Clay picked up the little ball of fur, it was over.

Clay named the cat General Patton because of the way he took command at Clay's apartment upon arrival. As only a cat can do, General Patton began his tenure as the purring potentate of Clay's flat as soon as he landed his white and orange paws on the carpeted floors of the one-bedroom apartment. The owner of the café where General Patton had been surviving told Clay an important thing about the little kitty. He said that upon inspection, General Patton had six toes on his front paws. Those cats are known as "Hemingway cats" because at Ernest Hemingway's house in Key West, all the cats have six toes, or carry the *polydactyl* gene in their DNA to mother or father six-toed kittens. The funny thing was, Hemingway named his six-toed cats after famous characters, the first cat being named Snow White. It was pure luck, or maybe pure fate that Clay Caswell named his little buddy General Patton, not even knowing that Hemingway cats have celebrity names from the start.

Clay was content. His mind fighting what would later be called PTSD, he found his only peace in two things: General Patton and the Bureau.

By 1970, Clay was fifty years old; the world was becoming more difficult to him with every change in America. It started with the escalation of the war in Vietnam and the protests on the Mall, only a mile from his flat. Clay began to experience the pressure vicariously, like a vise on his head. Although the war was thousands of miles away, the nightly news was a constant reminder of his soldiering days, and especially his time in Korea.

With no female companionship and no one to talk to except General Patton, Clay began to live more inside his head where things were more familiar. Clay Caswell was an American hero. And he was a victim of horrible "shell shock." Poor Clay's condition took a turn that no one could see coming.

Chapter 48

WATERGATE WENT ON for two full years before Nixon resigned as the President of the United States in August of 1974. Clay Caswell was shaken, Washington D.C. was devastated, and the world watched to see how America would survive. For Clay Caswell, who was getting older, lonelier, grayer, and more doubtful about his country, coping with life became harder. He became more withdrawn, more bitter, and more distrustful of his own country.

And then it happened. In 1976 there was Koreagate. For many Americans, this was another scandal in the seemingly endless stream of problems for the United States of America, but for Clay Caswell, it tipped the scale from sanity to insanity.

President Nixon, before he left office, had made a push to eliminate aid to South Korea and pull out the troops who had been there since 1953. South Korea didn't like that idea, so it bribed the powers-that-be in America.

Supposedly, the Korea Central Intelligence Agency (KCIA) funneled bribes through a Korean businessman named Tongsun Park to influence certain members of Congress to keep U.S. money and military in South Korea.

In other countries, bribery and corruption are accepted, but in America that's not supposed to be how laws and policy are made. A congressman named Richard Hanna was rumored to have been approached by Tongsun Park and made a deal to share in commissions from American rice sales to Korea and use that money to influence members of Congress. The country was still reeling from Watergate, Nixon resigning, Ford taking office, and then the election of Carter.When the Korea matter hit the newspapers, the media named it Koreagate. If it hadn't been for Watergate, it would certainly have been called something else.

As for Clay Caswell, he had managed to deal with the unrest of the 60s and the scandal that surrounded Watergate, but when he learned that Korea was taking over Congress with bribes, his disorder went into overdrive.

Clay never slept well, but as Koreagate was publicized, the memories of his imprisonment in Korea came to him in violent nightmares of human savagery. He lost more sleep than usual. Clay slipped from his nightmares of abuse to visions of Koreans taking over the country. Hundreds of Korean soldiers came to him, night after night, with bayonets, bamboo spears, surgical instruments, whips, bats, and vats of soup with a few pieces of rice floating on top. The rice, it turned out, wasn't rice at all, but maggots swimming in the large pools of tepid water. In his sleep Clay greedily swallowed them, only to vomit when he woke up in a bed that was soaked with his sweat and reeking with the odor of rotten eggs. In his dreams, he lost weight. Seeing himself from above, he saw his ribs through his back, his hips visible under the thin skin on his ass. In a recurring nightmare, he pulled himself through muddy water to a bed crawling with cockroaches, their antennae and barbed legs making their way into his nostrils, his mouth, ears and throat; Clay crunched the hard-outer shells of the cockroaches with his teeth.

That was what happened when he slept, so he avoided sleep. He tried his damnedest to stay awake. Just closing his eyes turned into hallucinations of barbarity. Without sleep, his head pounded, day and night. There wasn't enough aspirin in stores to stop the pain of each heartbeat in his head. He missed work; he had never taken time off before.

He'd been promoted to the number-two man in the security department of the Bureau. That status gave Clay a lot of leeway. He took two weeks off to plan how he could save General Patton and maybe, just maybe, some American would help him save his country. When he returned, some folks at work noticed his bleary eyes and his lack of focus, but no one knew what was going on in Clay's weird world. The fact that he had taken that much time off was unusual for *him*, but it didn't set off any alarms at the Bureau.

Clay's his entire persona wanted to save America while his mind was spinning, pounding, suffocating in heavy air, smelling fumes of his own burning flesh as he was branded by red-tipped bamboo, pulling at his yellow puss-filled armpit, starving to death—the new normal for Clay went from almost sane to completely bat-shit crazy.

He knew the Koreans were coming. And Americans in his hometown would need money to save America. And Clay's hometown, Ellenton, South Carolina, now the Savannah River Site, was where he had been most happy, the place where he grew up in the rustic life, playing baseball as a child.

Chapter 49

CLAY BUILT, ALONG with General Patton, a crate made of wooden slats to hold the money that would be needed to help America save herself. When he was ready, when everything was in place, Clay went to work and studied where the money from the Bureau was being sent via its own armored vehicles. He had credibility; no one paid attention to Clay's red eyes, pained look or sweating face. He was Clay Caswell, the model of security and safety.

He pulled a "surprise security inspection" on the three Bureau men as they pulled into the ramp at Richmond. The three of them stood down, backed off, and let Clay go over the truck, the tires, the doors, the keys, and the weapons they were required to carry. He told them he was going to check on something and that he would be back in ten minutes—for them to wait on the loading dock and he would return. And he drove the truck away. Simple as that.

Clay Caswell was their boss, the big guy. The three of them waited at the dock for two hours before they called the Bureau. Even then, they didn't suspect Clay had absconded with the money. They reported that he must have gotten lost.

Clay was a soldier. He was prepared. His black F-150 pickup truck was ready with a cover over the bed, the crate already built and in the truck. General Patton was in the front seat in a carrier. The two of them headed south, General Patton meowing and carrying on for a while. Clay didn't care if he got away or not. He was going to save America from herself. If his strategy worked, good. If not, he would still finish with his ultimate plan.

Clay Caswell had lost his *country*; he had given his life, his very being, and his every waking moment had eventually sacrificed his sanity.

And he buried that money, God only knows why, but he buried it in the outfield of Rhodes Field and headed to Key West. In the space of three days, he made it to Key West, General Patton happily in tow. In the next two days, he bribed the keeper of the cats at Hemingway's home, only after showing her General Patton's paws, and telling her that he (Clay) was dying of cancer and General Patton desperately needed a home. After a tearful goodbye to his only friend, Caswell walked to a ten-foot tall buoy that stands on a concrete waterfront harbor where land meets the Atlantic. The large buoy is a tourist attraction that says: "Southernmost Point, Continental United States." People have their pictures taken there every day. But at night the scene is less busy. Clay waited for the sun to set and he calmly sat himself down on the edge of the buoy, pulled out his thirty-eight-caliber pistol, pointed it at his right temple, and made a mess of where his head had been.

Chapter 50

In the Bureau of Engraving and Printing it was known as the "Caswell Matter." Things are called "matters" when there is a big mistake somewhere. It was a Matter. It sure was. The BEP had allowed their second in command to drive out of the Bureau with thirty million dollars in their own armored car.

He had been the most trusted, the most honorable, employee of the BEP. Those who had known him wondered why Clay Caswell would steal from his government. Had they known about his fractured mind, they might have understood. After finding his body on the pier next to the buoy, they thought it would be easy to find the money. Rather than report this major breach of security, the Bureau (BEP) sent two investigators from the BEP and looked all over Key West for clues about where Clay had been. They went to hotels, bars, houses of ill repute, and anywhere else they thought Clay might have gone spending lots of cash. The bills never showed up. They eventually gave up, creating a confidential document for the next Bureau Chief to figure out.

When the BEP found out that Clay was gone, the chief had two choices. One, he could follow the proper procedure, call in the Secret Service, and get the full force of the United States involved. That choice had some problems; they really didn't know if Clay was lost. Maybe he would be back at the end of the day. Two, they could wait.

The second choice seemed, in 1976, like a better option. Pretend. Don't tell. Sweep it under the rug. There were only seven people in the BEP who knew about it. Three of them, the riders in the truck, were told that Clay was captured, shot, and killed and they were never to speak another word about it. They didn't. Their jobs hung in the balance and there was no need to chat about Clay Caswell, the person who had tricked them into potential job loss.

The other four people in the Bureau were easily sworn to secrecy. There was a folder made that said, "eyes only" on it that was passed from Bureau chief to Bureau chief as they retired. When the money was found, the previous Bureau chiefs were dead. It all went to the attention of the current chief, Charles Madison.

Chapter 51

INSTEAD OF SENDING legions of investigators to Aiken, Charles Madison sent one investigator, a young man named Hank Stafford. Hank was from Ohio; he'd never been south. A single man enjoying the benefits of Washington D.C., he was interested in seeing some of the Southern belles and sampling some barbeque. The chief didn't give him any details. Hank's work folder contained a few pieces of paper, one of them with Hugh Buncombe's name and address on it. All he knew was there was some old dude who had passed some bills of great interest to the Bureau. Hank's job was to trace the money and report directly to the Bureau Chief. It was an easy job, this investigation. Travel south, good weather, barbeque, maybe meet a hot girl somewhere along the path.

The Bureau had already dug *its* hole. The Secret Service didn't know anything about the money. And like any other government agency, the employees of the BEP weren't exactly excited about doing *more* work.

When Hugh spent the money at Sullivan's Island, the Richmond office contacted the Bureau and informed it that their system said to call the BEP. The call was made; it was up to the Bureau to call the Secret Service. No such call was made. Madison wanted this to be put to bed quietly. His thinking, quite correctly, was to find out if there was more money, get it and return it. That way the whole matter, a forty-year embarrassment, would be over and the Bureau wouldn't have to make some report to Congress about it. Charlie found himself in a whipsaw. He could easily have ratted out his predecessors—they'd hidden the problem—that would make him look like an honest Bureau Chief. But if he did that, his former bosses and their families would be crooks. All the awards, the letters of commendation, the little plaques from the government would be better put in the attic than kept on the wall of some proud grandchildren's homes. Rather than become the rat, Charlie chose the path of continuation: to keep this whole mess under wraps. It seemed simple—go find that old man from the picture at High Thyme and question him. The videotape was reviewed. After a few weeks, with Charlie doing all the work, he figured out that some old guy named Hugh Buncombe lived in Aiken, South Carolina. Easy enough. Go to Hugh—he will tell the Bureau where he got the money, the Bureau gets the money and brings it back. A piece of investigative cake.

Charlie was kidding himself if he really thought it would be that easy.

Hugh had finished with his coffee klatch. And Kathy, Mandy and Max had all gone on to their respective spots of responsibility. Hugh was home with Bailey. He had been to Rhodes Field, but not to gather any more money. He'd managed to smuggle out of the hole every single dollar, a backpack load at a time, over the past two weeks. In all there was thirty million, minus the cash used by Clay Caswell.

Thirty million dollars, in packs, in Hugh's spare bedroom.

Hugh didn't know it was thirty million; he was counting it, figuring out how much was in each pack, marking it with a three-by-six-note card, and stacking it. Clay Caswell's letter, the three-page hand-written confession and declaration of war against Korea, was in his dresser, in perfect condition.

Hank had driven to Aiken in one of the older Bureau cars, a black Crown Vic that looked, smelled and had every sense of being a "cop car." He parked in front of Hugh's house on that bright morning of June 21, the day of the summer solstice.

A knock on the door. Bailey barked. Hugh, thinking it might be Kathy, closed and locked the door to the spare bedroom. When Hugh opened the door, he knew.

Chapter 52

HANK SHOWED HUGH his badge, saying a few things that Hugh never heard.

"I want to talk to my attorney."

"About what? I haven't asked you any questions."

"Doesn't matter. You've got a badge, and I've got an attorney. I don't know what you want, but you can talk to my attorney." Hugh shut the door in Hank's face.

Hank knocked again. Hugh opened the door.

"Yes?"

"Who is your attorney?"

"Maxwell Cooper." Hugh closed the door again. He watched through the sheers in the living room as Hank walked back to the car. Hugh saw Hank messing with his phone and punching numbers. Hank drove off.

In that two-minute scene, Hugh's body aged ten years. His face flushed, his fingers went numb, sweat ran down the sides of his body and his nose started running. He felt an urge to pee. He went to the bathroom, peed. And then he vomited.

"Max."

"Yeah, Hugh, what's up?"

"I need to see you right now."

"I've got an appointment at ten. How about eleven?"

"Cancel it. I need to see you right now. I'll make it worth your while. Cancel the appointment. I'll be there in ten minutes." Hugh grabbed Clay Caswell's letter along with a paper bag filled with some of Caswell's cash. In eight minutes Hugh Buncombe and Bailey were in the lobby of Cooper and Cooper.

Carla Robeson was in the middle office, next to Max's office, working.

Max had only finished canceling his meeting when he greeted Hugh.

"What is going on, Hugh?"

"I need to talk to you." Hugh, without an invitation, walked back to Max's office and tossed the bag of cash on Max's desk. "There's twenty thousand dollars cash. I want to retain you for the rest of the day. There's more money if you need it."

"Good lord, Hugh. What the hell?"

Before Max could close his door, Hugh started telling the story in his typical loud fashion. He told Max about the money, Rhodes Field, the digging, the wooden crate full of cash, the letter from Clay Caswell. It was a confession that had been building up in Hugh like floodwaters at a dam.

The phone buzzed.

"What Sharon? I'm busy back here."

"There's a man in the lobby. Says he needs to talk to you about Hugh Buncombe. He showed me a badge."

"Jesus."

"Should I show him back?"

"No. Tell him I'm busy and I promise to call him at two o'clock. Make him leave the office. Promise. Two o'clock."

Hugh fell into the client chair. Bailey, sensing something was wrong, whined.

"I'm going to jail, aren't I? I am going to spend the rest of my life in prison."

"Not if I have anything to do with it, Hugh. Not if I have anything to do with it. We gotta figure some stuff out. Let me see the letter."

Hugh tossed the letter on the desk as he grabbed Max's office phone.

"Is that guy gone? How do you talk to Sharon?"

"Hugh, sit down. Give me the phone. You've gotta get ahold of yourself. Take a deep breath." Max poked the phone a few times.

"He's gone. Sharon says he's outta here. This letter is hilarious."

"What's funny? What's funny about this?"

"The letter. Have you read this?"

"A hundred times."

Max started reading the letter aloud: "If you are from Korea, go to hell. I hope you burn in hell. And I hope you all eat maggots. I hope you die with chicken livers sewn in your armpits. My name is Clay Caswell and I didn't leave General Patton. A soldier never leaves another of his brothers behind, and I am taking General Patton to Hemingway's. He'll be safe there. I never, ever left a soldier behind. Me and Eddie Granville couldn't save those men."

Max stopped. "He's not a deserter. He must've fought with Patton."

"I don't think so. Keep reading."

The letter went on to tell Clay Caswell's story, every word of it true—about his service in WWII, his experiences in Korea, his fallen comrades, his service to The Bureau of Engraving and Printing. Clay wrote about Korea taking over America and how he wanted to save her.

"Holy shit, Hugh. This is unbelievable."

"Keep reading."

Max, again reading out loud: "My grandparents and my parents were born and raised in Ellenton. The best memories of my life were when I played baseball on Rhodes Field. I love baseball. I was a very good baseball player. I played center-field. I hope whoever finds this money likes baseball and is not Korean. Clay Caswell."

"How much money, Hugh?"

"I've cataloged over twenty-five million. Clay Caswell said thirty million, but there's some missing, I think."

Max shouted. "Thirty million dollars! Good god, Hugh!"

Hugh shrugged. "It's my money."

"It's not your money. It belongs to the United States of America. The best I can do is maybe get you a finder's fee and keep you out of jail. Where's the money?"

Hugh Buncombe was feeling better. Just being around Max, telling his story, sharing the letter with someone made him feel like he wasn't so guilty.

"I'm not telling you where the money is."

"On second thought, Hugh, don't tell me. I don't want to know. I don't want to be considered an accomplice."

"Call that guy back and tell him I'll give him a hundred thousand to go away."

Carla Robeson appeared in the doorway.

"I've got a better idea."

"Who are you?" He looked at Max. "Who is *she*, Max?"

Chapter 53

CARLA ROBESON, DRESSED in black heels and a Nina McLemore dress, stood in the doorway.

"She's Ms. Robeson. I'm helping with her father's accident."

"And you've been listening?" Hugh exclaimed.

"You've been talking loud enough for the people walking on the street to hear you. If you have a secret, you should try whispering." And then she put her right index finger to her lips. "Like this," she said quietly.

"Max," she said, "call the man with the badge."

"I said I'd call at two. It's only ten."

"Call him. Ask him two questions. Ask what department he's with and if he has a partner."

Hugh put his hands out to Max. "Call him. I don't care."

Max hesitated and looked at Hugh.

"Go ahead, call 'im."

Max dialed. "Hello, this is Maxwell Cooper. I wanted to confirm my call with you at two o'clock. And I want to have a meeting with you and your co-worker at three o'clock. Is that good?"

"And your co-worker will be here?

"You don't have a partner? And what department of the government are you with?

"Ok. I'll call you back at two o'clock."

Max hung up.

"He doesn't have a partner. He's with the Bureau of Engraving."

Carla had moved from the doorway into the seat next to Hugh. "And there is nothing on the Internet about a man named Clay Caswell except some testimony at a Congressional hearing in 1954."

Hugh and Max looked at Carla.

"You were both talking so loud."

She continued. "I looked it up. Max, you can look."

Max moved the mouse around and typed.

"She's right."

"What difference does all of this make?"

Carla took over again. "Because the Secret Service investigates missing money. And they always, *always* work in teams. It keeps people from getting bribed, like what you were thinking of doing. The Bureau of Engraving has to turn over all investigations to the Secret Service."

"Who are you again?"

"Carla Robeson. I know a few things about the government."

It was Max's turn. "How do you know so much about the government? I thought you were a Wall Street person."

"I'm older than you, Max. I've done a few more things than you. I smell a rat."

"I do too," Max responded.

"I'm not a rat," Hugh said.

"Not you, the government. There's nothing anywhere about thirty million dollars missing from the government. Clay Caswell worked for the Bureau. If this had been reported, it would've been in the papers, the news, the Internet for the past thirty years or so. Clay Caswell doesn't exist except as a war hero. Don't you see what's going on here?" Carla Robeson was on a roll. With one hand on her hip and the other on her chin, she looked at Hugh. "How old is the guy with the badge?"

"Young. Maybe thirty, probably under thirty."

"That's what I thought. The Bureau sent a guy with no knowledge, hoping to pick up the money, threaten jail and get out of here. I bet he doesn't know anything about Clay Caswell."

"What difference does any of that make?"

"A lot of difference."

Max was still sitting in his chair, watching Carla.

"I need to talk to you Maxwell," she said, "in private."

"Without me?"

"Yes. Without you," she said. "Maxwell, follow me to the conference room. Mr. Buncombe, you stay put."

Carla walked out of the office, Max close behind. She stepped into the large conference room and closed the door.

"I've got a plan," she said, "but I need to tell you some things in confidence. Are you in?"

Max looked at Carla. She was still standing, her eyes darting back and forth. Max sat down. "I don't know. It depends on what you tell me. I can't hide secrets from Mr. Buncombe. If it impacts him badly, he could come after me."

"Get over it, Maxwell. Grow a pair. What I'm going to tell you will get that Mr. Buncombe out of trouble, but you're going to have to trust me. And you're going to have to convince that old codger to trust me."

"I'm a lawyer. I don't trust people."

"Then you're screwed and so is he. But I'm telling you, if you do what I say, your trust won't be misplaced. You've gotta let me take this thing over. If not, I'm out and you can deal with the government and try to save Mr. Buncombe. You don't know what you're dealing with. I do."

Max looked at Carla, still standing. Now her eyes weren't darting; they were like lasers, red lasers drilling a hole in Max's own eyes.

"Come on, Max. I don't have time to play with you and Mr. Buncombe. Either trust me or not. It's up to you."

"An hour ago, life was easier."

"Jesus Christ, Maxwell. Pick."

Max thought about his dad, about what he would do. He wished, for the thousandth time, he wished he could call on his dad. What would he do? Life was suddenly a mess. He looked back at Carla, still drilling his face with those eyes.

"I'll trust you. You'd better not screw me."

"What I'm about to tell you is in confidence. It is protected by the attorney-client privilege. Do you understand?"

"I know all about the privilege."

"So do I."

Carla sat down at the conference table.

"You might want to get a cup of water," she said. "The first thing you need to know is exactly why I hired you."

"Oh my god." Max picked up the Styrofoam cup with water at the brim.

Chapter 54

"I WAS VERY successful on Wall Street, that much is true," she said, "but a few years ago I became a sacrificial lamb in a corporate struggle. I pled guilty to a crime I didn't commit and was banned from trading on any exchange for a period of five years. I have some unusual knowledge of the stock market." She stopped for a moment. "I need to get some water, too."

Max stood up, stepped down the hall and brought back another full Styrofoam cup.

"I needed a place to trade, an IP address that wasn't traceable to me. I've been trading stocks here at your office for six months. The trading has been in my father's social security number. That violates the terms of my probation, but with the knowledge I have of the market, it was irresistible."

"You're like your great-grandfather. You cheat the system with no regrets."

"No. I admit I'm a maverick, but I have no apologies about my ancestors. I don't cheat anyone. Let me finish."

Max leaned back in the chair, shoulders slumped. He'd never paid attention to her briefcase or the extraordinary amount of time that she spent at the office. She needed help with her father's accident. It didn't hurt that she was rich as Croesus; she'd proved that by where and how she lived. Max felt duped. He took another sip of water.

"Mortgages have become commodities. Like corn, or orange juice. Any thinking person could find trusts, mortgage-backed securities and buy the insurance on those mortgages. For the past six months, I've shorted seventy-five million dollars' worth of mortgage-backed securities. The return will be three hundred million dollars. I'm ready to take the profit now. It's luck, *pure luck*, maybe with some theurgical influences that Hugh Buncombe has come across this cash. It will allow me, it will allow *us* to take this profit with impunity."

"What in God's name are you talking about?"

"Don't you see it? The government is at our door trying to hide something that happened over thirty years ago. If this hits the newspaper, the Bureau will be embarrassed; the country will suffer another black eye. Jokes will be made on late-night television; the twenty-four-hour news cycle will go on for days about this hidden money. Congress will have hearings. There will be severe consequences to the Bureau of Engraving and Printing. This is huge, Maxwell.

"I didn't think of this in those terms."

"I know. Don't worry about it. I've got this. We have power, Mr. Cooper. With a little negotiation, I can take my profit and not have some investigation into my trading. You've got to let me take the lead here."

Max sipped the last of his water and set the empty cup in front of him. He stared at the cup in a reverie of thought. How could all of this happen under his nose? What could he have done differently? Carla watched him for those few moments, letting it all sink in. She continued.

"After all, the stock market trades were done at your office. You might be investigated for wrongdoing. You have something to lose, Maxwell, if this goes the wrong way. Let me take the lead here. I've got a plan." The cadence of her speech, her tone, was truncated in sharp, spare tones. She had done this before; it was in her bloodstream, the same blood of Leland Brunswick, swimming in her veins with the cold calculation of an alligator about to pounce on a puppy at the edge of the pond.

"What have I done wrong? I didn't find this money. I didn't trade any stocks."

"You haven't done anything wrong, but you might spend the next five years trying to prove that you didn't. I'm telling you I know how to handle this and keep everyone, including you, out of danger, and away from any investigations."

Maxwell Cooper was angry and trapped.

"I want to hear your plan. How can you keep Hugh Buncombe out of jail?"

Carla folded her hands in front of the empty Styrofoam cup. "Oh, I can keep Hugh out of jail. That's the easy part. The government will let him out if he doesn't talk about it. And they'll pay him something for that. There's whistleblower money, but we don't want it. The government will have to approve of that disbursement. But I intend to get the most out of the government for our little treasure hunter. The trick is going to get them to allow my stock trade. That's where the money is." She stopped again. "I got this, Max. I got this. Sit back and watch the show."

Max was defeated. "I don't want to jeopardize my law license."

"Don't be so fatalistic. I've got a back-up plan; I'll take the fall. I'm not going to let you get into any trouble."

Carla Robeson enunciated the plan in astounding detail. Max had no choice. He was like his own clients, stuck in fore-closure, a bank holding the power and the money, with no way out. If the plan failed, Max's only option was to wind up standing in front of some judge, some committee, trying to explain how he had no options. He could only pray that Carla Robeson's creative, but spur-of-the-moment plot would keep him and his client safe.

The first part of the strategy was to send Hugh Buncombe home. It would keep him from knowing too much. Max told Hugh to get the money in some storage boxes. Hugh complied. Max had Sharon cancel all his appointments for the rest of that day, and the next. And then he sent Sharon home. Sharon hung a sign on the door of the office that said there was a death in the family and the office was closed for two days. The phone was put on automatic voicemail. All the business with the money was going to be done from Carla's cell phone.

Chapter 55

CARLA SAT IN Max's chair to make the call while Max watched from the client's seat. She'd already let Hank know she "worked with Maxwell Cooper."

"Let me talk to your boss," Carla told Hank.

"I'm supposed to talk with Hugh Buncombe."

"Look here, I want your boss to call me from his cell phone. You get that done. That's how you're going to get to talk to Mr. Buncombe." Carla gave Hank her number.

Twenty minutes passed. Carla never looked at Max while she worked on the computer, madly pounding the keyboard.

Carla's phone rang.

Someone said a few words when she picked up. She became intolerant right away.

"I work at the office of Cooper and Cooper, Attorneys. My name is Carla Robeson. You can look me up in the Wall Street Journal archives. Do that and call me back." She hung up.

She went back to the computer, not looking at Max, pelting the keyboard. Thirty minutes passed. Max could no longer sit still. He roamed around his own office like a stranger, looking at pictures on the walls, picking little pieces of paper off the Persian rug that covered the hardwood floor. Carla kept pecking away.

The phone rang again. "Yes." Carla listened. "What do I want?" she asked. "Before we get there, let me read you something." She grabbed Caswell's letter.

"My name is Clay Caswell. I am an American soldier. I was second in command in charge of security for the Bureau of Engraving and Printing. I believe that America is being taken over by Koreans. I have taken thirty million dollars from the Bureau and put it here for the good people of Ellenton to protect themselves against the Korean invasion."

Carla stopped for a moment. There was silence on the other end.

"How come I've never heard about Clay Caswell before, Mr. Madison? You would agree with me, wouldn't you, that someone from the Bureau stealing thirty million dollars is a major breach of security? Wouldn't you?" More silence.

"Okay. So, we agree by your silence. And you would agree with me, wouldn't you, that the Bureau, and your failure to communicate this to Congress or the American public, has committed a major breach of law?"

"What do I want? It's simple. You have the power to get an order from the United

States Attorney for the Southern District of New York. Tell him that Carla Robeson has been instrumental in an investigation concerning money laundering and that she has been so helpful that her stock trading prohibition needs to be lifted. It needs to be done today."

Max couldn't hear what Mr. Madison said, but Carla made faces while she listened. Apparently, there were some protestations on the other end of the phone. Carla went back to the letter and read some further incriminating things to Charlie. Then she asked a few questions, like those darts that she was so good at throwing. Her shots hit unprotected territory and the answers were slow, followed by silence. More darts. More unfortified spots were struck. She had Charlie in a corner. She stopped and let it sink in. A full minute passed.

"You have the power to get this done. I've seen the government work very fast when it needs to. Make the call. The United States Attorney isn't too busy for your phone call. You are the Chief of the Bureau of Engraving and Printing. Carla Robeson has been very helpful. All I need is a signed order relieving Carla Robeson from her probation. The channels can be cut. This is a matter of national urgency. Carla Robeson has saved millions of taxpayers' money. I want the signed Order by four-thirty. You've got my cell number. Call me and I'll give you the email address where you can send the Order. Don't disappoint me. And tell your boy down here to stand down. Tell him to go to The Willcox and get an adult beverage." More talk from Charlie elicited a small smile from Carla.

She pushed the red button on her phone, walked past Max and out to the lobby where Hank Stafford was reading a magazine.

"Your boss is going to call you. He's going to tell you to go have a liquor drink at The Willcox. Have a nice day."

Hank's phone rang.

"Yes sir, that's what this lady just said." And Hank left. Liquor before noon was awesome.

Carla, very much in charge, came back to Max, still seated.

"We've got to go get the money."

Chapter 56

It was Max's time to take this task by the horns. Hugh had been told to stay put in his house and to take no calls or visitors. He answered the door and peeked behind Max and Carla.

"Is that guy with you?"

"No," Max said, as he and Carla stepped past Hugh into the foyer, "we've got him at bay." Max and Carla moved past the living room on the left, the dining room on the right and headed straight toward the kitchen. Hugh got a clear sense that Max was in control, Carla right behind him. Max and Carla stood around the kitchen table as Hugh followed.

"We've got a deal cooking to keep you out of jail, Hugh," Max said, "but we've gotta have the money. We need it now."

Hugh, still standing, looked straight at Max.

"I need a guarantee I'm not going to jail."

Carla took over. "Max has cut you a deal with the government. We've been working on it for the past two hours."

"Who are you again?"

"I'm Carla Robeson. I know more about how the government works than both of you. The bigger thing though, Mr. Buncombe, is not *who* I am, but *what* I'm going to do for you. I'm going to see that you get clean money for the filthy bills you tried to give to Maxwell. I'm the reason the government is not going to prosecute you. In exchange for the money, I'm going to get you whistleblower money, one fourth, seven million five hundred thousand dollars in the next ten days. If you keep making unreasonable demands, I'm out and you and Maxwell are on your own. He can't promise that he'll keep you out of jail. You either trust me and Mr. Cooper or I'm telling you that you will spend the rest of your rotten days in a federal penitentiary." When she said the word penitentiary, she made it into the full five syllables, stressing the syllable *pen*. "Tell him, Maxwell. He's your client."

Max knew she was lying about the deal being completed. It was *being* made. He thought about the absolute certainty of an investigation, about how he let a client into his office and illegally trade stocks while there. If Carla was going to screw Hugh, the worst thing was that Max gave bad advice to a criminal.

Hugh sat down at the table and rustled the money like a dealer in Vegas shuffling cards.

"You're going to guarantee me that I am not going to prison, Max? That much has been done?"

"No. But you don't have any choice, Hugh. The safe thing to do is give up this money."

Max didn't lie to his client.

"I need to know if the deal is one hundred percent."

"The deal's been made, Mr. Buncombe," Carla said, stepping forward. "I'm the one who made the deal. You can hold me responsible."

"You both heard me," Hugh said, "if I serve one day in prison, it's on you, Max."

"Get the money, Hugh," Carla said, "we need the money, all of it, now."

Max sat in the car while Carla and Hugh loaded the boxes in Max's SUV, all of it. It was one o'clock. On the way back to the office, Carla, in the passenger seat, eyes on the road, told Max: "You didn't lie back there Mr. Cooper. Good job. You can continue to be my lawyer. Very good. Now, get them on the phone."

Max dialed Jimmy Nash. "Are you and Lucretia ready to go?"

Chapter 57

As Max and Jimmy confirmed the rendezvous point, Carla called her contact at the Augusta airport.

"Is the plane ready? Good. How about the uniforms? Good. We'll be there in an hour."

Max looked at Carla, her eyes still dead ahead. "What about the Order? What if it doesn't come through?"

"It'll come, Maxwell. You call me and let me know when you get it. This airplane has cell service. We'll be landing before 3:30. The Order should be there by that time. Have some confidence in your government, Maxwell." Carla smiled.

Thirty minutes later, Jimmy Nash and Lucretia met Carla on the tarmac of the private runway at the Augusta Regional Airport, a Gulfstream V waiting for them. The jet was in a private fleet that Carla leased occasionally; she hated commercial airlines. This plane had room for sixteen; the seats were black Italian leather, two seats facing a wide, hand-made table with two more seats across from the table. There were four such tables, sixteen seats in all. If needed, the seats folded down into a double bed allowing eight to sleep comfortably.

There was a fifty-five-inch flat screen TV mounted on the wall near the cockpit.

"Here's the money you were promised," Carla said, handing Jimmy and Lucretia each, two thousand dollars in cash. The money she gave them was clean money, not the poisonous paper that Hugh had found. Jimmy, dressed in his finest khakis and a light-blue shirt, stuffed the money into his front pants pocket. Lucretia looked at the cash and put it into her handbag, finding the zipper on the side and closing it.

In the next fifteen minutes, they were in the air. Jimmy and Lucretia, sitting next to each other, held hands as the plane took off. The leather seats were the softest leather they'd ever felt; Jimmy wondered to himself how they kept the leather so clean.

"Your first flight?"

"Yes ma'am," they both said, gripping each other's hands.

"Flying private is the best way to go. You don't have to put up with all those other people and flight attendants rolling those things up and down the aisle. You're going to like this."

Lucretia and Jimmy looked out the porthole windows, Lucretia sitting next to the window, Jimmy leaning sideways, sometimes resting his chin on Lucretia's shoulder. They relaxed and whispered to each other, pointing out things on the ground before the plane reached its cruising altitude and only the puffy clouds could be seen below.

Carla was charmed by their innocence, but she had things to do. She had her Mac on board and continued to press buttons as Jimmy and Lucretia became acclimated to flying. The jet had a maximum speed of six hundred miles an hour; there was no turbulence in the air. To Jimmy and Lucretia, their first flight, the hour and a half seemed to go by faster than a good sermon preached by Pastor Duplin. When they landed at Westchester County Airport, Greenwich, Connecticut, at 3:30, Carla's phone buzzed.

"Yes, Maxwell...? What did I tell you? Call your client. Let him know he's safe. I'll call you in an hour." The plane had taxied to a private part of the airport. Within the next sixty seconds, the three of them were back on the tarmac.

"Here are two uniforms," she said to Jimmy and Lucretia, "go put them on in the bathroom just inside the building there. And don't tarry. Use the bathroom if you must, but we're on a deadline."

Jimmy and Lucretia followed orders, moving quickly into the one-story annex used for those passengers and crew who flew private.

"What did she mean by tarry?"

"I think she wants us to hurry. For this kind of money, I'll run as fast as she wants."

Five minutes later Lucretia and Jimmy emerged from the building dressed in brown, the same color brown as UPS drivers, in fact, in uniforms *identical* to UPS drivers. Carla waved at them from a brown panel van, the same color as a UPS panel van. "I'm driving this part. Jimmy, you can drive when I tell you."

"Ok."

Thirty minutes later they were a block away from their destination.

"Jimmy, you drive up to that gate right there. I'll be in the back of the van. Lucretia, do just as I've told you. Do you understand?"

"Yes ma'am."

When the camera in the house picked up the van outside the gate, an alarm beeped.

"Yes?"

"UPS delivery," Jimmy said.

The gate swung open. Jimmy drove down the quarter mile circular drive lined with hundred-year old sycamore trees with peeling gray and white mottled bark. The front entrance to the home had two hand-carved Brazilian hardwood doors with an opaque, oval, thick glass pane.

Lucretia, a brown hat covering her head, hopped out once Jimmy got the van parked so the back of the vehicle was at the front stoop. Lucretia loaded the two thirty-pound brown boxes onto the hand truck. A man stood at the front door. Lucretia had a receipt for him to sign, just like the UPS drivers. The man, barely looking up, signed as Lucretia wheeled the box into the foyer.

"Thanks," the man said.

Lucretia, on strict instructions, kept her head down, saying nothing.

Twenty-four seconds later they were out of the gate, riding back to the airport, Carla Robeson grinning.

"I can't believe he was home," she said. "I can't believe it."

"Your friend is gonna be surprised, isn't he Miss Carla?" Jimmy said.

"Yes," she said, "yes he is."

"I guess this is what rich people can do," Lucretia whispered to Jimmy. "They can pay a lot of money to surprise a friend with a birthday gift."

Carla, still smiling a smile for which she had been waiting a year and a half, looked at the receipt that Lucretia had gotten signed.

Birthday or not, Ralph Lousteau would be *very* surprised.

Chapter 58

CARLA ASSUMED DRIVING duty after leaving Lousteau's home. She asked Jimmy to get out of the van and drop a letter in the box on a Hickory-shaded street in the neighborhood. Jimmy didn't look at the letter; he was so happy to have two thousand dollars in his pocket and a plane ride with Lucretia, he didn't care where the letter was headed. It was important to Carla, though, that the letter be sent from a post office in Greenwich.

Before they had landed at Westchester County Airport, Carla was ready to sell her seventy-five-million-dollar investment and put three hundred million in her pocket. After receiving the good news about the Order from Maxwell, while Jimmy and Lucretia got dressed at the airport, she covered each of her positions in the market. The money would arrive in her accounts over the next few days.

There were still some details to wrap up, but for this day, this incredible eight hours, Carla had time to talk to Jimmy and Lucretia. They had changed back into their airplane attire, stuffing the brown suits in a bag that Carla would later burn in her favorite fireplace at the Brunswick Cottage.

Jimmy and Lucretia, seated across from Carla as before, were holding hands and occasionally kissing.

With the plane in flight, back at cruising altitude, Carla was curious about her guests.

"Tell me, how did you two meet?"

Lucretia told her all about how Jimmy took her heart at the *Magnolia Café* by being so charming and clean.

"And the newspaper says you're in the compost business?"

"Yes ma'am. Since I got bit by the snake, everyone wants me to pick up their trash. Derek, the man who saved my life, has become my partner. We got a bank loan and we're buying a real truck to haul everything. We're even looking at a piece of land where we can double or triple our production. Derek says the world is going organic. Says we can capture the market on this stuff and move into other cities. Derek is good with managing. I'm pretty good with numbers."

"Tell me, Jimmy, if I bought something for five hundred dollars and sold it for six hundred dollars, what would be the percentage of profit?"

"Twenty percent. Like I said, I'm pretty good at numbers."

"I understand."

Jimmy rubbed Lucretia on the cheek with his little finger. She smiled.

"How old are you, Jimmy?"

"Twenty-seven, ma'am."

"And you, Lucretia?"

"Twenty-four."

"Children, marriages?"

"We've never been married, ma'am."

Carla was like a data processor, absorbing information, storing it away in some cloud for future use. She continued with her interrogation.

"Tell me about your grandfather's house. Who was he?"

"He was an accountant for a bunch of rich people. He saved his money and built the house right off Hitchcock Woods. He outlived my grandmother. I took care of him until he died. I was the only grandchild who looked after him. He left me the house, but I've had a time keepin' it up. Things are getting' better, though. Derek and I have got some good things goin'." Jimmy rubbed Lucretia's hand as he spoke.

"And you, Lucretia?"

Lucretia told her story about being the black sheep of the family, her working at the café and going to church every Sunday with her mom.

Carla Robeson had in front of her, on a plane ride at thirty-one thousand feet, two people in love. Sure, she'd seen it before, but this young couple was so impressive, so genuinely *American* with their work ethic and dedication to family—Carla was touched; she sat back in the cushioned black leather seat and watched them. It was almost uncomfortable.

"And you've never been on a plane before, right?"

"No ma'am," they both said.

"You know, there's something very romantic about you two; there's something very special about being above the earth at thirty-thousand feet, there's something very heavenly about seeing the sun set from this angle," Carla's hand moved gracefully to the porthole where an orange and yellow glow flowed below them. "Ever think about proposing to this beautiful woman, Jimmy?"

Jimmy blushed a full-blown red, his white skin from his neck to the top of his head, crimson.

"Yes ma'am."

"There's no better place on earth. In fact, we're not even on earth. We're above the firmament here. Maybe with the sun setting, on this private plane..."

Lucretia was already tearing up as Jimmy got on his knees in that Gulfstream V and asked her to marry him.

The answer was in a squeal—and more tears. Jimmy and Lucretia hugged, moving back and forth in each other's arms. With tears in their eyes, they looked at Carla, who sat back in her black-leather seat. A few minutes later she pulled Jimmy aside and told him to pick out a ring at Windsor's in Augusta; she told him to ask for Donnie, her good friend. She would pay for it. Jimmy smiled.

Carla liked Jimmy and Lucretia a lot.

Chapter 59

BY THE TIME the plane landed, Hugh Buncombe was a nervous wreck. He had no idea that there had even been a plane ride. All he knew was that within four hours that morning he'd given up almost thirty million dollars and all he had was a promise that he wouldn't go to jail—and a pledge from a well-dressed woman that she'd make sure he got a tip or something. As much as he thought he trusted Max Cooper, his common sense told him he'd been screwed. Maybe the whole thing was a scam by his lawyer to get the money. Maybe Max knew about him finding the whole stash and he had set up some guy to come to his house pretending to be with the government. Max hadn't called him back except to say he had the assurance from the government that he wouldn't attend thirty years of remedial training behind bars. It was now 10 p.m. Hugh called Max's cell phone.

"Where's my money?"

"Here at my office like I told you. The government is picking it up in the morning. I'm spending the night with it. And my gun. You want to join me?"

Hugh and Bailey arrived at Max's office fifteen minutes later. Hugh had his gun in his truck, choosing not to threaten Max until he felt the time was right.

"Where's my money?" Hugh was sure it had disappeared.

"In the conference room."

Hugh spotted a pistol on the coffee table.

"That yours?"

"My dad's. I've never fired it. Figured I'd kill anyone who tries to come here.

Hugh felt better. "Can I see my money?"

Max waved him toward the back as he looked out the front windows, fearing that someone had followed Hugh.

Hugh opened the door to the conference room and peeked at the stacks of boxes. He didn't need to count each one. It looked like Max wasn't lying. He came back to the lobby. "Where's the letter from the government? I'd like to see it. I don't want to go to jail."

Hugh read the letter three times. It was simple. Hugh wasn't to be charged with anything, but the money had to be returned immediately.

Hugh was reading it a fourth time when Max spoke. "I've gotta keep that letter, Hugh. You can't have a copy."

"It's the only thing I've got to protect me."

"I know. I'm gonna keep it in my safe deposit box at my bank. I can't give you a copy. The government does not want this getting out. The way I see it, there are four people on the planet who know about this. The Chief of the Bureau, you, Carla Robeson and me. The guy they sent to talk to you doesn't know squat. All he was told was to ask where you got the money. He's clueless."

"I can't get a copy?"

"No. If the government ever comes after you, we'll get it out of my safe deposit box."

"What if they kill you? What if you're dead?"

"I'll write a letter that gives you access to the box. It's the best I can do. Charles Madison was very clear about this."

Hugh sat down on the couch in the lobby. Hugh looked down the hall. Beyond that, just in the large conference room, the money was neatly stacked. He'd worked so hard. He'd dug with his bare hands; dug with a small shovel, he'd dug so much—and now he had to give it back. And he had to be quiet about it.

Max watched Hugh for a minute. "Carla said she was gonna take care of you, Hugh. She said she'd call in the morning. So far, she's done everything she said she'd do. The letter is there from the government. Hugh Buncombe is not going to jail. Now we've got to trust her to get you some legitimate cash. That money back there stopped being legal tender years ago."

"I hope we haven't misplaced our trust."

Max liked the fact that Hugh used the word 'we.' He felt bad enough making Hugh give up the money, but since Carla had a plan, a plan that she didn't fully disclose, Max was practically forced to convince Hugh to trust her.

"You can spend the night here with me if you want. I want you involved in this."

Hugh was good with that. "Bailey says he can sleep anywhere. I'll put these two chairs together."

"I've got the couch. If anyone comes along, you can shoot first."

"Damn right."

Hugh Buncombe and Max Cooper didn't say much the rest of the night, Max trying to sleep and Hugh nodding off occasionally. It had been a long day.

As for Hank Stafford, the uninformed patsy from the Bureau, his trip had been lovely. He knocked on the old man's door and the next thing he knew, the Bureau Chief told him to go get a liquor drink and use his per diem on a nice dinner. He walked around Aiken, taking in the charm of the place, the tack shops, the greenery, the quaint storefronts, the absolute true Southern charm he'd only read about in fictional stories. He ate a scrumptious lunch at the *Magnolia Café,* where he picked up a copy of *Garden and Gun* magazine.

He was already checked in at The Willcox and, after spending a few hours by the pool reading his magazine and a book titled *On a Street Called Easy, In a Cottage Called Joye*, (a book by some Northerners who fell in love with Aiken), he had dinner. His per diem covered the meal of shrimp and grits, another treat that he'd only heard about. Call it the charisma of Aiken, the lovely allure of the South, Hank decided to splurge outside his daily stipend and have a drink at the quiet bar at the inn where he could watch some sports and continue reading if he wished. It was there he met a nice woman—an attractive and older, but very seductive woman who engaged his eyes and ears. She was delightful, a southern treat, her accent dripping with words like y'all and 'pshaw' that she pronounced in two full syllables. She was so well dressed and seemed to know everyone in the place—she made him feel at home.

At the end of the evening, after a night of small talk and cute jokes and stories, the nice woman asked Hank to walk her to her car, a black Mercedes S63 AMG 4Matic. She asked Hank if he was going to be around for another night, maybe they could have dinner. Hank had not exactly been the luckiest young man in the love department. Although the woman was a little older than the women he was accustomed to hanging with, she was so sweet it seemed almost offensive to turn down an invitation for a meal. Hank wanted to stay another night. He didn't realize that the nice woman had gotten everything she had come for.

Chapter 60

In the morning Hugh and Max drank coffee at Max's office, speaking little to each other.

At 8:30 sharp, Max's cell phone rang.

"Hello."

Hugh couldn't hear the particulars—Max spoke some yesses before he hit the red button.

"The truck from the Bureau should be here within the hour. Then we can put this behind us, Hugh."

"And trust Carla."

"Yeah. It's all we can do."

Hugh and Max watched, mainly in silence, as two men loaded the cash into an armored truck that said Garda Global on the side. They'd given their IDs, and Max confirmed their identity with Charlie Madison before he allowed them to begin carting the cash out the back door. Hugh couldn't bear it, peering out of the windows of the old house-office, watching his money drive off. Before ten o'clock, it was over.

Hugh and Max had missed coffee with Kathy and Mandy for two days in a row. That was bothering Hugh as well as Max. They'd grown accustomed to their morning habit and this whole money thing had interrupted their routine.

Max's cell phone rang again. It was as though Carla Robeson knew the money was gone.

"Hello."

"I need you to come to my house. Call Mr. Buncombe and bring him with you."

"He's standing right here."

"Come now. Don't bring anyone else. Take two cars."

While Max and Hugh drove to Carla's, the agent Hank Stafford made a deal with Charlie to spend another night in Aiken. Hank looked forward to a tour with a pleasant woman, Judith Burgess, the hometown, homegrown, tour guide. He decided to splurge on a horse-riding lesson in the afternoon. He was also excited about his dinner date with the lovely woman who owned the black Mercedes.

When Max and Hugh pulled up to Carla's house, she was standing in the doorway.

"I've sent my maid on an all-day errand to Augusta. We've got a lot of business to tend to. Get some coffee. I've got sweet rolls on the kitchen counter. Get settled and follow me."

Carla walked with great purpose toward her downstairs office. The room was mahogany paneled, dark, luxurious and formal.

Overnight, Carla's accounts had been clicking like one of those slot machines in Las Vegas. Account after account was piling up with money, three hundred million in all. It was legal, all of it.

"Sit down, gentlemen."

There were two chairs in front of her desk, just like at Max's office. Max and Hugh sat down, Bailey behaving, but sniffing everything.

"Mr. Buncombe, I told you I would give you the amount you might have earned from the government." Carla leaned forward, drilling Hugh with her eyes.

Hugh looked at Max, fearing the truth, the ugly lie he'd been told and now she was going to screw him. Max felt the stare coming from Hugh's eyes.

"I'm still going to do that," she continued, "but I'm going to give you a little guerdon, a bonus if you will. I've been very lucky in my life and your little find has made my life even easier. You would normally be entitled to twenty-five per cent of the find, or about seven and a half million dollars. Under the government rules, you'd have to pay taxes on that, which means you'd have to pay almost four million. I'm going to wire transfer twenty million dollars into whatever accounts you tell me. At twenty million, you should be able to keep more than you would have gotten from the government." She waited.

"How can you do, I mean, why would you…?" Hugh stopped.

"Have you ever lost anything, Mr. Buncombe? Have you ever really had something *taken* from you?"

"I lost my wife. She was taken. God took her; something took her. I miss her every day."

"Can't get her back, can you?

"No. What does this have to do with giving me money?"

"Nothing. Everything."

"I don't understand."

"You see, Hugh, I don't need money. I have money, lots of it. But what I lost, what was *taken* from me, was my *reputation.* I lost that. How does a person get that returned to them?"

Carla pushed her chair away from the large desk.

"I've thought a lot about this, gentlemen. I lost my reputation on the street because of someone else, something unrelated to any errors of my own. You also did nothing wrong. You *found* money. You didn't *steal* it; you *found* it. And if it weren't for Maxwell here and some luck, you'd have probably gone to jail for something you didn't do. But back to my question—what if you lost your ability to hold your head high among your friends, your colleagues? What if they considered you a dishonest person, a person who couldn't be trusted? I submit to you that is worse than not being able to pay your bills, worse than making an honest mistake."

"I still don't understand why you're giving me more than you promised."

"It doesn't matter. Just understand that you have helped me in ways that I could not have accomplished by myself. Things are now in play that will partially restore my reputation. That wouldn't have happened without your fortuitous find and your trust in me. For that, I am eternally thankful to you. When I see you on the street, I want you to remember me as a person of high character. I did more than I promised. I've always done that, but because of some bizarre circumstances, my reputation was tarnished. In the coming months, it will be radiant again; I have you to thank for that. So, keep the extra millions. I want you to have it. From where I sit, you deserve it."

Carla turned her attention to Max.

"Maxwell, you've introduced me to a very enterprising young man. Jimmy Nash is doing good work in an organic recycling business. He's got a house, his grandfather's house over off Hitchcock Woods, a beautiful spot. It's in disrepair. I'm going to get some contractors out there to renovate the place. I want to make sure they do the work and do it right. Since he's sort of your client, I want you to get him in for a meeting. I'm going to pay for the entire rehab. We don't need to sign anything with him, but I want him protected from contractors, plumbers, electricians, whoever. You prepare those agreements; I'll pay the costs."

Hugh spoke first: "Holy cow."

"I had no idea. I…"

"I've been living under a cloud for the past year, Maxwell. I'm out. There are some very deserving folks out there. In fact, there are three more. I want to buy a house for Jimmy's partner and his wife. Her name is Patsy. She works at the hospital. Tell them they can spend a half million on a house and whatever else they want. I'll pay. And the man that took them all in—the man you represented in court—I want to pay off that place and give him three hundred thousand—as long as these nice folks each get five-hundred thousand dollars. Maxwell, I want this done anonymously. Just say a client of yours did all this, I don't care. Just don't say a *man* did it. Men get too much credit."

"I'll tell them a client did it."

"They'll probably figure it out, especially with me being out there wearing a hard hat at the grandfather's place, but I don't want my name gratuitously tossed about, are we clear on that, Maxwell? Hugh, are we clear? No word of this to your buddies, whoever they are."

Hugh and Max looked at each other and then back to Carla.

"Clear."

Chapter 61

THEY SPENT THE next half hour getting Hugh's account numbers to Carla, calling the banks and investment companies on the phone. Carla handled most of the calls with a matter-of-fact business voice, speaking in clipped phrases that were well understood by the person on the other end of the line.

While the money was pouring into Hugh's accounts, Carla sat back in her chair watching the double monitors on her desk. By noon, Hugh Buncombe had twenty million dollars in his bank accounts. Carla looked like she enjoyed the whole process.

"Hugh," she said, looking across the desk, "you can go now if you wish. I need to spend some more time with Maxwell here. We have some ground to cover on the disbursement of funds to his clients."

Hugh looked down at Bailey.

"Can I stay?" he asked.

"Yes. But don't bother me with a bunch of questions. I've got checks to write and some lecturing to young Maxwell here."

And she wrote checks. And lectured Maxwell. She told him he needed to stop his pursuit of concupiscence and get serious about his personal life. Max told her he'd found the woman he was going to marry.

Carla smiled. And then she lectured him some more. She couldn't help it.

After thirty minutes of dressing Maxwell down, she put a check into an envelope. "You had to close your office for two days," she said, "I've enclosed a little something extra; this ought to take care of your trouble." And she smiled again.

Thirty minutes later, Max and Hugh stood on the front steps of the Brunswick Cottage, Carla inside. Max started down the front steps. Hugh pulled Max back up, wrapped his arms around him and hugged him, a manly bear hug that came from Hugh's heart.

"You are a good man, Maxwell Cooper. A very good man."

"That means a lot to me, Hugh," Max said.

Although Max and Hugh had spoken on the phone to Mandy and Kathy a few times in the past thirty-six hours, Max and Hugh hadn't been to coffee at the *New Moon*. Hugh and Max agreed to keep the past events a confidential matter. Each called his girlfriend and promised they would be at coffee the next morning.

While sitting in the front seat of his car, Max opened the envelope. A check for two million dollars was enclosed.

Chapter 62

MAX KEPT THE two-million-dollar check in his desk drawer for a few days before calling his banker friends. A meeting was scheduled. Max, at twenty-six years old, knew he needed some advice.

Thomas Boswell and Lisa Kaminedes, the bankers, were pleased to have a meeting. They had been handling Calhoun Cooper's affairs for years; Max trusted them.

"Have you not been receiving the notices from us?" Boswell began.

Max turned red. "I've had a hard time dealing with dad's estate. I haven't even started the paperwork in probate court. Did dad owe some money? I'll be glad to pay."

"You've not opened the notices, not even bank statements?"

"Just the ones to the law firm."

"Lisa and I were going to call you, Max. Your father has an estate, a combination of stocks, bonds and cash in excess of three million dollars. The certificates of deposit have matured and we need to do something with those. You didn't know he had a rather large estate?"

Max stared at them for a moment. And then he put his head on the big conference table.

"No," he said to the oak table. He sat in the chair, looking at his hands in his lap. "I didn't know. We never talked about what he had. We liked talking about work. I had no idea."

"Your dad was a good investor, a very good saver of money. I'm a little surprised he didn't tell you, but then again, he wasn't planning on dying..."

An hour later, Maxwell Cooper walked out of AllSouth Federal Credit Union with five million dollars in his accounts. He called Mandy. Lunch was scheduled at the *Way Café*.

When Mandy arrived, Max hugged her and held her tight for a moment. She pulled back and looked at him.

"Everything ok?"

"Let's get a table away from everyone."

They sat at a four-person table near the back door of the café where other diners seldom sat.

"You're going to be my wife. I want to share everything with you."

"And?" Mandy was a little nervous.

Max told her about Carla's two-million-dollar tip, not disclosing why or anything about Hugh Buncombe. He stopped for a moment, took a sip of his iced tea and told her about his father's estate, the three million that he'd inherited. He stopped again. Mandy knew enough about Max to wait.

"I've got some decisions to make," he said, "I don't really have to work, Mandy. I can do whatever I want."

"So, what is it you want to do?"

"I want us to go on a six-month tour of the world. They did that in the old days, you know. I want us to have an unbelievable honeymoon."

"And then what, Max? What do you want to do with the rest of your life now that you don't have to work? Is that what you're struggling with?"

"No. That's just it. I know what I want to do."

"What is that?"

"I want to keep working. I love practicing law. I was made to do it. My dad had all this money and he worked every single day. I didn't grow up at his elbow, watching him work, so I can lie around and do nothing with my life. I want purpose in my life; I want meaning."

Max looked at Mandy and continued. "You have given my life meaning. I never thought, I never knew how much I could love a person, and you've done that. You've given me something I didn't know existed." Max stopped and took a deep breath. "But with this money, as crazy as it sounds, I want to do more. I can choose what kind of cases I want to handle. I'll probably do a bunch of *pro bono* work. I like working, Mandy, and I want to make sure it's okay with you if I still bust my ass as though I don't have any money. It's weird, but that's what I want to do. I know exactly what I want, and that's two things: I want to marry you and I want to work. It's what I was born to do. Love you and work."

"And you're asking me if it's okay that you keep working?"

"Yeah."

Mandy had a choice. She could disclose her wealth or continue to guard that part of her life. At this moment, she chose to guard it.

"Max, I'm good with you working. This town, this little city has a long history of people who came here with more money than God and continued to work. I'm proud that you are going to be one of them. And think about this. I'm going to keep working at *The Standard* as long as I find it interesting. And I'm going to write my novels. Are you okay with that?"

"Yeah, I'm good with it." Max took another deep breath. "I thought you might think I was nuts. This makes me feel better."

"Good. Are you going to eat that turkey sandwich or do I take it home? I'm not going to waste good food no matter how rich you are."

Max smiled and took a big bite. With food still in his mouth, he said, "you are one funny woman. And I love you."

"It's mutual."

Max laughed while she sat up, taking a bite of her sandwich, stifling her laugh.

Later that afternoon, Mandy called Max. It was a little after five; Max was still at the office.

"Can we talk?"

"Yeah. What's up?"

"Let's go to The Willcox."

Max, worried that something was unraveling, showed up in five minutes. Mandy was already there at a corner table. She had coffee in front of her. Max figured this wasn't going to be good.

"You know how you told me we should know everything about each other?"

"Should I get a liquor drink?"

"Get coffee. We need to talk."

Max pulled the wooden-backed chair closer to the table and waved at the waiter, pointing at Mandy's coffee.

Before the coffee arrived, Mandy started. She told him about her grandparents, about the hotels, about the family net worth, about the trust fund that she had, about everything. When she finished, she leaned forward and sighed, a full-blown sigh. It was a relief to her.

"Are you now going to tell me that you're breaking up with me?"

Mandy grinned; she didn't smile. "You told me something today that made me love you even more. You said you wanted to work, despite your financial security. That's what my family has always done. We work. We don't display our wealth. The fact that you want to work means a lot to me. I've chosen the right partner. No, I'm not breaking up with my fiancé. I'm telling you I love you even more. And *now* we can get a real beverage."

Max leaned forward, looking at Mandy, putting his hands over hers.

"I love you," he said, "but I don't have time for a drink. I've got to get back to the office." And then he laughed. Mandy gripped his hands.

"That's my man."

They spent the night at Mandy's garage apartment next door to the ten-thousand-square foot cottage where she grew up. After all, it was all in the family.

Two days later an article appeared in the *Wall Street Journal.*

Chapter 63

ANOTHER BLOW BEFALLS LOUSTEAU

The Wall Street Journal has learned, according to people familiar with the matter, that Ralph Lousteau, the CEO of Gocows Mortgage, who is under federal investigation for manipulation of stock prices and selling securitized mortgages that were known to have no value, has had another legal difficulty thrust into his path.

The Secret Service, it was reported, according to sources, has received a letter from Mr. Lousteau's former maid stating that she saw Mr. Lousteau emptying the safe in his home office. People familiar with the matter have learned that Mr. Lousteau had received a subpoena for him to testify about the location of his assets, which are said to be disappearing. Mr. Lousteau, who has been a frequent commentator on many television shows regarding market conditions, at first, had no comment. After several days, however, Mr. Lousteau held a news conference where he told reporters that he never had a maid by the name of Eldora and that he had no idea how three million dollars in cash showed up at his residence in Connecticut. The maid's letter, according to sources, said Mr. Lousteau had been receiving visitors at his mansion for several months, each carrying a large brief case.

Mr. Lousteau, at the news conference, informed those listening that he had a safe in his office, but the safe was one foot tall and ten inches deep. He said this: "if the money wouldn't fit, any jury would acquit." The investigation continues.

The news articles for the previous months had been brutal. Ralph Lousteau had gone from Wall Street darling to Main Street crook. It started when Gocows was discovered to have sold a pool of twenty-five hundred mortgages to *two* separate investors. One, the Minnesota teacher's pension fund, bought the mortgages for two hundred million dollars. Lousteau's company made a quick ten million dollars on the sale. Then, it was reported, the same mortgages were sold to an investment group in Iceland for another two hundred million. The 'error' wasn't discovered until the Minnesota Trust began a foreclosure action and learned that the Iceland Trust had already started foreclosing. It's always harder to say something is an 'error' when the corporate hand is found in the cookie jar, and on this "mistake" Gocows looked more like it had jumped inside the jar, eating the cookies as it made its way to the bottom. Then, once the investigation started, another 'error' was discovered. It turned out that Gocows had sold another set of mortgages to another "Trust" and also sold them to Greece. And Greece, a country that was already in the news every day with news of its money problems, had to explain to the Greeks that a man in America who looked like a mad Einstein had had them. Gocows had come up with the money to pay for the "errors," but Lousteau was no longer asked to offer any commentary on the market. In fact, he quit granting interviews.

There was even a cartoon that appeared in the *Wall Street Journal* with a caricature of Lousteau, a protuberant belly squeezed against a dining table of plenty. Mouth opened wide, he was eating a heaping spoonful of Greek people. The cartoon showed a large belch erupting from his pie hole. The caption was simple: Gocow's Lousteau has a nice dinner: devouring Greek souls.

The media put the news on TV. Interviews were requested from Gocows and Lousteau; none were granted. Lousteau cut his hair so that now he looked like he had the mange. He wore sunglasses and a hat everywhere. His face no longer shone with brilliance; his fat smile looked more like a cushion with some teeth barely visible. He was an outcast, tossed into the dustbin of irrelevance.

And that's why he was at home when the cash arrived. He had immured himself in his own house when Carla brought him three million dollars in cardboard boxes. And those dollars were part of the money that Hugh had unearthed. Lousteau would have more explaining to do.

When the article came out in the paper about Lousteau claiming the money wouldn't fit, Carla read every word of it to her father. She read it aloud four times, accenting some words with great emphasis and then reading it again with different emphasis. She laughed, tugged at her father's arm and told him how her reputation was on its way to restoration.

Two days later, Leland Brunswick, III, passed away.

Chapter 64

"MAXWELL," SHE SAID, "my dad didn't make it."

"I'm sorry, Carla, I wish he'd been here to see what has happened."

Carla smiled. "He is here. He let it go. He knows about everything. I've kept him informed. I talked to him every day. Although he was in a coma, I *know*, he heard me. It wasn't a coincidence that he died right after my stock suspension was lifted. He knew I was okay and he let it go."

Carla was seated in the navy wing-backed chair in Max's office. "It's okay, Maxwell. He's here with me now. I feel a certain peace about it all. Quite frankly, it's a little strange, but I have peace. I want you to do the best you can with the lawsuit. After your percentage of the settlement or jury award, I want to take the rest of the money and establish a trust. The funds, the interest from the trust, will be given to the needy people in Aiken. I'll figure out whom I want on the board, the committee. It won't pay a penny, you know, but I want you on the board."

"We have an offer of five million."

"I know. Tell them we'll settle for seven and call it a day. If not seven million settle it for what you think is right. I trust your judgment. I don't care. He's watching now; he's at peace and so am I. It's a good feeling."

Carla stood up. The appointment was over. Max had his orders and she, Carla Robeson, had done everything she could do to save her father. She had no regrets, especially since her dad *knew* that she was justifiably restored.

Justice comes in different forms, various ways, and Carla was pleased with the outcome, regardless of the money. Money isn't everything, she would say to herself, but it sure helps. And the cash that fell in her lap from a war-decorated soldier via a nuclear chemist was a sign from the heavens that justice worked in mysterious ways. She was pleased. And now she was going to help people, something her father would enjoy from his lofty spot.

Chapter 65

ONCE GRANDDADDY'S HOUSE was fully restored, a photograph was taken. Jimmy, Lucretia, Quentin, Derek and Patsy stood on the front porch in between the gleaming four white columns.

Carla was the camerawoman. The entire band of them had figured out that Carla was the benefactress and requested she come to their Sunday afternoon brunch. It was after church, of course. Quentin, Jimmy and Lucretia never missed attending.

And the Sunday brunch at Granddaddy's house was something this group did for the rest of their lives. They only missed if there was an out-of-town event for one of them.

In the picture, Lucretia was turned toward Jimmy, kissing his cheek. Her belly showed a bump, in the next two months there would be a healthy little girl added to the family.

While the photo didn't show it, Patsy was also pregnant. A little boy would be born eight months later. That little boy would have a long life. And, later, a brother and a sister, everyone healthy, would join him.

Quentin would marry a woman he met in church.

Lucretia and Jimmy framed the picture and hung it in the kitchen. It was a constant, wonderful reminder to all of them, every Sunday, to how their lives were intertwined in the most bizarre and purposeful way.

Quentin reminded them of that in his blessing every Sunday at the brunch.

Hugh moved into Kathy's house, but they never married. They were both happy with the arrangement. That's right, even these "old people" were okay with "living in sin."

Chapter 66

MAX COOPER HAD been sworn to secrecy about the treasure found and all the things that happened right after Quentin Cleveland's foreclosure trial. But he was married. It seemed that Mandy should know *something* about it, especially if he told half-truths.

It was October; they were at the beach house on Sullivan's Island. They had had their coffee out on the veranda. Mandy was dressed in a white cotton robe; Max wore a pair of sweatpants and a long-sleeve T-shirt. Max went the kitchen while Mandy took in the scenery, the calm waves barely rippling before they landed on the shore.

Max came out to the deck with a bottle of champagne and a carafe of orange juice. He said nothing as he poured the drinks into crystal glasses.

"No Solo cups?"

"This is a formal occasion. It's our six-month anniversary."

Mandy nodded. She knew.

"I want to talk to you about an idea I have for your first novel."

Mandy took a sip of the mimosa, and listened.

He told a story in some detail, taking poetic license here and there, telling her about a woman who found millions in an Aiken Cottage that was formerly owned by a CIA agent. Mandy listened for fifteen minutes, rarely interrupting.

"Are there some lovers in your story?"

"Of course. I thought the book should have you and me in there. You know ..."

"Ideas for a title?"

"*Lost and Found.*"

Mandy put her drink down and stood up next to Max. "I like the story, but I've got my own idea for a title. How about: *Everything I Was Looking For.*"

And she kissed him.